WHEN THE EARL FALLS IN LOVE

JESSIE CLEVER

WHEN THE EARL FALLS IN LOVE

Published by Someday Lady Publishing, LLC

ISBN-13: 978-1-7372120-3-4

Cover Design by EDH Professionals

Edited by Judy Roth

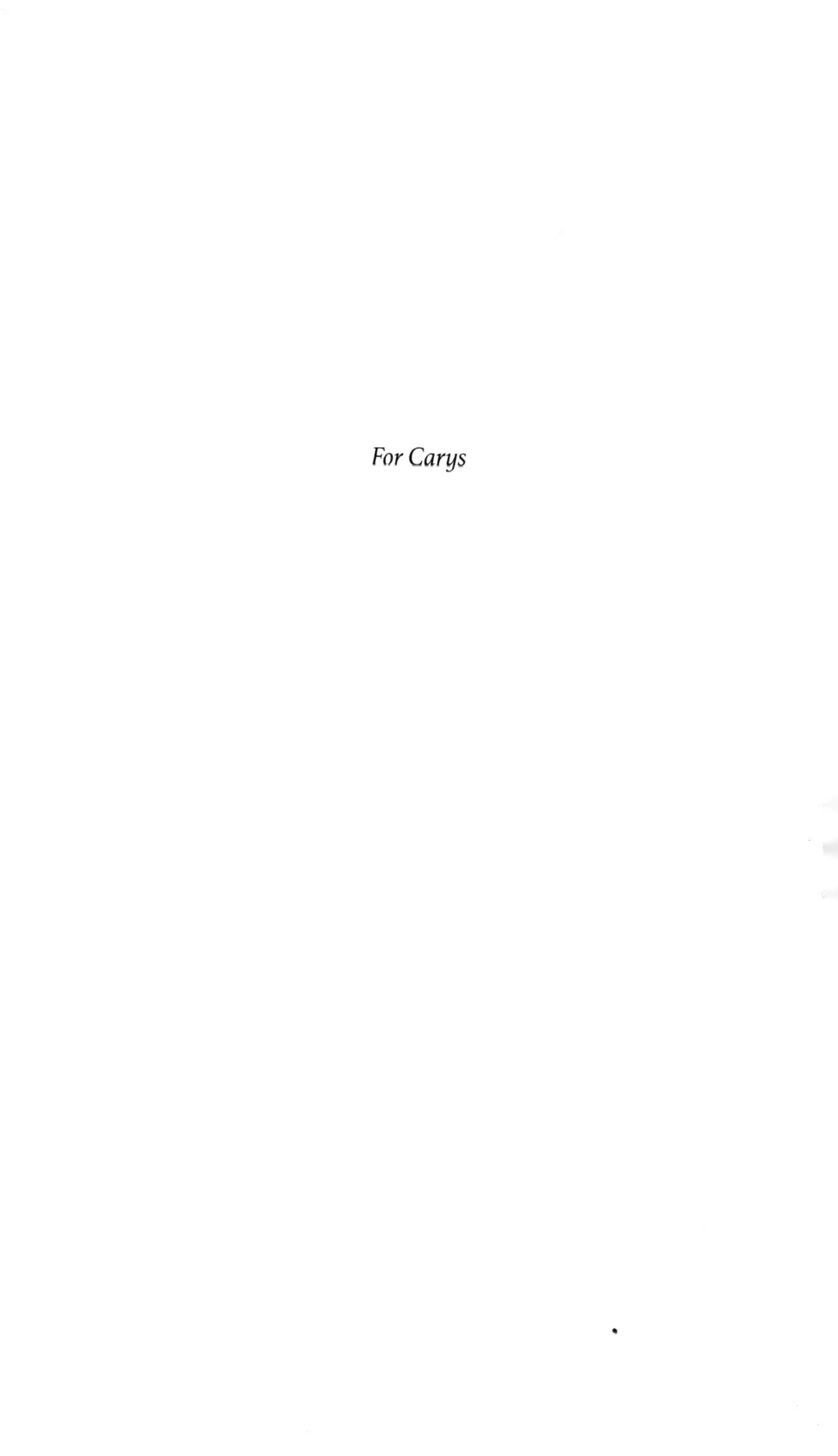

For Carys

1

When she looked at her mother, she was reminded of all the things she might have been and wasn't.

People said it was cruel how it happened. They said other things as well, Audrey knew well enough as she had overheard from time to time in the four seasons she had been out, but she had learned to ignore those things. The bold features of Lady Eugenia D'Arcy had tipped too far when it came to her daughter, and in Audrey, they had become distorted and mismatched. While Audrey had the same wide, expressive eyes, on her they had been rendered rather sunken, which in turn had accentuated her overbite, which she had in place of her mother's wide smile. And this was without even mentioning her small, pert nose that seemed to go with none of her other features.

Audrey's hair, mouse-brown, frizzy, and unwilling to form either curl or wave, was never spoken of.

When Grandmother Regina had requested Audrey fetch her handkerchief she had mistakenly left in the pocket of her cloak, Audrey was only too happy to flee to the cloakroom if only to escape the whispers and knowing glances from around the ballroom.

The first three seasons she hadn't minded. It was nice to sit on the edge of the ballroom with Grandmother Regina and Aunt Verity. Grandmother Regina didn't talk much since the stroke, but when she did, she said kind things to Audrey and smiled softly. Aunt Verity, who took care of Grandmother, was much the same.

But this was her fourth season. *Fourth.* And she was rather tired of the quiet smiles and kind words. She was rather tired of all of it.

As she left the bustle of the ballroom behind her and the quiet of the corridor descended upon her, she couldn't help but wonder.

When could it be assumed that she was firmly on the shelf?

She thought of it. Often, in fact. The word *spinsterhood* was richer than chocolate on her tongue. To no longer be required to stand at the periphery of ballrooms appearing keen and delighted at any attention given one, to no longer feign interest in the insipid conversation dandies conjured with stunning banality every season, to no longer...

Be reminded every day how she had failed as a lady.

She shivered at the thought and rubbed her hands up her arms.

She hadn't failed as a woman. At least, she tried to tell herself that. It wasn't her fault society held standards for women she had somehow not met by magic of her birth. Audrey had other qualities to recommend her. Her brothers were always saying what wit she had, what guile.

But wit and guile did not display themselves well in a ballgown.

This part of the house was quiet now as all the guests had made their way into the ballroom, and she slowed her step, wishing to prolong the time she had in such solitude yet knowing she must hurry to return Grandmother Regina's handkerchief.

She stepped into the cloakroom only to stop abruptly. There was no maid in attendance, and Audrey wondered if the woman had wandered off as soon as the last of the guests were seen into the ballroom.

For a moment, she stood and blinked at the spot where the maid should have been, and she couldn't help but allow her thoughts to run wild.

Had the maid slipped away for a daring assignation with a footman? Privacy was likely more easily discovered when the staff and family were engaged in entertaining guests. Or perhaps she'd slipped out the back for a gossip with the other maids and a quick puff on someone's cheroot.

Audrey wrinkled her nose at this thought. She didn't care for her father's pipe, and she knew a puff on a cheroot would make her ill, but the rest of the picture she'd conjured would do nicely.

It would be a far cry more exciting than her own life.

Properly depressed by her rambling thoughts, she eyed the racks and stands of coats, cloaks, and wraps that filled the entirety of the room. The night was incredibly well attended, and the mounds of cloaks she must sift through to find Grandmother Regina's was daunting to say the least, and she suddenly felt the urge to sit down.

She plunged ahead instead, poking through the first stand she came to. Grandmother Regina wore her amethyst velvet gown that evening, which meant she would have paired it with her emerald and lavender cloak. It should not be difficult to find amongst the more reserved fashions of black wool and brown furs. But after several minutes pawing through other people's outer garments, she realized the task was going to be a great deal more arduous than expected.

She had reached the back of the first row of stands when she heard the footsteps. It was darker in this part of the room as the only wall sconces lit were near the door, and she stilled, allowing her other senses to take over as she couldn't see quite well.

"Lady Channing."

She nearly bit her tongue.

The voice was sing-songy and sweet, cloying almost in the way it beckoned this poor Lady Channing.

"Lady Channing, where are you?"

Audrey's fingers curled reflexively around the cloak still in her hand.

Oh God. She had unwittingly stepped into the middle of an assignation.

She pivoted, wrapping the cloak in her hand partway around her body as if she could make herself disappear.

"Lady Channing, I do hope we may continue our—"

The last word was lost on her as she turned, still wrapped in the cloak as if she may see the man's approach through the stands.

Continue their what? What had they been doing?

A thrill raced through her body so unexpectedly, she squeaked. She pressed a hand to her mouth, pulling the edge of the cloak up higher by her face as if this may stop the noise from emerging, but it was too late.

"Lady Channing?" The voice was closer now, deeper, and—

Seductive.

She swallowed. This man's obvious game of charm was not meant for her, and she lectured her body to behave. Not in four seasons had it shown any interest in a gentleman, not that there had been many that had expressed interest in her, but now was not the time for it to explore its desires.

She didn't know who this gentleman was, but he was obviously of low character if he were to engage in such activities in the middle of a ball. She had no business having such a reaction to a man, and to only his voice no less. She had more sense than that.

"Lady Channing?"

Heat flared low in her stomach, and she pushed her hand against it. Oh, dear God, what was happening to her? How could a man's voice be so...alluring?

She shook her head, her hair rustling against the cloak she still held wrapped around her, and the noise was amplified in the small, dark space.

It was all a game, she told herself. This man was obviously skilled at the pursuit of women, and she was only falling victim to his—

A gentleman stepped from between the racks of cloaks opposite her, and even in the dim light, she could make out his impressive frame and his wide smile.

"Lady Channing?" He dropped his voice to a near growl now, and she whimpered. He moved instantly in her direction, and she pulled the cloak higher across her face although she couldn't be sure how much of her he could make out in the dark. "Are you playing games with me now, love?"

The words weren't meant for her, but that didn't mean her body didn't betray her and thrill at the sound of them.

He moved so quickly she didn't stand a chance of

dodging out of the way, of telling him he'd made a mistake. He pounced, his arms going around her, pushing aside the cloak as if it were no barrier at all. She let out a sound she thought might have been surprise but as his arms closed around her, it cut off her air, and it sounded far more like a moan.

A sultry moan.

Her eyes went wide as he swept her against his chest—his hard, massive chest—and unwillingly, her hands spread across the flat, muscled planes.

Oh. Dear. God.

She could feel so much of him. Under her palms, along her thighs, against her stomach.

This was what it felt like. To be touched, to be held, to be—

He turned again, and suddenly she was pressed against a wall. His head bent to hers, and she thought he was going to kiss her, but no.

"Lady Channing," he whispered, his lips so terribly close. "Where have you been hiding?"

The words were not meant for her. She tried to tell herself again, but her body wasn't listening. Her heart thundered, and her knees weakened. He lowered his head, and she watched it happen. She couldn't close her eyes against it, because...well, because...

This would be the only time she'd ever be kissed, and it would all be a lie.

The thought had enough power to split her in two, and she thought she would collapse if he weren't holding her up. Her body ached with the realization that the only kiss she'd ever have was because the man thought she was someone else, but she wanted that kiss.

She wanted that kiss more than anything, and the

strength of her conviction surprised her. After four seasons of boredom and fatigue, being trapped in a cloakroom with a stranger bent on kissing her was the most thrilling thing to happen to her, and she *wanted* it.

Her eyes drifted shut just as his lips touched hers, and everything else fell away.

His lips were soft, teasing, and she yearned toward his kiss, but she didn't know what it was she was supposed to do, so she held back, letting him come to her. He brushed his lips against hers, once, twice, and then his arm tightened around her back as the other traced a blazing path up her torso, over the mound of her breast—oh God, her breast!—along the delicate skin of her collar, the column of her neck, until he cupped her face in one hand, tilting her head back as he deepened the kiss.

That was when he hesitated.

She felt it like a blast of cold air from the ocean at Norfolk.

He knew she wasn't Lady Channing.

How could he tell from just a kiss? Was it the feel of her lips? Was she not making the appropriate noises? Was it the shape of her body?

It didn't matter because that was it. That was all she would get. The soft brush of lips and the passing caress of his hand across her breast.

Pain sliced through her, but she didn't move, and neither did he. Seconds passed, but they might as well have been hours. It was as though she could feel him making a decision, could almost hear the thoughts in his head tumbling one over the other.

Her heart ached with anticipation and knowing. He wouldn't choose to continue the kiss. He wouldn't choose her. They never did, and they never would. Despair fell over her even as she stood pressed against the wall, his body enveloped around hers.

His lips still touched hers, hovering over her as if on the edge of a kiss, and it was the most excruciating torment she'd ever endured.

She felt the first burn of unshed tears when his lips descended on hers with a force she hadn't expected. A whimper caught in her throat as his arm tightened at her back, lifting her up and against him. Her hands slid up his chest, wrapped around his neck as if her body knew instinctively to hang on.

The kiss was thorough, ravishing, and brutal.

It was the most glorious thing she'd ever experienced.

And over before she knew it had begun.

He released her, his hands slipping to her shoulders as if to steady her. She didn't open her eyes at first. She couldn't bear to. He was much closer to her now, and she was certain he could make out her features without the cloak obscuring her face, and she didn't want to see the look of recognition on his face.

For surely he would know the wallflower that was Lady Audrey D'Arcy.

Slowly, she let her eyes open, gathering her courage with every breath until she met his gaze.

She had braced herself for the contempt and despair. She had prepared herself for rejection. But she didn't find any of those things in his face.

Instead she found him smiling. No, grinning was more like, with his mouth tipped up on one side, his eyes soft with recent pleasure.

"Do you always meet gentlemen in cloakrooms, or do I have the pleasure of being your first?" he whispered, his eyes passing over her face with a familiarity that sent a shiver down her spine.

"You're the first actually, and I must say I did not intend it." She was surprised at how steady her voice was as she curled her toes in her slippers to steady her watery legs.

She wished this conversation over. She wanted to keep the kiss they shared unblemished by words, and at any moment, she knew he would say something horrid. She had to end this.

She moved to step around him, but he stopped her with a single finger against her cheek. He wasn't wearing gloves, and the callused fingertip sent a tingle along her skin that rendered her useless. Her eyes flashed to his.

"Tell me your name." His voice was as demanding as his statement, and while she wanted to balk at his high-handedness, her senses tingled at his masculine authority.

What on earth was wrong with her? What sort of spell had he cast over her?

She swallowed. "Why must you know my name?"

His smile turned almost devilish. "Because I wish to know what name to whisper when I make love to you."

He knew it was a touch too far, but he wanted to see her reaction play across her glorious face.

He couldn't make out many details in the dimness of the cloakroom, but her eyes—God, her eyes were so wide and expressive. He could get lost in them.

The thought seemed silly. How many women had he encountered in situations just like this? A stolen kiss in a garden? An embrace in the shadows of a terrace?

It was never anything more than that unless the lady were willing and a widow or resolutely unhappy wife, and then it had only been a handful of times in the past ten years. Because for him, it wasn't about that, the end result. It was about the chase.

And this mystery woman who had responded so passionately to his clandestine kiss in a dark cloakroom was proving to be a delectable opponent.

"I should think such an occasion unthinkable."

She had a cute nose. It was small and pert, and when she was particularly indignant as she was now, the end of it twitched up in irritation.

"Pity." He kept his voice low, both out of necessity to avoid discovery but also because he found such a relaxed tone irked her.

Her gorgeous mouth flattened into an agitated line until she said, "I hardly think so. You may find other women who enjoy such assignations, but you will find I am not one of them."

He raised an eyebrow at this. "I have a distinct memory of a kiss that would suggest otherwise."

Her lips parted—did she have an overbite? He couldn't be sure in the dark—and a small sound of disbelief escaped.

"You have no such thing. I was accosted and left with no choice in my actions."

He crossed his arms over his chest, enjoying this banter far too much. When was the last time he'd bantered with a woman? There were kisses and fondling for sure, but banter? Never.

"One is always left with a choice of one's actions. You could have simply asked me to stop. I would have, you know."

She blinked, the movement exaggerated in the dimness.

"How could I have asked you to stop when I wasn't aware what you were going to do?"

He looked about them. "We're alone in a cloakroom at a ball. Even for a debutante I would think you would know what happens in such places."

"I'm not a debutante."

The words were fast and firm, and he understood far more about her from that single sentence than anything else that had occurred in the last ten minutes.

He took a small step toward her. "You're not?"

She took a small step back, but the wall was still behind her, impeding her movements.

"I am not. I am—" She stopped, those larger front teeth worrying her lower one with unwitting appeal.

He smiled. "Ah, you almost gave yourself away there, didn't you?"

She shifted, and he could almost imagine her driving her feet into the floor in frustration, although he couldn't see to be sure.

"I am well past the age of being considered a debutante, my..." she left off, her eyes wide and her chin up as if waiting for a response.

He couldn't help but grin. "Lord," he supplied and said nothing else.

She eyed him, her head turning slightly as if she were studying and assessing. He wondered what she saw.

He was careful when he played these games, and the facade he assumed had been perfected over the years. The object was to win the lady's affection, not find amusement for himself. Sometimes even now he forgot he was an earl that never should have been.

To her, this mystery woman in a cloakroom, he would

appear the privileged rogue and nothing more. He preferred it that way.

"You would not do me the dignity of telling me who it is that accosted me?"

He laughed softly. "Accosted? I am afraid we shall not agree on this point, my lady." He took another step closer and now she was backed up against the wall. He leaned in, dipping his head until it was dangerously close to her ear, so close in fact he heard her draw a quick startled breath. "I'll never be able to forget how you felt in my arms," he whispered. "I've never held someone so...responsive." He dared to dart out his tongue and lick the soft lobe of her ear.

She shoved him, hard, as he'd expected her to, but what he didn't expect was that she kept hold of him. Her hands were tangled in the lapels of his dinner jacket as she held him at arm's length, her face open and hard as she stared at him. It was almost as though she were considering something.

"Responsive?" she finally asked, her voice soft and almost timid, entirely unlike how she had spoken in the few minutes of their acquaintance.

He nodded. "Yes, quite."

She tilted her head. "Your tone would suggest responsive is a good quality."

He studied her, wishing suddenly to know the color of her eyes at the same time her words sent a tingle of anticipation through him.

He swallowed. "Yes, responsive is very good."

What was she playing at? The missish debutantes the season usually presented were timid and anxious. But hadn't she just said she wasn't a debutante?

She let go of him, dropping her gaze to the floor as if she had come to a conclusion.

"I suppose you say that about all the women you meet in dark corners." When she raised her gaze, he found her eyes bright and focused. "Someone like you would know exactly what to say to get what you want."

He didn't know why, but he was feeling affronted now. "Someone like me?"

She gestured weakly. "You know. A rogue, a rake, a..." Those teeth worried her lower lip again, and his stomach clenched in response. "That's not it." She set a fisted hand to her chin as if she were set on contemplating just exactly what it was she meant to call him. "A rogue or a rake would have seduced me by now, but you've demonstrated remarkable restraint. You seem rather more delighted by wordplay." She dropped her hand and met his gaze. "Are you a serial charmer, my lord?"

He laughed, the sound louder now as he couldn't have stopped it. "You make it sound like an accusation."

"It is." She shook her head. "I can't imagine one aspiring to be a charmer. Your words would always be false, and no one could ever trust your meaning."

He sobered. "I beg your pardon."

"A charmer by definition would be skilled at affecting the desired outcome through flattery and platitudes. Both of which I am not susceptible to, I should add." She paused as if to assure he'd heard her. "But how could a person then trust you if all you say is deliberately manufactured?"

"You're a wallflower." The words escaped his lips before he knew he was going to speak, but suddenly all of the clues slipped into place at once.

He was conducting a clandestine interlude with a wallflower.

Her face closed. He watched it happen, and even in the dark, he could make out the change in her features.

"Excuse me," she uttered and made to move around him, but for some strange reason, he stopped her, putting his hands to her shoulders.

"Please. Wait."

She didn't resist his touch. Instead, she sent him a glare that spoke volumes of her displeasure.

He didn't know what to say though. He'd never met someone like her. Someone who gave more than the usual quips young ladies were schooled in. It was a relief to talk of something more substantial than the weather and spaniels, and he suddenly wanted her to stay.

No, it was more than that.

He wanted to get to know her better.

The thought had everything inside of him coming to a standstill. He had spent years perfecting his game. He had won over any number of reluctant debutantes, charmed widows, and lonely wives. But none of those conquests mattered now.

For some reason, he thought he had hurt this mysterious woman's feelings, and it saddened him.

"I don't mean to suggest being a wallflower makes you in any way—"

"Deficient?" Her eyes lit up at the word. "Because I hate to remind you that that is exactly what society is suggesting when they created the label."

"But you yourself just gave me a label."

"Yes, one that is regarded with inexplicable respect. If I exhibited the same talent you're revered for, I would be called something far more unsavory." She tilted her head, those beautiful eyes wide and her smile one-sided. "Funny how that works, isn't it?"

She was right, and he hated it. She pushed against his hands as she made to move around him.

"It doesn't mean I would view it as such," he said quickly, and she stilled.

"Well, that makes one of you in the scope of about fifteen thousand others. Pardon me if I don't applaud."

He let go of her then, his arms dropping uselessly at his sides. "You're funny," he said, his voice softer than he had thought it would be.

She watched him, her eyes guarded. "I can't ever tell when you're being serious and when you're simply being charming. You're rather vexing, my lord."

He'd been called a great many things in his life but never that.

"I beg your pardon, my lady." He held up both hands. "I mean that seriously."

She blinked, but he could still see the doubt in her eyes.

"How about this?" He scraped a step backward to give himself room and bowed properly before her. "Dashiell Evers, the Earl of Amberley. It is most definitely my pleasure, Lady..." He raised only his eyes to her expectantly.

She chewed her lower lip for several seconds and finally shook her head. She crossed her arms below her bosom before saying, "No, I don't think I shall give you my name. I don't think you can be trusted with it."

He straightened. "Trusted with it?"

She nodded at the room around him. "For you, this is another conquest in what I'm beginning to understand is a long line of them. For me, this is the utter ruination of my reputation. Another stark inequality in this game we're playing, my lord. I don't like such odds."

Her chin went up at her last words, and he understood just how much pride and courage she contained.

"I would never ruin you."

Her smile was forced. "You already have."

Her words cut with alarming truth, and suddenly he realized just how different it was for him and the women he charmed. She was right, this mystery woman. While he was given the buoyancy of triumph, the lady was left with the vulnerability of complete destruction with only a single word uttered by him. He had never really understood that before now. To him, it had just been a game, a harmless one. He never ruined any of the debutantes he pursued. He gave them only pleasure and a respite from the unending balls, dinners, and socials.

Now he saw it differently.

He took a step back, affording this woman more room in a sign of goodwill.

"You're right. I do beg your pardon, my lady. I didn't truly understand what this may mean for a debutante. I thank you for pointing out the truth of the matter."

She shook her head. "There you go again. I have no idea if you're being honest or not. It is infuriating to speak with you." She never raised her tone, yet he felt properly scolded.

"I swear I am in earnest. I only ask that you allow me to make it up to you."

Her eyes narrowed. "How do you propose to do that?"

"I should like to court you. Properly." He had felt it building inside of him, this need for more of her, and had it been only minutes earlier, he would have set about charming her, but he knew now that wouldn't work. She was too smart to play the game, and he would need to resort to honest methods if he were to have more of her.

For he wanted more of her. He wanted all of her. Her passion, her wit, her intelligence. She was like a storm, powerful and sweeping, leaving behind a sense of freshness and possibility. He wanted more of it, and he would use any means he must. Including proper ones.

She blinked, her lips parting in disbelief. After several seconds, she spoke, and the tone of her voice cut him with its despair. "You mustn't be cruel."

This time when she pushed past him, he let her go. He didn't need to chase after her because he knew something else with absolute certainty.

Wallflowers tended to grow at the edges of ballrooms.

2

She returned to Grandmother Regina after an unforgivable amount of time had passed and without the wished-for handkerchief.

"I'm terribly sorry, Grandmother," she said as she took a seat next to the old woman's chair. "The maid overseeing the cloakroom seems to have wandered off, and despite my efforts at locating your cloak, I must admit I was not up to the task. The room was practically filled with cloaks and wraps, and I couldn't find yours for all the Crown Jewels."

Grandmother Regina's smile was accompanied by the soft twinkle and absent eyes that had become her characteristic expression after she'd suffered the apoplexy several years earlier. Now she simply patted Audrey's hand.

"It's all right, darling. We'll find the Bible some other time. I'm sure Eugene has simply misplaced it."

Audrey slid her glance to Aunt Verity who sat beside Grandmother Regina, but her aunt shrugged softly and leaned forward to touch her mother's shoulder.

"Mum, do you see the colors that are fashionable this year? I do love that peach."

Grandmother Regina's eyes came back into focus as she surveyed the ballroom before them, her smile more genuine as she took in the swirling colors in front of her.

"Oh, I do love when the girls wear a little more color. You would look so very nice in that peach, Verity." Her grandmother's voice was stronger, more certain, and it was as if she'd never slipped and mentioned her dead husband.

Grandfather Eugene had passed away nearly a decade previously. Audrey mostly remembered his laugh, his scent of mint and tobacco, and the way he would look at Grandmother Regina when he thought no one was watching.

Even at such a tender age, Audrey had known what that look meant.

Love.

Something powerful swept through her at the memory, and she now, too, looked out at the dancing couples to distract herself.

What she had just encountered in the cloakroom was far from love, but it was also the closest she would ever come to it. Unconsciously, she raised her gloved hand to hover above her lips as if she could feel Amberley's kiss.

She dropped her hand to her lap. There was no point in dwelling on it. It was not as though it would ever happen again.

Once more she slid her gaze to Aunt Verity as her head bent close to Grandmother Regina's while they chatted about the season's fashion. Audrey felt a swell of envy at Aunt Verity's relaxed features. Soon, Audrey promised herself. Soon she, too, would be a spinster and freedom would be hers.

No more balls to attend. No more fake smiles to master. No more pretending to feel nothing when matrons asked her, yet again, why she was not wed.

Freedom.

If it were a food, it would be a Madeira cake, and she would eat the whole thing in one sitting with a fork and an entire pot of tea.

This thought as usual brought immense satisfaction, and she turned her attention back to the ball, pleased with herself.

This, however, lasted mere seconds when she remembered how his hands had felt pressing her body against his. He was so *firm*. Solid and comforting while at the same time hot and dangerous.

She hadn't realized she had shaken her head until Aunt Verity asked, "Audrey, are you well?"

She flashed her aunt a smile. "Perfectly fine. It was just a little warm in that cloakroom. Perhaps I shall fetch us some lemonade."

She stood before either could respond and turned in the direction of the refreshment table only to stop dead in her tracks.

The first thing she registered was his smile. In the dark, she had seen the white of his teeth, and now, under the warm glow of a thousand candles, she saw the rest of it as he stood mere feet in front of her.

She opened her mouth, ready to reject his overture. They were not properly introduced, and if he spoke to her now, there would be questions. Her heart raced, the blood pumping wildly through her veins.

People would know.

They would know something had happened because he would dare speak to her in public without a proper introduction, and somehow, they would find out. Find out what had happened. What she had done.

But then—no overture came.

He merely smiled at her from where he stood, and it was then she became aware of their hostess, Lady Chamberlain, stepping neatly between them to curtsy before Grandmother Regina.

"Regina, my love, I'm so glad you've come this evening." The woman held a champagne glass absently in one hand as she smiled serenely. "I truly wasn't expecting such a turnout. After all, Margaret is having Sawyer's coming out tonight. I would have thought more people would have attended that."

Lady Chamberlain was closer in age to Grandmother Regina than she was to any of the rest of those in their small circle, but she had taken care of herself, and one would swear she was no more than forty. Audrey involuntarily touched the skin of her neck, her eyes unmoving from Lady Chamberlain's unlined flesh.

"Of course I came, darling," Grandmother Regina said. "I wouldn't miss it."

Lady Chamberlain's smile was small, and Audrey realized the habit had probably saved the woman wrinkles over the years.

"If you would allow me," she turned her arm extending to Amberley, and Audrey feared she might actually swallow her tongue. "Have you had the pleasure of meeting Dashiell Evers, the Earl of Amberley?"

Grandmother Regina's smile was quick. "Oh, you must be little Matthew's son. I'm so very sorry about your father."

Audrey's eyes flashed to Amberley's face. The man she had encountered in the cloakroom had seemed incapable of suffering hardship, and now she saw his face did not change at her grandmother's pronouncement.

"Thank you for your kindness, Lady Hodge." He gave a small bow. "It's a pleasure to make your acquaintance."

"So terrible," Grandmother Regina went on with a small shake of her head. "And especially after what happened to David." Another small shake, only this time it was accompanied by a sound of remorse and sadness.

Audrey hadn't been able to take her eyes from Amberley's face even though she knew she should, and now, finally, she saw a reaction. It was small and had she not been fixated on him it would have gone unnoticed. But his eyes narrowed as if he were stopping a flinch. She couldn't stop her own curious tilt of her head.

Lady Chamberlain pressed a hand to Grandmother Regina's shoulder, her gaze already moving on through the crowd. "Do excuse me, Regina. My guests need me."

Grandmother Regina raised a shaking hand as the woman wandered off before gesturing beside her. "This is my granddaughter, Audrey, Lady D'Arcy. She must be about your age, I should think."

Amberley's face changed again, his gaze sliding over her with predatory satisfaction. She straightened her shoulders in response, swallowing nervously as her stomach fluttered with heated memory.

Lud, what was wrong with her? Her body had turned into a confused mixture of stormy emotions.

"Lady D'Arcy," he said with a bow—was there a smugness to his tone now or did she imagine it?—but even though he bent forward, his eyes never left hers, boring into them until she felt the heat rise inside of her again.

She swallowed and curtsied on suddenly unsteady legs. "My lord."

"And this must be your sister." He turned that enigmatic gaze on Aunt Verity so quickly it snuffed out the small flame that had begun to smolder inside of her at the intensity of his stare.

Grandmother Regina laughed. "Oh, dear boy, no. This is my daughter, Verity."

Grandmother Regina's smile was now filled with pride. People often mistook Verity for one of the Hodge family cousins. She was after all a great deal younger than Audrey's mother and Uncle Reginald.

Amberley's eyes widened. "You don't say. Well, I do beg your pardon, Lady Hodge."

Aunt Verity curtsied. "It's no matter," she said with a polite smile.

Grandmother Regina leaned forward conspiratorially. "Do you want to know something, boy?" she asked, her gaze sliding between Aunt Verity and Amberley. "She's named Verity because she's the proof of the love Eugene and I shared."

Aunt Verity shot out a hand to close around Grandmother Regina's shoulder, but there was no stopping the woman. This was her favorite story.

"I was thirty-nine when Verity was born." Grandmother Regina gyrated her eyebrows, and Audrey closed her eyes and turned her head away. She only wished she could do the same with her ears. "We still had it even then, and Verity is proof of it!" Grandmother Regina clapped her hands together in triumph.

Audrey opened one eye a slit to see if Amberley had run from the ballroom, but what she saw had her opening both eyes.

Amberley had gone down on one knee before Grandmother Regina so he could look her in the eye as she told her story, and his face was alight with mirth.

"If only everyone were so lucky, Lady Hodge," he said with as much triumph as Grandmother Regina.

Audrey looked to Aunt Verity who held the same

stricken expression on her face as Audrey thought she sported. Aunt Verity had been the victim of Grandmother Regina's retelling of this story many times over, and Audrey didn't know how the woman survived it. But even through the disbelief on her face, Audrey saw her struggling to hide a smile.

"Well, you know, young man, you could be just as fortunate. I have two beautiful women by my side at this moment. One of them could be yours."

Audrey's face heated with her hidden shame, but in her mind, she felt the echo of Amberley's kiss, the pull of his hands, the hardness of his body, and she didn't feel shame at all.

She felt power.

Exhilarating, life-altering power.

It was what she had wanted for so long, and yet she hadn't realized it for what it was even when it had reached out and grabbed her. Quite literally. But now she knew, and her skin tingled in anticipation, wanting more of it.

She sucked in a breath. This was not a part of the plan. She was still confined by the rules of society, and until she was safely on the shelf, she couldn't tempt fate.

The irony of her thoughts should have been amusing, but they only made her sad. She wished for the relative freedom the mantle of spinster would give her, and yet she wanted the same things now, but because she was still "out" they were forbidden to her.

She squared her shoulders.

She need only wait. That was it. Time mattered little when most of it was spent at the periphery of ballrooms.

Amberley stood. "That's actually why I'm here, Lady Hodge. I should very much like to ask your granddaughter to partner me in a dance."

Audrey didn't know how her face didn't just burst into flames.

Her gaze riveted to Amberley's smile, his friendly smile, and wide, trusting eyes. Grandmother Regina—no, any woman—was likely to eat it up.

"Oh, that would be wonderful. I don't know why the gentlemen don't ask Audrey to dance more often." She leaned forward again as she had when she told Amberley the origin of Aunt Verity's name. "She's got quite a wit, that one." She straightened. "If only the gentlemen knew."

Amberley's gaze moved slowly to her, his smile kicking up on one side in a grin. "I assure you, Lady Hodge. I have some suspicions about this acclaimed wit."

Grandmother Regina laughed as Audrey's heart pounded furiously now.

"Oh, I'm so very glad. It's about time someone knew." She made a shooing motion with her hands as the orchestra struck up the first notes of the next dance.

Audrey swallowed, and her hands curled at her sides. It was a waltz.

"Go now, children. You mustn't waste the evening."

Now when Audrey caught Amberley's gaze the playfulness had dissipated, replaced by a hunger she knew only too well. She had meant to take a step forward, place her arm on his, but she was stopped by the naked emotion she saw in his eyes.

He'd come after her. He'd found her. And he'd made a proper introduction by bringing their hostess with him.

No one had ever gone to such effort for her.

It was all so...new.

The word sent a ripple of excitement through her, and she stepped forward, allowing the Earl of Amberley to lead her onto the dance floor.

He hadn't expected her to come along so easily.

He worried, not for the first time, that perhaps he had developed his skill at charm too well. Was it possible to be too charming? Echoes of his past pierced him like an accidental prick of a pin against one's skin. Not enough to draw blood but certainly enough to make one twitch.

"Your grandmother is delightful," he said as soon as they had taken their spots amongst the other dancers.

It was to be a waltz then. How opportunistic.

He found the waltz to be most conducive in his attempts at seduction, but when he took in Lady D'Arcy's face under the soft light of the chandeliers, he no longer felt so triumphant. Honestly he felt rather tired.

Another ball. Another eligible young woman. Another potential conquest.

But even as the litany of thoughts passed through his mind, it didn't sit quite right with him.

It wasn't like that.

Not with Lady D'Arcy.

Something was different. Something was just a little bit...dangerous. What a ridiculous word, but somehow, he felt it suited the situation. He sensed Lady D'Arcy was going to be trouble for him, and he yearned toward the sensation.

He swallowed, stepping forward to place his hand along her back, open his opposite hand to receive hers.

And then it happened.

That zing of sensation he had experienced earlier in the cloakroom. It was acute and visceral and unlike anything he had felt before. When he charmed a young lady, it was all about calculations and expected human response. It was never about...feelings.

But he had feelings when he touched Lady D'Arcy, complicated ones, and they scared the hell out of him at the same time he wanted more.

He watched her, his suspicions growing as she slid her hand into his, her chin tilting casually as if to say it were every day she danced with the earl with whom she had just had a clandestine encounter in a dark cloakroom.

"Grandmother Regina is rather a delight, isn't she?" Her tone was as casual as her mien, and his growing pleasure surged at the obvious gambit she laid before him.

"And your aunt, Lady Hodge, is she forced to endure that tantalizing retelling of the origin of her name on a regular basis?"

Lady D'Arcy's smile was as pleasant as if they were discussing the opera. "She must endure it a great deal. She's cared for Grandmother Regina since the apoplexy three years ago."

"I'm very sorry to hear that about your grandmother."

Lady D'Arcy shook her head as they swung into the first turn of the waltz.

"Thank you, but as you can see, Grandmother Regina has fared rather well. She forgets things from time to time, and she has some difficulty walking. Her right leg tends to drag. But it does nothing to dampen her spirit."

She never moved her eyes from his even as her feet traced the steps of the dance. She was competent and confident, and his heart squeezed at the notion.

What was he doing? What was he doing here with her? She was a wallflower. He prided himself on never dallying with wallflowers. It just wasn't fair. A woman so desperate for attention would fall for anything, and it simply wasn't fair game.

Except...

He had kissed this one. He knew her taste now, and the feel of her in his arms, and it was—

Well, he didn't know what it was. Perhaps that was why he had followed her back to the ballroom, why he had so rashly proposed courting. She hadn't given him enough time to decide how he felt about her.

"I am glad to hear of that then." He opened his mouth, ready to launch into his usual witty banter that had successfully entranced many a young debutante, but she cut him off.

"Why did you follow me?"

He closed his mouth.

She gestured around the room with her head. "All of the eligible young ladies here tonight and that—what was the name you said? Lady Channing, was it?" She blinked as if giving him a pause in which to confirm her statement, but he found he was unable to speak. "Why did you follow me of all people? Surely there are more interesting prospects here for you tonight?"

"Prospects?" He didn't like the sound of that word.

She shrugged softly. "I didn't mean any offense by it."

"That's what people say when they make offense."

Her smile lifted into a grin, and he realized she found this humorous. His heart thumped as his emotions swirled into a greater mess.

"I truly didn't. You may come to learn that I'm hardly one to judge. I have my own ideas about my future that do not exactly align with the expectations of society."

There was much in that sentence that caught his attention, but the one he found most appealing prompted the question, "Will I be seeing you enough then to draw such a conclusion?"

Her grin faltered. "God, I hope not. It's exhausting having to keep my guard up around you."

Now it was his turn to grin. "Is that what you're doing? Guarding yourself against me?"

Her eyes narrowed. "I've heard of your reputation, my lord."

"Please. This is hardly the time for such formality. Dash will be fine."

One eyebrow shot up. "Dash?"

He nodded, spinning her about the floor. "Dash. It's short for Dashiell. I'm sure you've heard of it."

"I have heard of it, but I cannot be expected to call you such."

"Why not? It's my name. Would you call me something other than my name?"

"I would call you Lord Amberley, I should think."

He shook his head. "How terribly boring."

Something shifted in her eyes then, and he thought he might have struck a sore spot. But what could it have been?

"Whatever it is that I shall call you, I do hope I shan't have the opportunity to employ it often. Can I assume you will not be pursuing me after this dance?"

"Why would you assume that?"

Her eyes drifted to the edge the dance floor.

"Because I am a wallflower. I had heard the charms of the Earl of the Amberley were reserved for ladies of a more refined nature."

"I find these ladies you speak of have grown rather tiresome. I think it's time I should seek something...more daring."

Her eyes widened ever so slightly, but a light flashed in them that he latched on to.

Lady D'Arcy wanted something. He wasn't sure what it

was, but her face moved with the emotions she tried to hide from him.

"More daring?" She swallowed as she spoke, and her upper lip danced over her slight overbite.

"Do you know your face is the epitome of captivating?"

She faltered in her step, and only his arms tightening about her kept her from falling completely. Her eyes were even wider now, her lips parted.

He shook his head slowly, taking his time to find the right words. He was an expert at words. He could find exactly the right ones any young woman wished to hear, but it had never mattered before which ones he chose. But now it did. It mattered to *him* and not the woman to whom he spoke. It mattered that he get it right. That he convey to her the torment of emotion her very face caused within him.

"It is," he breathed as the rest of the ballroom dropped away, as his focus narrowed to just her face. "Every ounce of emotion is captured in those wide eyes and that generous smile. I can't look away for fear I might miss something beautiful."

She watched him, her eyes guarded, for two more steps of the dance, and then without warning, she pried herself from his arms, stumbling into the pair of dancers beside them. This set in motion a disturbance that rippled through the rest of the dancers, but Lady D'Arcy had already picked up her skirts and disappeared into the crowd around the edge of the dance floor.

He watched her go even as he stepped out of the way of the remaining dancers as they resumed their steps.

He wasn't sure how long he stood there, studying the place where she had disappeared while he tried to understand the tumult of feelings that had tumbled through him in the past hour since he had encountered her in the cloakroom.

This woman.

This *wallflower*.

She was right. Lord Amberley did not spend his time on wallflowers, and yet he hadn't had enough of her. His mind was already scrambling to find a way to see her again.

"Your conquest not go as planned?" This bald question was followed by a rankled laugh as Dash turned to see who had spoken.

He straightened his shoulders. "Lord Breedlove. What a pleasure. I haven't seen you since Spader's fox hunt. Was that nearly a year ago now?"

Breedlove's lips spread, revealing yellowed teeth, likely from his overpowering cigar habit.

"It must have been." He gestured with his champagne glass in the direction Lady D'Arcy had fled. "Wallflowers aren't your usual type, are they, old chum?"

Dash's skin crawled at Breedlove's suggestion of friendship. They had been at school together and nothing more, but Dash found himself oddly protective of Lady D'Arcy, even when this wastrel should merely mention her.

"Tell me, Breedlove, is your mother here? Did she give you a list of suitable brides? I'm sure it's nearly imperative that you secure a rich heiress by now, isn't it?"

Breedlove's father's gambling habits were notorious, and the betting books of the clubs all contained wagers of when the old duke would require his son to marry.

Now Breedlove's champagne glass lowered as his eyes narrowed. "I don't believe that's any concern of yours."

"And neither is my social proclivities any concern of yours." He made to step away, but he was too late. Breedlove spoke again, and this time, no amount of fortitude could stop the lightning bolt of emotion that seared through him.

"Just like your betrothal was no concern?" The man paused long enough for Dash to turn and meet his gaze. "Tell me. Does the wallflower know of your broken betrothal? I only ask because she seems too young to have been out in society when it occurred. Poor girl. It is only fair that she know, don't you think?"

"The wallflower's name is Lady D'Arcy, and you will do well to remember it." He made his tone flat, and Breedlove's mouth tightened at the obvious warning.

"Lady D'Arcy. Please tell me you're not thinking of offering for her hand as well?" Breedlove made a tsking noise as he shook his head. "Lord Amberley, you do have a terrible habit of falling in love with women who do not wish to marry you. Judging by what I just witnessed, I'm afraid you're headed for the same disaster."

He should have walked away. He shouldn't have allowed this wanker's barbs to stick in his skin, but Breedlove knew only too well where to press.

"You know one should never assume such things. It exhibits the baser qualities of a person."

Breedlove's lips became a flat slash across his square face. "You speak of the quality of a person? Are you really in a position to judge? You're not David after all."

His heart stopped for an instant in his chest. He could feel it. One moment it was beating, and the next it wasn't. It hung there like a boulder; his body struggling to keep him upright. But then the next beat happened, and it was as if nothing were amiss.

He stepped closer to Breedlove and lowered his voice. "What is it you really want?"

Breedlove's lips tipped up in a malicious grin. "I wager

you won't make it to the altar with this one just as you didn't make it with the last."

"There's no need for such a wager," Dash said with a small shake of his head.

"No need? Are you so certain of the outcome then?" Breedlove's eyes flashed with greed, both for the winnings of a wager and any opportunity to pummel Dash into the mud.

"There's no need because I wouldn't disrespect a lady by betting on her freedom of choice."

Breedlove's laugh was startling and harsh. "Oh, Amberley, it really is a pity."

He should have left. He shouldn't have spoken another word, but the guilt he had carried around with him for the whole of his life scratched mercilessly at him until he said what he shouldn't have.

"What is a pity?"

Breedlove's lips twitched into a sneer. "It's a pity your brother died, and your parents were forced to have you." His eyes traveled up and down the length of him as if assessing the specimen. "It's obvious the goods are not an adequate replacement."

It was only by the thinnest of margins that Dash kept control of his emotions. As it was, he leaned forward, his jaw cracking with restraint.

"I will marry Lady D'Arcy. Mark my word. And then, when I have the right as her husband, I will call you out." He turned on his heel and disappeared into the crowd.

3

"Did you hear a choir singing?"

Audrey looked askance at her cousin. "Did I what?"

Caroline shrugged. "I always thought my first kiss would be accompanied by the sound of a choir singing in angelic tones."

"Surely not."

Caroline studied the rest of the party assembled in Grandmother Regina's drawing room. "It's the one flight of fancy I allow myself. After all, what can it hurt? If there is a choir, then I should be pleasantly surprised. If there isn't one, it shouldn't be anything less than I would expect."

Audrey had confided in her cousin about her encounter with Lord Amberley in the cloakroom because, well, Audrey simply had no one else with whom she could share the experience, and she very much wished to share it with someone. After all, it had been her first kiss. It had been her first anything, and she was still so unsettled by it. She wished she could name a feeling for it, but she couldn't. She was just...suspended somewhere between what she had been before and what she was now, but she didn't know what she was now.

Caroline was beautiful with the perfect heart-shaped face and delicate features and golden hair that society lauded, and yet she was an utter and complete pessimist. Audrey had hoped her cousin's negative slant would help ground her in her feelings about the encounter with Lord Amberley, but she found herself further perplexed instead.

"You're saying you've even set disastrously low expectations for your first kiss?"

Caroline turned her intense gaze on Audrey then. "Of course. One must be prepared for such things. You wouldn't wish to be caught off guard in such a critical moment."

Audrey blinked. "That's precisely what happened. I was caught off guard. I didn't expect to be accosted in the dark by a marauding Romeo."

Caroline's eyes narrowed in study. "Was he a Romeo though? He sounds like nothing more than a common rake."

"Who's a rake?"

They turned at the sound of Philip's voice and found him shifting from a conversation with Audrey's brothers to hovering protectively over his sister at the sound of such a potentially dangerous word.

"Oh, not someone of my acquaintance," Caroline assured him. "It's a fellow Audrey met."

"What?"

Audrey flinched at the near roar of her eldest brother's voice as he forced his way into their small group.

"Sorry," Caroline muttered.

Audrey smiled and tilted her head, a tactic she often employed to calm her brother's nerves.

"It's nothing, Ethan. I promise. It was just a dance at

Lady Chamberlain's ball. It was days ago now anyway, and I haven't heard from the gentleman in question. Nothing more than normal social doings." She slid her gaze a couple of inches to the left to take in her other brother who hovered just over Ethan's shoulder.

Gavin had been born three minutes after Ethan, and one could always find him standing just behind his brother. That was how Audrey had thought of them when they left for the continent nearly five years previously. It was the only way she could bear it when she thought of them fighting against Napoleon. Somehow, she knew Ethan would be all right because Gavin would always be right behind him.

Now though, she wished neither of her brothers were so close.

She hoped her paltry explanation was enough. Ethan didn't engage much in social endeavors since his return, and she hoped his unfamiliarity with the subject would prevent further questioning.

"Does this fellow have a name?"

Audrey and Caroline pressed similar annoyed glances in Philip's direction.

"He was an earl of some name," Audrey muttered before taking a sip of her lemonade to forestall further explanation.

"An earl?" Ethan growled. "Which earl?"

There was no use for it. She might as well get this over with. She lowered her glass and looked directly at Ethan.

"The Earl of Amberley."

"Hell's teeth," Ethan spat, scraping his booted foot along the carpet like an enraged bull. "What in God's name were you doing accepting Amberley as a partner?"

Audrey gestured across the room to Grandmother Regina. "Grandmother insisted. How was I to refuse?"

Ethan's focus shifted only momentarily to his grandmother seated across the room before it came blazing back to Audrey's face.

"You will not dance with him again. The man is a confirmed rogue."

"Mmmm."

The noise was small. So small, in fact, that the lot of them looked around as if someone might have accidentally trod on a mouse.

It was Gavin who spoke from behind them.

"Do you have an opinion on the matter?"

They turned their attention to the woman standing at the periphery of their group. She was rather tall and willowy, her soft brown hair gathered plainly at the nape of her neck in a simple chignon, and she wore a gown of nondescript gray or lavender. It was hard to tell in the soft light.

She seemed startled to find Gavin speaking to her as her eyes widened and flittered away from the group as if she had not been eavesdropping.

"I do beg your pardon. It's only that...well, from what I've heard that is...it's just—"

"Spit it out, woman."

Audrey put a hand on Ethan's arm that he regaled with a ferocious glare, but he subsided under her touch.

The woman grew more nervous, wringing her hands together and blinking furiously. Audrey knew most of her grandmother's acquaintances as this dinner was to be mostly a family affair, so she was surprised to find someone with whom she was not more familiar standing in her grandmother's drawing room.

"It's only the application of the word rogue is ill-used. Lord Amberley is not a rogue."

Audrey could see Ethan grinding his teeth from the twitch in his cheek, but Gavin did all he could to hide a smile.

"Is that so?" Gavin asked, obviously struggling to contain said smile.

"Yes." The woman nodded, seeming to grow taller as she regained her confidence. "The word rogue would suggest he's a ruiner of young, unattached females when in fact, he does nothing of the sort. He is, if anything, the most proper of gentleman."

Audrey grew concerned that Ethan's jaw may snap clean off, and she squeezed his arm.

"What do you mean?" he ground out.

The woman met his gaze directly, and Audrey found a growing appreciation for her forthrightness.

"Lord Amberley is a charmer. Not a seducer. Everything he does is most proper and free of scandal. It's merely that he can lure a woman into his presence with the simple use of his charm."

"Charm?" Ethan spoke the word as if he were discovering a new way of speaking of horse manure.

The woman nodded. "Yes, charm. It's all rather harmless. It only serves to make a woman feel..." Her voice suddenly trailed off and two spots of color sprang to her cheeks.

Audrey keened forward, feeling somehow that the poor woman had tripped upon some uncomfortable personal experience.

"It can make a woman feel cherished," Audrey supplied before the woman could step farther into her accidental embarrassment.

The woman shifted her gaze, meeting Audrey's eyes with a kind, knowing smile. "That's it precisely."

"I don't want you to feel cherished," Ethan growled.

Audrey turned a frown on him. "Thank you, dear brother. I shall keep that in mind."

Gavin swallowed and shook his head behind his brother, sharing a glance with Audrey before turning to the woman.

"You will pardon the impropriety, but I should think at this point introductions are in order," Gavin said softly and kindly even though the woman had not balked in the least at Ethan's grumpiness.

The woman started, her hands wringing once more at her waist. "I'm terribly sorry. I'm Miss Pippa Holloway." She gestured behind her, but as they could not see anything from their small, clustered group, the gesture meant little until Miss Holloway turned back and realized she was blocking their view. She stepped several inches to the left. "I'm Lady Spader's new companion."

Now they were able to take in the diminutive woman seated behind Miss Holloway.

The group as one drew an understanding breath. Lady Spader had been friends with Grandmother Regina since before America was its own country.

"Lady Spader, how nice to see you," Caroline intoned for the group.

"What's that, girl?" Lady Spader held up a hand to her ear.

The assembled group merely waved in the woman's direction, and she waved back, an absent smile on her lips before she returned to plucking the dates out of the biscuits she held on a china plate in one hand.

They turned their collective gaze back to Miss Holloway.

"Are you acquainted with Lord Amberley's abilities then?" Ethan asked, and Audrey surged forward at the impertinent question, but Caroline seized on it first.

"Do I hear the dinner gong?" she cried with a strange twist to her voice.

"I think Grandmother Regina mentioned we are to have pheasant this evening. How delightful," Audrey spoke over Caroline until Ethan was properly distracted.

Gavin, however, was not, and he kept a steady soft gaze on Miss Holloway. Audrey noted it at the same time she tugged on Ethan's arm to leave the poor companion alone.

"I don't hear a dinner gong. Surely you must be—" But Philip never got to finish his sentence because Caroline let out a noise then that was close to the most inhuman noise Audrey had ever heard, which could only mean one thing.

She turned her gaze to the door, a smile tripping at the corners of her lips as she attempted to hold back a laugh. She was not the only one overcome with mirth, and she averted her gaze to find Gavin and even stoic Ethan holding back their laughter.

"Stonegate," Caroline seethed.

Hawkins Savage, the Earl of Stonegate sauntered up to the group.

"Philip, old boy. It's been an age."

Audrey watched Caroline, waiting for the woman to erupt like a boiling teakettle.

It happened when Hawk turned his gaze, and his smoldering smile, on her.

"Hello, pet," he said.

Caroline's only response was a sound somewhere between a growl and a moan. She grabbed her skirts in tight handfuls. "What are you doing here?"

Hawk had the audacity to look offended. "Doing here? Why you know more than anyone how much Grandmother Regina loves me."

"Don't call her that." Caroline stabbed a finger in Hawk's chest. "You don't *get* to call her that."

Hawk's offended expression deepened, and he placed an innocent hand against the same chest Caroline was still attempting to stab through with her finger. "But she asked me to. I would never dream of offending—"

But it was too much, and Caroline strode away with an angry twitch of her skirts.

Hawk's expression folded into satisfied glee. "I do always relish an opportunity to speak to your sister, Philip."

Philip drank lazily from his glass and muttered, "At least someone enjoys speaking to her."

Ethan grumbled something and moved off then to speak with Uncle Reginald who was holding court by the fireplace. Audrey didn't miss how Gavin seemed to linger, his gaze surreptitiously traveling to the unexpectedly entertaining Miss Holloway before drifting along in the wake of his brother.

Philip and Hawk had moved off somewhere, and Miss Holloway had returned to Lady Spader, leaving Audrey suddenly alone. She made her way over to Grandmother Regina and bent to give the woman a kiss on her cheek.

"I thought this was to be a family affair, Grandmother," Audrey said, her gaze traveling the width of the nearly full drawing room.

"What's that, dear?" Grandmother Regina shook herself as if having just woken from a nap even though her eyes had been open the whole time.

"Nothing, Grandmother," Audrey said and cast her gaze around for Aunt Verity.

The woman appeared as if summoned by Audrey's very thoughts, carrying a glass of lemonade she handed to Grandmother Regina.

"Oh, is this wine, my pumpkin?" Grandmother eyed the glass with immense hope.

"No, Mother. It's lemonade. The sweet will be restorative."

Grandmother Regina sneered. "I don't need to be restored. I'm robust as it is. Look at me." She held out her arms, the hand holding the glass of lemonade shaking violently. Aunt Verity snatched the glass away with a sigh that would have been imperceptible had Audrey not been standing directly next to her.

Audrey looked at her aunt sharply, studying her as if for the first time. The sigh had suggested an unpleasantness Audrey could not fathom. Aunt Verity held such freedom as a spinster. Why should she be unhappy?

Before Audrey could ponder it further, a low murmur traveled through the assembled guests as another gentleman entered the drawing room. She slid her glance to the door, wondering who else her grandmother may have invited, only to feel her stomach drop cleanly to the floor.

Dashiell Evers, the Earl of Amberley, was smiling.

Directly at her.

She swallowed and looked swiftly down at her grandmother.

"Grandmother," Audrey nearly hissed. "What is he doing here?"

Grandmother Regina's vacant gaze skittered around, and it was Aunt Verity who answered, her voice flat and unusually tired. "We needed to even the numbers."

Grandmother nodded at this pronouncement. "Can't have a lady going unescorted into dinner, can we?"

Audrey would happily have gone into hell than to face dinner with the alarmingly charming Lord Amberley.

HE THOUGHT it would be a great deal more difficult to find himself seated next to her at dinner, but he was surprised to find Hawk at the seat adjacent to Lady D'Arcy's.

"Hawkins," Dash said with some surprise.

"Dashiell." Hawk turned a critical eye on his friend. "What are you doing here?"

Dash nodded toward the end of the table. "Lady Hodge invited me. I seem to have made an impression."

Hawk's grin was quick. "You always make an impression."

He would normally have been buoyed by such an assessment, but now the words only left him feeling hollow.

Ignoring the words and the accompanying feeling, Dash pointed to the chair still under Hawk's hand. "Tell you what, mate. I'll buy you a drink at the club this week if you let me have this chair."

Dash knew Hawk wouldn't miss a ploy when he saw it, and now his friend slid his gaze to the chair beside his. Lady D'Arcy had already assumed her seat, and it was obvious she was doing her best to ignore what was happening beside her. Dash knew this because he caught her gaze sliding over to them and darting back before she thought she was caught.

Dash was surprised when Hawk's expression turned somber. "I'm not sure I can do that, old chum. I know you might be harmless, but Lady D'Arcy is a friend of mine. A good friend. I shouldn't like to see anything untoward happen to her."

Something warm spread in his chest at his friend's protectiveness over Lady D'Arcy, but he couldn't as yet name what it was.

Dash gave a small nod. "I wouldn't wish anything untoward to happen to her either, old friend."

Hawk hesitated, but finally gave a nod, releasing his grip on the chair. "I look forward to that drink," he said before slipping away down the table to the next vacant chair.

Lady D'Arcy continued to stare at her empty plate as he assumed his seat, and he regretted not being able to see the face that had so enraptured him. He had struck upon the very thing when he had said her face was captivating. Her features were animated even when she didn't speak. Her eyes were bright and focused as if whatever caught her attention had earned the whole of it.

Never before had he found such a woman so pleasant to look upon, and yet they called her a wallflower.

He tugged at the lapels of his jacket as he settled in, his mind flashing on his own grievances with what society had deemed acceptable.

He was pleased to see it was a crowded table. Attentions would be captured elsewhere, and should he decide to spend a socially inappropriate time speaking with his dinner campion, no one would be the wiser. He couldn't help the small smile as he settled his napkin in his lap.

"I trust you are well this evening, Lady D'Arcy."

He imagined he could hear her teeth grind.

"I am quite well, Lord Amberley. I wonder if the same could be said of you."

He looked quickly at her to find her eyes fastened on the candelabra set before them, its widespread arms shielding them from the occupants opposite. The entire room buzzed with conversation interlaced with the clinking of dishes and the intermittent clank of silver serving utensils against platters and urns.

"Should I be unwell?"

She turned to face him, her lips pursed. "I think you must be mad if you think to be my dinner companion this evening."

He couldn't stop the small smile from growing. "Then perhaps you do not know me well at all."

Her expression turned lethal. "I think that is exactly the point."

He shifted to allow a footman to pour the wine and when the servant had slipped soundlessly away, Dash bent his head back to his companion.

"I plan to change that, Lady D'Arcy. This evening being the first of many occasions I think we can both look forward to."

She dropped her spoon against her soup bowl. The noise was lost in a small eruption of laughter at the other end of the table, and Dash was decent enough to ignore her falter by spooning up some soup of his own.

When she had properly recovered and dabbed at her lips with her napkin, she said, "Many occasions? My lord, I do not see how there would be an opportunity for such a thing."

"I think that is how we differ, my lady. I see plenty of opportunity."

She set down her spoon, and this time when she faced him, her expression bordered on murderous. "How is that?"

Again he plied her with his most charming smile. "There will be plenty of time when I court you."

It was a good thing she didn't have an implement in her hand because he was fairly certain this time she wouldn't have simply dropped it against her soup bowl. She would have used it to stab him in the eye.

"Court me?"

The words came out as hardly more than a whisper, but

it wasn't the level at which they were spoken. It was the hard edge of fear he heard in them.

His smile faltered for the first time.

"Yes, Lady D'Arcy." He pitched his voice low so the other occupants of the table might not overhear. "I plan to court you."

There had only been one other woman to whom he had spoken those words. While he might have earned the reputation of a charmer, he did not sink so low as to toy with a woman's emotions. When he was serious about pursuing a lady, he made his intentions clear.

He remembered her reaction to those same words that night in the cloakroom, but he had thought her reaction was one of surprise. She'd had time to think on it now, and surely, she would find his intentions promising. She did not, however.

"You will not."

He sat up straighter. "You would refuse my suit?"

He wasn't arrogant by any means. It was the simple facts of the matter. He was an earl with ample coffers and excellent social standing. She was the daughter of an earl, and it could be argued she couldn't have wanted for a better match. Especially considering this was not her first season.

"Of course I would." Her fingers trembled as she picked up her soup spoon, but he knew it was from an overwhelm of emotion. And not a favorable one.

For some strange reason, she obviously found the idea of courtship entirely repulsive.

"You do not wish to be courted?" He nearly whispered this question.

He could see plainly on her features how much the thought vexed her, and he didn't wish for any other members of their dining party to catch on that he'd upset her. Especially not about a subject so enticing to society gossips.

"No, I do not." These words were pushed out through her clenched teeth.

He took a sip of his wine, averting his gaze for several seconds, hoping it would give her time to calm down.

"I didn't mean to upset you," he said after a space.

She turned so quickly he nearly upset his wineglass.

"Upset me?" This was spoken a great deal louder than any of their previous conversation, and they both immediately looked away from one another, casually observing those around them.

But the table was fitfully engaged in a deep discussion of pheasant hunting on one side and the new soprano debuting at the Royal Theatre on the other.

"Upset me?" she repeated after a space at a much lower volume. "Is it not obvious that you upset me just by being here?"

The words cut, but she couldn't know why. He dabbed at his lips with his napkin, keeping his movements overly controlled.

"I'm terribly sorry. I didn't realize." Something twisted in his chest as he spoke the words, and he wondered if the pain would ever lessen. He had thought it would have by now, but he supposed perhaps it never would.

Only he never suspected a wallflower would have the power to prod at the old wound left by his dearly departed brother. No, not his brother. By those his brother had left behind.

He took several more spoonfuls of soup to cover his reaction as he worked to settle his mind and regain his confidence.

The footmen began to serve the salad before he spoke again.

"Are you holding out for a better match then?"

She stabbed a piece of lettuce with her fork. "You are most obtuse, Lord Amberley."

He glanced in her direction to see her spear a stalk of asparagus. "Am I? It seems a perfectly valid question."

She set down her fork. "I am a wallflower, Lord Amberley. You know that perfectly well. Must you remind me?"

"You are a wallflower only because society said you were. I don't feel the same way."

Her eyes flashed to his face, and the bright quality that had been there earlier disappeared, to be replaced by blatant disbelief.

"I told you the truth that night at the ball. I find you utterly captivating." He studied her face, taking precious, stolen seconds to drink in the sight of her.

Did his presence truly upset her or was she only unused to such attention? He hoped it was the latter.

The look of disbelief faded from her eyes as cold acceptance settled in.

"You are simply charming me, my lord, and I'm afraid I'm not susceptible to it."

He returned his attention to his plate. "I will admit charm can sometimes be rather unsubstantial. I would never trust one's words if they were not backed by clear and supportive action."

She poked at the lettuce on her plate. "And what action would that be? Forcing one's place at a dinner table?"

He laughed softly. "That's rather amateurish, I'm afraid."

He could feel her heated glance on the side of his face. "You prefer to display your abilities in cloakrooms then?"

He couldn't help the thrill that raced through him at her

boldness. He would expect an unschooled debutante to never mention what had transpired between them that night, but Lady D'Arcy seemed to shy away from nothing.

Except courtship, which was rather curious.

"I'm pleased to inform you my abilities extend beyond cloakrooms."

She set down her fork and placed her hands neatly in her lap. "I regret to inform *you* I feel no remorse that I should not see said abilities for myself."

"Who said you wouldn't?"

He picked up his wineglass and focused on taking a small slip. He knew he was convincing because she started at the first touch of his fingertips against the palm of the hand she had nestled in her lap. Unlike him, she was not practiced in the seductive arts, and she turned a startled gaze on him before catching herself and turning her attention to the table before her. She blinked furiously though, and had anyone been paying attention to more than their plate and the gossip spreading down the table, they would have noticed an unexpected change in Lady D'Arcy.

But as it was, only Dash was aware of the sudden change, and he was busy taking a drink of his wine, his lips curving against the glass as he took note of one important point.

Lady D'Arcy had not pulled her hand away from him.

It lay exactly as he had found it with his fingertips, and now he traced the lines of her palm, the softness under her thumb, the delicate arch of first one finger and then another.

He outlined one knuckle and then the next, marveling at the smoothness of the skin, its creamy texture against his rough fingers.

He had nearly reached the final finger when he noticed

her chest had begun to rise and fall in rapid succession. He took another casual sip of his wine and slipped his fingers through hers until he cradled her hand in his.

She swallowed, the sound so loud and yet undetectable as the conversation around them turned to the races at Ascot. He slowly returned his wineglass to the table.

Only then did he slip his fingers from hers and for the smallest moment, he no longer touched her. He allowed her breath to even out, her eyes to blink several times. When he could be sure she believed his torment of her to be over, he took two fingers and pressed them to the pulse at her wrist.

She jumped, her shoulders going back against her chair, but then he was already turning his head to the companion on his right, a young man likely just out of Eton who was speaking of the prowess of his father's Arabians to the lady next to him.

"I hear Arabians can be of the finest horseflesh," Dash intoned seriously, and the lady on the far side nodded appreciatively as the bloke next to him smiled in understanding.

Dash heard none of the resulting conversation. His attention was snared by the rabbiting pulse beneath his fingertips. He waited several more seconds before sliding his fingers along the fine skin of her wrist, torturing both her and himself with the exquisiteness of it until his hand suddenly stilled of his own volition.

He enjoyed touching her.

The charm conquests of late had been nothing more than that. Conquests. A game he played with himself to see if he could conjure the reaction he believed himself capable of, but it had never occurred to him whether or not he *enjoyed* doing such things.

But right now as his fingers pressed to Lady D'Arcy's

wrist, he knew he did enjoy it. With *her*. Very much so. His blood sang with a sudden heat, and he picked up his wineglass a little less casually this time, allowing his hand to slide away from her wrist.

And when the footmen brought out the next course, it was as though nothing had happened at all.

But something had happened.

His reaction to the captivating woman beside him was more than he had bargained for, and an old fear came crawling out of his memory.

A fear of falling in love.

4

"Do you know what I don't understand about promenading?"

Audrey blinked into the warm sunshine, trying her best to remind herself she was still in her body regardless of how her mind wished to wander, and currently, her body was walking through Hyde Park with her cousin, Caroline.

"What is that?" she found herself asking although she wasn't entirely sure what Caroline had said.

"What is the point?" Caroline answered, and it took a moment for Audrey to comprehend.

"You mean, what is the point of promenading?"

"Exactly." Caroline twirled the handle of her parasol between her hands, making the shadows that just barely outpaced them on the ground before them dance in disturbing contortions. "What are we supposed to think? A gentleman will decide he wishes to court us because he's seen us promenading?" She looked about them at the couples and groups scattered along the path. Now she deepened her tone as if imitating such a gentleman. "Oh, right then, I couldn't even imagine marrying her, but then I saw her walking, and righto, she's definitely the girl for me." More head shaking. "I mean really. Is that it? They've confirmed we can promenade and suddenly we're eligible for marriage? I shouldn't like to think my merit is based on something so insubstantial."

"I rather think the ability to walk shouldn't be taken for granted. Look at Grandmother Regina."

Caroline cut her a swift glance. "Of course I would never take it for granted. What I'm saying is a woman is judged on such silly merits in this society. I'd like to be judged for my weightier attributes."

"And what are those?"

"My intellect for one," she said, nodding at a passing mother and daughter with whom they were acquainted. "I should say I have remarkable composure."

"Is that what was on display last evening when Hawk arrived?"

This earned Audrey a scowl.

"You know very well I cannot stand the man. After what he did to Philip."

Audrey pulled her wrap more tightly around her even though the sunshine of the day was nearly making her too warm. It was nice to have something with which to busy her hands.

"I don't believe Hawk did anything to your brother. I think your brother simply grew up. He had his wilder days while at school, but that's all behind him now."

Caroline turned a sharp eye on her. "But what if it isn't? What if Hawk just cajoles him into more dangerous things? What if—"

"Caroline," Audrey said only to stop her cousin before she spiraled into despair. "Philip is a grown man and has shown a remarkable ability for sound decisions. Perhaps you need only trust him a little more."

"I am more than happy to trust Philip. It's Hawk I do not trust."

Audrey shrugged. She couldn't very well fault Caroline for that one. Hawk was known for his wilder days, more so than Philip, and Audrey was not well enough acquainted with the man to suggest whether or not he'd outgrown them the way Philip had.

"Then perhaps you can be civil with him when you are forced to mingle."

Caroline made a scoffing laugh. "The way you were civil with Lord Amberley?"

Audrey faltered in her steps. "I *was* civil with Lord Amberley." The words came far too swiftly, and heat climbed up her neck.

"Were you? I saw you speaking to one another for quite a while. What was so terribly interesting?"

Audrey's lips parted, and the truth of what had occurred made its way to her throat, but no words came forth. Caroline had always been her confidante, but Audrey had never had something so scandalous to share. Now that she did, she found she didn't wish to share it. She wanted to hoard it for herself.

Lord Amberley's fingertips had been so coarse against her skin; her fingers shook against her wrap with the memory of it. The daring of it, the secrecy, the...*boldness*. Her heart thudded in her chest from the mere memory of it.

It was the single most courageous thing she'd ever done, and not only did no one know of it, but she hadn't really meant to do it.

She'd let it happen to her, but she hadn't initiated it. How could she? She hadn't known such things were done.

But Lord Amberley had carried it off with aplomb, and this thought had her excitement dimming.

He was obviously skilled at such seduction. She should have known. But what had Miss Holloway said? Lord Amberley was only a charmer; he didn't actually damage the reputations of the women he pursued.

Fluff and nonsense. Lord Amberley had certainly damaged her.

"I scolded him for taking the seat from Hawk. It was rather rude after Grandmother Regina had gone to so much trouble to arrange the seating. It just isn't done."

"It's Aunt Verity who arranges the seating. I know because I asked specifically not to be seated next to Hawk before we went in to dinner." Caroline paused to nod to a passing woman and dog. "I'm sure no one noticed. They were too occupied with Hawk's retelling of the time he and Philip stalked that deer across the Highlands. Do you remember that?" She shook her head. "Philip could have been killed."

For once, Audrey was grateful Caroline was easily consumed by her own worries, and the attention was so swiftly off of her.

That was until they turned the bend in the path, and they both spotted Lord Amberley at the same time.

Caroline stopped dead, a puff of dust coming up around them as her boots dug into the path leaving Audrey to stumble a few steps ahead, making it more than obvious how much his very presence had confounded them.

"Lord," Caroline whispered. "The man is relentless."

Audrey seized Caroline's arm. "Don't leave me."

"What?" Caroline's brow folded in concern. "Whatever is the matter?"

Audrey's heart thumped louder the closer Lord

Amberley drew to them, and she whispered frantically, "He said something last night about wishing to court me. I cannot let him—"

"Court you?" Caroline said far too loudly, turning fully to face her and letting go of her parasol with one hand to grip Audrey's. "Well, that's wonderful. Audrey, you must—"

"I don't wish for him to court me," Audrey hissed.

Caroline waved this bit of information away. "Oh, of course you do. It's simply nerves." She returned her grip to her parasol and spun about at the same time to greet the earl. "Lord Amberley! So splendid to see you again so soon."

Amberley bowed. "Lady Hodge, a pleasure as always. I trust you are well."

"Oh, quite splendid. I'm always one for a good promenade. Love the fresh air." She was rambling, her eyes darting around them.

Audrey narrowed her gaze on her cousin, trepidation stealing over her.

"Lady D'Arcy," Amberley bowed again but kept his eyes on her. He hadn't done that with Caroline. She pursed her lips and refused to look away.

"Lord Amberley," she muttered.

"Oh my, look at that," Caroline said far too brightly. "Hedges! I think I shall have a look. Just over there. Several steps away. I won't be able to hear a thing." And with that Caroline tottered off, doing an admirable job of pretending to be absorbed in nothing more than the hedges along the path.

"Is your cousin all right?" Amberley said as they watched her go.

"No. She's quite deranged actually." Audrey turned to the earl. "What do you want?"

He had the audacity to look taken aback. “Lady D’Arcy, I would never—” He held a hand innocently to his chest.

“I will walk away in an instant if you do not get to the point.”

He dropped the hand. “Why do you not wish to be courted?”

The question came so swiftly it knocked the air from her lungs.

“That is a personal question.”

“It’s a personal affair I wish to have with you, so if you do not answer the question, we’ll never get very far. So, tell me, Lady D’Arcy. Why are you opposed to courting?”

That was too much.

His voice had turned to molten heat, and it thrummed through her with a speed and tenacity she’d never before felt. How could someone’s voice hold such power?

Affair? Why would he use that word? What did it mean? Was he suggesting something...improper?

She had to remember what kind of man he was.

She straightened her shoulders. “I’m terribly sorry if I have given any other indication, but I do not wish to have such a close acquaintance with you, Lord Amberley.”

He stepped closer. The movement was nearly imperceptible, and they were still a proper distance apart, but she could feel that step as if it were a physical touch, and her stomach tightened.

“A close acquaintance with me or with anyone?”

She could see his eyes clearly now, and they were bright green even in the shadow cast by the brim of his hat. They bore into her, and she wanted to squirm away, but his gaze held her.

“With anyone,” she heard herself whisper.

He took a step back, and the trance was broken. She

wanted to shake her head to clear her thoughts, to shake the mental power he had over her, but it would have given her away.

"Anyone?" He tilted his head as he studied her. "But... why? Why would you condemn yourself to a lonely life?"

She tugged so hard on her wrap, she feared she might rip it. "It's not a lonely life. It's a free one."

"Free?" He spoke the word as if it might be a disease. "Free from what?"

She looked about them as if she might find the answer in Hyde Park. But the answer was in Hyde Park. It was all around her. The ladies promenading. The gentlemen taking note. It was all a manufactured idea that determined a person's worth, and Audrey could never compare to such standards.

She stood in the middle of it, failing entirely without ever being given a chance to succeed.

"Free from all of this." The words flew from her lips as her hand flew from her chest to take in the space around them. The gesture was wild and overt, and she snatched her hand back, tucking it against her and hoping no one had noticed.

Amberley looked about them. "Promenading? If you do not wish to promenade, then you simply—"

She let out a noise then, one composed of frustration and weariness.

"Good day, Lord Amberley." She had hoped he would have enough sense to let her go, but he didn't. What else had she expected?

He stepped in front of her, blocking her retreat.

"Help me to understand. What is it that you wish to be free from?"

There it was again. That intense green stare boring into

her. She had never held anyone's attention. Why did she have to claim his and why now? Why couldn't he just let her slip away unnoticed like everyone else did?

"You can't understand," she whispered, and her words were soaked with the despair she could feel to her bones.

He could never understand. He could never understand what it was like to be a woman who didn't meet society's standards when her future depended on those very standards to find a suitable husband. There was so much that Audrey would never be good enough for no matter how hard she might try. Her future was doomed before she had even had a go at it.

But he couldn't understand that. A gentleman and an earl, no less. He could never understand what it was like to be judged without merit and sentenced to a life of ineptitude.

"I can't understand if you never give me the opportunity to do so." He spoke the words softly. It was not a threat. It was not meant to persuade her into confiding in him. It was a simple truth.

She wanted to tell him. She wanted to say exactly what she felt.

But then Caroline was at her elbow, tugging furiously.

"It's Gavin! If he sees you, he'll tell Ethan."

Audrey's gaze flashed in the direction in which her cousin was looking and spotted her younger brother almost immediately as he was a head taller than most men.

"I'm so sorry," Audrey managed.

"Who's Gavin?" Amberley called after her, but she was already too far away. He couldn't have heard her. Their conversation was over.

So why did it take so much to tear her eyes away from him?

JUDGING by the stormy expression on Hawk's face when the man found Dash at the club later that day, this would not be a jovial visit.

"Have I heard correctly that you wagered Viscount Breedlove that you would marry Lady D'Arcy?"

Dash's thoughts had been consumed by his interactions with the lady in question, and it was a moment before he drew himself out of his reverie to understand what the Earl of Stonegate had just said to him.

"A wager? What are you talking about?" He pushed himself straighter in his chair as he contemplated the man.

Without waiting for permission, Hawk took the seat next to him. "The betting books are full of it, I'm afraid. The odds are not in your favor it would seem. I had a look after your insistence in sitting next to the woman last night."

Dash shook his head, nearly upsetting the glass of liquor he'd forgotten was still in his hand. "I don't know what you're talking about. What wager? Why on earth would I make a bet with Breedlove? And it's preposterous to think I'd bet on a lady's honor."

Hawk considered him with narrowed eyes but was prevented from speaking when a footman came to ask if Hawk should wish for something to eat or drink. The man ordered, and the footman slipped away.

"Then you didn't make the wager?" Hawk asked, settling into his seat.

Dash opened his mouth to deny it and snapped it shut. "Oh no," he whispered.

Hawk raised an eyebrow. "You did bet on the woman. You know that is grounds for calling you out, Dash. I had hoped to avoid the matter."

Dash blinked as the memories of that night fell back into place, but he was momentarily distracted by something else.

"*You* would call me out? I should think one of the lady's formidable brothers would see to the deed."

He hadn't forgotten the tall gentleman striding toward them in the park. He vaguely recalled the man from Lady Hodge's dinner along with the another strikingly similar man if not for the scars on his face.

Hawk's drink arrived and he sipped it meditatively. "You will find I'm rather protective of Lady D'Arcy. She's a dear cousin to someone very important to me."

Hawkins Savage, the Earl of Stonegate, had never been one to divulge his personal life, and since Dash had known him since their days at Cambridge, he had come to know this fact quite well. He also knew that his friend took loyalties very seriously, and if he should feel a need to protect Lady D'Arcy, there was a strong reason for it. Dash would not ask which cousin it was whom Hawk held so dear. He would respect his friend's privacy.

But Breedlove was another matter.

"I'm afraid I lost my temper in Breedlove's presence, and he must have mistaken my threat for a wager."

"A threat? What could the man possibly have threatened you with?" Hawk's tone was dull as they both knew Breedlove to be no more threatening than a kitten.

Dash heard the man's words playing over and over again in his head, but he couldn't bring himself to speak of it. Instead, he said, "He impugned Lady D'Arcy's honor, and I told him I would call him out for it when I had the right to." Dash paused before taking another sip of his drink. "I suppose there's a lot of threats of dueling going about."

"You threatened to call him out?" Hawk's smile tipped

into a knowing grin. "For Lady D'Arcy?" He shook his head. "The woman seems to have made an impression." These last words were soft and beguiling, and Dash understood that his friend was remembering another woman from another time.

He set down his glass and faced his friend. "This isn't like Nicole, Hawk. I can't say what it is, but Lady D'Arcy seems to have cast a spell over me."

Hawk swirled the drink in its glass. "I can recall a time you said just the same thing about Nicole."

He didn't speak the words accusingly, but Dash felt it all the same.

He pushed a frustrated hand through his hair. "It isn't like that. It's…" For a moment, he wanted to say this was real whereas last time was something else entirely, but saying as much would admit a truth he still didn't wish to. So instead, he said, "It's deeper with Lady D'Arcy." He glanced at his friend. "I know that sounds absurd, but it's as though I'm standing on a boulder now when I was standing on dry sand with Nicole." He shook his head. "Much longer and I'll be speaking like a bard."

Hawk's smile was soft now. "I think it makes perfect sense. I only worry that your attraction to Lady D'Arcy is based on the right reasons."

Once more the past hung between them, and Dash wished he had another drink.

"We're not getting any younger, I'm afraid, and the title would require I marry soon and produce an heir." He spoke to the empty glass beside him as he sifted through his thoughts. "I can't see myself doing that with anyone other than Lady D'Arcy. Not after…" but he couldn't finish the sentence. There was too much to pack into simple words.

Hawk set down his glass and leaned on the arm of his chair as he considered Dash.

"Does she know?"

Dash raised an eyebrow. "You'll need to be more specific."

Hawk cringed even as he gave a commiserate smile. "Does she know about Nicole?"

Dash gave a shrug. "I would think everyone knows about Nicole. It wasn't as though she was discreet when she ended our betrothal."

"You forget Lady D'Arcy was not out when the matter occurred. She may not have heard of it."

Dash shook his head. "Wouldn't her mother know then? Wouldn't she advise her daughter on the matter?"

Hawk's laugh was sharp. "Now I do understand Breedlove mistook your words for a true wager. You know nothing of the woman at all."

Dash leaned back and studied his friend. "I would beg you to elaborate."

"Lady D'Arcy is a wallflower, and I mean that in the simplest form of the term. I find the woman singularly entertaining in her intelligence and humor. She's wonderful company. But the fact of the matter is she doesn't live up to society's standards for women, and because of that, her mother, the famed beauty in her time, has found her daughter to be unworthy."

Something familiar and painful dug into Dash's chest at his friend's words. "Her mother finds her to be lacking?"

"In every way," Hawk mumbled with a shake of his head. "The Countess of Dartford is not good at seeing what really matters in a person, and she is not one to abstain from criticism. I've witnessed enough of her disdain for her only daughter, and if it were at all possible, I would do more to protect the lady. She doesn't deserve the way her mother treats her."

"I can understand that all too well," he heard himself whisper.

Hawk's face tightened as he leaned closer. "I thought you might."

Hawk's words rang inside of him. "What of her father? Why doesn't he attempt to deflect the woman's scorn?"

"The man is absent more than he's present. He has a penchant for loose women and drink, and he's more likely to be found in a brothel than spending time with his dear family."

Dash wasn't surprised by this. "What of her brothers? Why don't they protect her?"

Hawk's expression turned inward, and Dash wondered at what wound he had inadvertently poked.

"Ethan and Gavin," Hawk said now at not more than a whisper, and when he finally raised his eyes, Dash saw in them an unspoken hurt. "They were at Waterloo. It's...complicated."

Dash recalled the two men from the dinner party once more. The one with the deeply scarred face and the other trailing after him like a shadow. He suddenly understood more about Lady Hodge's outburst on the promenade that morning.

"They are a close family then," Dash said, feeling a hollowness ringing inside of him.

Hawk only nodded.

There was a beat of silence as Hawk finished his drink before saying, "What are your intentions when it comes to Lady D'Arcy?"

"I had wished to court her."

Hawk's eyebrows went up. "So proper. What is the

cause?"

Dash settled back against his chair. "I find your assessment of Lady D'Arcy rather accurate. The woman is intelligent, witty, and humorous. I enjoy her company. I'm not sure there is more that I could ask for in a wife."

Hawk was already shaking his head before he'd finished. "She'll never court you, I'm afraid."

Dash stared. "I'm beginning to understand that. However, I would like to know why."

Hawk finished his drink and set the empty glass down on the table between the chairs.

"Are you familiar with the aunt? Lady Verity Hodge." Dash nodded, and Hawk continued. "I think Lady D'Arcy views her as a paragon of feminine freedom. As much as females can attain these days."

Dash recalled the young woman with the dark circles under her eyes and the faded complexion tending to the woman they all referred to as Grandmother Regina.

"She seems more a prisoner to me," Dash said even as he flinched from the heartlessness in his words.

Hawk nodded in agreement. "She is a prisoner. Condemned to a life on the shelf because she happened to be born so long after her older siblings. When Lady Hodge suffered her stroke, it was assumed Verity would care for her. Now she's stuck."

"But she's still young. Surely someone might marry her."

"But then who would care for Grandmother Regina?"

Another familiar stab of pain rang through him, and he could understand all too well what it meant to be burdened with the expectations of others.

He considered his friend, understanding suddenly how much valuable knowledge the man held of the Hodge and D'Arcy family.

"Do you have any advice about how I could convince Lady D'Arcy to accept my suit, or is it hopeless?"

Hawk's expression was chagrinned. "I'm afraid you may have more luck winning Lady Wilson back than you do of getting Lady D'Arcy to accept your suit."

Even the suggestion of being once more engaged to Lady Nicole Wilson had his insides churning. His past with Nicole was complicated by more than a lost love affair. Somehow David had managed to wind himself into Dash's engagement. His brother had amazing reach for a dead man.

"So, you're telling me it's hopeless?"

Hawk shrugged and gained his feet. "I suppose there is always the chance for a miracle."

Dash didn't know why this statement should feel like a boulder careening down on him. He had told Hawk the truth. He enjoyed Lady D'Arcy's company, and she would make a good wife. The title demanded he seek a partner and produce an heir, but there was so much more he hadn't said. Things he hadn't figured out himself.

Like the explosive physical reaction he had to the woman when he so much as laid eyes on her. Like the realization of how much he enjoyed touching her when he'd caressed her hand the previous night. Such a simple touch and yet he thought it might undo him completely.

For someone so skilled at charm, he had thought himself immune, but Lady D'Arcy was proving herself the antidote to his defense.

"I'm not keen on miracles," he murmured.

When Hawk met his gaze, an understanding passed between them.

"When is your mother arriving in town?" Hawk asked softly.

Dash gained his feet and looked at the floor as he answered, "I'm afraid she arrives today." He looked up and pasted a false smile on his lips. "That's why I'm hiding here."

"You've no more luck on getting her to agree to rebuilding the stables at Evers Park?"

Dash gave his friend a quick glance. They hadn't spoken of the stables in some months, and Dash was surprised Hawk remembered. But then he shouldn't have been. Hawk was a good man and friend.

Dash shook his head. "Much as everything, she insists on Evers Park remaining the way it was when David was alive." He forced a smile he didn't feel.

Hawk did not allow the false expression to sway him. Instead, he reached out and put a hand to Dash's shoulder. Dash twitched under the contact, not one used to such shows of solidarity and compassion.

"I'm going to say something, Dash, and it's going to be rather unmanly, but I want you to hear it." Hawk's gaze narrowed until Dash felt like the only person in the room. "You're a grown man. What your mother thinks of you, what society has placed upon you, can't determine your worth. Only you can."

Dash had heard such platitudes before and just as before, the words sluiced off of him like a downpour on a hard-packed earth.

Dash smiled all the same to show his friend he appreciated the attempt.

"I'll be sure to tell my mother that at the first mention of David's name."

Hawk shook his head and bid him farewell, but Dash didn't miss the look of pity in his friend's eyes before the man turned away.

5

"Was he truly so persistent?"

They were standing at the edge of another ball in yet another ballroom that looked remarkably like the last ballroom they had stood in...was it only three days ago? Perhaps four?

Audrey couldn't tell anymore. Her days were so monotonous; they simply blended one into the next. Promenading with Caroline in the mornings, calls in the afternoon, perhaps an invitation to tea or a dinner, and then to the various rounds of balls. Day after day after day...

She slipped her foot from its slipper beneath the skirts of her dress and flexed her toes. She repeated the process with the other foot. It was something she had come to do when the boredom grew too great. Would anyone notice that her foot was out of its slipper? Not likely in the least. But Audrey knew, and that was at least something.

"Apparently. I'm not sure where the charm aspect is supposed to come in. Currently I'm mostly just annoyed."

Caroline studied the assembled dancers as the first notes

of the quadrille washed over the crowd. "Do you think he'll ask your father for permission to court you?"

"He's in Dartford at the moment, so that may be rather difficult."

Caroline slid her a knowing glance but didn't speak. At some point long ago, through some kind of mutual understanding that only happens when two people are connected as closely as Audrey and Caroline were, it was determined that should Audrey's father be in Dartford it would not be further discussed. Because Audrey's father only went to Dartford for one thing. To avoid his wife and entertain a series of mistresses.

Or sometimes other gentlemen's wives. Depending on what he was interested in at the moment.

Audrey had few encounters with her father. This was likely why her relationship with her mother was so pronounced. There wasn't another parental relationship with which to dilute her mother's well-meaning if hurtful intentions.

Caroline's brow folded, her gaze narrowing. "You wouldn't consider courting him then? Not even for the fun of it?"

Audrey looked swiftly at her cousin. "For the fun of it?"

Caroline shrugged, gesturing weakly at the ball around them. "You could continue to do this every night until you're officially on the shelf or..." She shrugged again. "You could find out why Lord Amberley is so adamant in his pursuit of you."

"You make me sound like a prized piece of horseflesh."

Caroline smiled and tilted her head coquettishly. "Oh, you're much lovelier than a piece of horseflesh." She blinked innocently. "Even your teeth are much nicer."

Audrey nodded exaggeratedly. "Thank you, my lady."

Caroline straightened. "But aren't you the least bit curious? What would Lord Amberley want with you? You're far too practical for his tastes."

Audrey's own brow wrinkled at this. "What do you mean?"

"Haven't you noticed the pattern of the other ladies he has charmed?" She waved a hand at this. "I can understand if you haven't. He has a rather robust track record. But they are all young debutantes with hardly a thought in their head." She pointed directly at Audrey now. "You on the other hand are extremely bright and engaging. I would think it would be harder to charm someone who can think for herself."

Audrey hadn't considered this. She folded her arms across her stomach.

"Perhaps he sees me as a challenge. I suppose charming is like any skill. It requires practice. Maybe he believes it's time to pursue a more difficult prospect."

She hated how this made her sound, but she'd heard worse things about herself from the gentlemen in society.

Caroline wrinkled her nose. "I would hope you're not some sort of game to him."

"But what if I am?"

They held each other's gaze for several seconds before shaking their heads in mutual understanding.

"We'll never know unless you ask him. You might just discover it's not at all what it seems." Caroline went back to studying the crowd.

Did Audrey wish to ask him? In truth, she hoped she'd discouraged him enough to send him into retreat, but she thought it unlikely. Her face flamed when she thought of him, and she swallowed and looked about them as if to distract herself.

How could she have created so many powerful memories with a man she had known for so little time?

It was ridiculous.

She wondered if she would need to start fanning herself when a woman bumped into her, sending her neatly into Caroline. They exchanged a series of startled noises only to discover it was Miss Holloway who had collided with them.

"I'm so very sorry," she chirped as soon as they had all straightened.

Audrey studied the woman to see if she were all right and noticed her brother standing behind the companion, his gaze intent on Audrey.

"Miss Holloway was just saying what a lovely stretch of weather we've been having." Gavin's voice was oddly pronounced as if he were forcing a note of joviality into his speech.

Audrey eyed him. "Are you all right? Is there something wrong—"

"Hasn't it been lovely, Caroline?" he asked in the same monotone, his eyes furiously intent on Caroline's face.

Caroline's lips parted. "Gavin, what on earth—"

"Yes, it's quite lovely," Audrey interrupted and more, she pulled Miss Holloway's arm through her own. "Caroline and I were just commenting on the...loveliness of the...uh... lovely weather."

A multitude of messages were exchanged through the glances shared between brother and sister in that moment, and finally Audrey patted Miss Holloway's arm, turning her attention to the crowd.

"Is Lady Spader all right? Is she in need of anything?"

Miss Holloway looked back over her shoulder in the direction from which she had come. "She's fallen asleep. It's not unusual for her, but she should nap for a while now."

Audrey kept her grip on Miss Holloway's arm. "That must be dreadfully boring for you. I'm glad you've found us." She turned to Caroline. "Aren't you glad, cousin?"

"Oh very," Caroline added and shifted so she stood between Gavin and Miss Holloway. "Why don't you fetch us some lemonade, dear cousin?" she announced with a grand tilt at the end of her question as if in mockery of his own forced tones from earlier.

He slipped into the crowd without further comment.

Audrey tugged on Miss Holloway's arm. "What's the matter with him? I hope he wasn't bothering you."

Miss Holloway's delicate features were flushed. "It's quite all right. I assure you. It was only a slight misunderstanding. Your brother is rather determined when he makes up his mind, isn't he?"

Audrey frowned. "I'm sorry. Gavin can be protective at times. It's hard for him. What with what happened to Ethan and all." Her own words made her pause as she realized how odd it was to see Gavin without his twin.

Miss Holloway shook her head. "It must be hard for him. I can't imagine what it's like to be a twin. That must be an incredible bond." She looked about them. "Is your brother Ethan in attendance tonight?"

Audrey shook her head. "Ethan doesn't attend balls. Not after…"

Waterloo.

She didn't have to say the word. It hung amongst them like it so often did in many gatherings these days.

"I understand," Miss Holloway murmured. "I must admit I still find balls overwhelming myself."

"Are you not familiar with them?" Caroline asked.

Miss Holloway shook her head. "Oh no. I grew up in Sussex, you see. We had the odd assembly now and then, but my father—" Strangely, Miss Holloway seemed to choke on the word. She licked her lips and tried again. "He didn't approve of such frivolity, so I have not had the opportunity to engage in such gatherings until now."

Caroline's smile was bright. "Oh, then I'm glad you've found us. We'll save you from the boredom."

Miss Holloway laughed, a pleasant soft sound, and Audrey found herself liking the quiet companion.

"How long have you been with Lady Spader?"

Miss Holloway's expression dimmed. "I've only been with her a couple of months. My father...I mean I came to London to seek employment in February. The agency placed me with Lady Spader almost immediately."

"You're fortunate to have found a posting so quickly," Caroline said. "You so often hear of ladies who are not so lucky."

Miss Holloway nodded furiously. "Oh, I'm terribly grateful. And Lady Spader is so..."

"Sleepy?" Audrey offered.

Miss Holloway laughed reluctantly as if she wished to not disparage her employer. "Yes, that's it."

There was a pause in the conversation then, and it was enough for Audrey to realize she was enjoying herself. The trepidation she had felt earlier at having to attend yet another ball in which Lord Amberley might have a chance to seek her out and rekindle all of those emotions she was trying so desperately to ignore had faded. Caroline's company was always welcomed, but Miss Holloway was proving a right distraction.

This is what Audrey wished for. The ease that came when there were no expectations placed on her. She wanted the banter between friends. Was Miss Holloway a friend? Audrey eyed the woman and thought she just might be.

Perhaps they could be spinsters together. The thought was somehow thrilling.

Her elation was short lived, however, because the Countess of Dartford appeared through the crowd.

"Caroline, lovely to see you." Her smile disappeared immediately upon setting eyes on Audrey, her only and disappointing daughter. "Audrey, why are you skulking over here? I told you to stand next to the dance floor if you hope to fill your dance card. You'll never do so—" Her mother stopped abruptly, eyeing the woman whose arm still hung through Audrey's. "I'm sorry. I don't believe I've had the pleasure."

Eugenia D'Arcy, the Countess of Dartford, had mastered the art of condescension, and she focused it into her gaze, which she had locked onto the poor Miss Holloway.

Audrey let go of the woman's arm long enough to pat it. "Mother, this is Miss Holloway. She's Lady Spader's companion."

Audrey thought it rather neat that Miss Holloway had gainful employment. What must that be like? To be responsible for one's own future? Having the power to earn one's own income?

Judging by how much Lady Spader fell asleep Audrey wasn't sure if it was any more exciting than her own existence though.

Her mother's face folded into a pinched look of disdain. Mother enjoyed looking down on others a great deal, and Audrey was sure she was finding fresh prey in poor Miss Holloway. It was not to be avoided, and if Audrey wished to have Miss Holloway as a friend, it was best to get this bit over with now.

"Companion? How unfortunate." She moved her gaze to

Caroline, her smile returning. "I'm sure your dance card is full already. Isn't it, dear?"

Caroline lifted a single eyebrow. "It's empty actually. I don't like anyone here, and I refuse to dance with idiots."

Audrey's mother's face fell. "Oh, I see." Her lips pursed again, and with a sigh, she turned her gaze back to her only daughter. "Come with me. Now. I will not let you stand over here for a minute longer."

Her mother held out her hand as though Audrey was still a small child to be led around by leading strings. All at once, she felt the weight of her life settle directly on her chest, robbing her of breath and hope and happiness. If only she could escape this.

Soon.

Soon, she would be safely on the shelf. A spinster. Free to do as she pleased without her mother's constant disparagement.

Audrey cast a warm smile on Miss Holloway as she moved to follow her mother. She did not take the woman's hand, by God. Audrey would never stoop that low.

But she was prevented from moving when a voice reached their small group.

"Lady D'Arcy, is that you? Well, what a pleasure then. I didn't know you'd be here this evening."

She didn't need to turn to see his face. She had it memorized. The way his eyes fluttered closed when he kissed her. The way his smile kicked up on one side when he teased her. The way those green eyes could pierce her very heart.

She would wager he knew bloody well she would be there and had purposely sought her out. But worst of all, she saw him for what he was in that moment, and it upended her entire world.

Lord Amberley was her means of freedom in that moment.

But before she could respond, her mother did it for her.

"Lord Amberley, I didn't realize you were acquainted with my daughter. Perhaps you'd like a dance?"

"I'M NOT DANCING WITH YOU."

"Your mother seems to think so."

She turned so swiftly it sent him back a step.

"My mother seems to think a lot of things. Most of which are untrue or silly."

He couldn't help but grin. "Which one am I?"

He loved the way her eyes flashed when he riled her.

They had stalked to the other side of the dance floor away from her mother, but even though he held her arm through his, it was clear who was doing the directing.

She stopped behind a cluster of debutantes and peered through the crowd behind them as if ascertaining whether or not her mother could still see them. She must have been satisfied because she turned on him.

"I am not dancing with you."

"You already said that. Why exactly are you not doing so? Your mother seems keen on the idea." He glanced over his shoulder in the direction in which they had left the Countess of Dartford. He looked back at Lady D'Arcy. "This doesn't have to do with your repulsion of courting, does it?" He wrinkled his brow in concern.

He knew very well of the tension between mother and daughter thanks to his run-in with Hawk earlier that week, but he wanted to see what she would say for herself.

Her frown was fierce. "I don't particularly set value in

what my mother deems worthy and not worthy. She's superficial, narrow-minded, and judgmental."

So that's how it was then. At least she didn't harbor false expectations of her mother's love. He flinched inwardly at his own hypocrisy.

"I'd hate to hear what you think of me."

Interestingly two spots of color appeared on her cheeks, and she looked quickly away.

"I will not dance with you because I've already been seen dancing with you once this week, and people will talk if we're seen together again."

"And that would be a terrible thing?"

"Yes." The word was spoken with such force he didn't know how it didn't blow him over.

A niggling at the back of his neck had him looking around, and it was several seconds before he realized he was looking for Breedlove. He gave himself a mental shake. What the man thought of Dash held little consequence. Dash's pursuit of Lady D'Arcy had nothing to do with the old nemesis no matter what Hawk had suggested. But why did Dash wish Breedlove could see him with Lady D'Arcy now?

He studied the woman at his side with a more critical eye, and she squirmed under his perusal.

"What is it?" she asked after shifting from foot to foot for several seconds.

He shrugged, feigning nonchalance. "It's nothing really."

She turned a sharp eye on him. "Nothing?"

He shrugged again. "It's just that I didn't take you for a coward."

Her eyes widened in that gorgeous, captivating face, and it was all he could do to remember his trajectory here.

"Coward?" she whispered.

"After our initial encounter, I wouldn't have guessed that you would be so afraid of what others thought of you."

"I'm not afraid." Her words were quick and strained.

He leaned the smallest of degrees closer to her. "Then why won't you dance with me?"

She tugged her arm from his. "You're just like my mother. Are appearances all that matter to you?"

His grin was one-sided. "It's not appearances that I'm worried about."

The color brightened in her cheeks, and he felt a measure of success when she took the smallest of steps away from him. He did affect her, but she was trying her darndest to hide it. Why?

She averted her gaze. "Well, I have no concern for appearances...or other matters," she muttered out of the side of her mouth as she poked at her hair with a trembling finger. "Soon I shall be free of all societal trappings."

He crossed his arms. "About that, we never did finish our discussion from earlier."

She looked back at him. "What discussion?"

The soft candlelight did marvelous things to her deep brown eyes. "The one we were having on the promenade. I worry, Lady D'Arcy, that our relationship is doomed to consist of snatches of conversation that preclude real meaning."

"We don't have a relationship."

His smile was slow. "And you claim not to be a coward."

Her chin went up at this. "What are you proposing, Lord Amberley?"

"We've already moved onto proposals, have we, Lady D'Arcy?"

She only frowned.

He dropped his arms and faced her. "I would like to

know why it is that you refuse my courtship." He dropped his voice, but in the crush around them, he doubted anyone would overhear them.

Her eyes darted about them anyway. "I told you. I do not wish to be courted."

"That's not an explanation."

"It is to me."

He narrowed his gaze. "Are you concerned about what you've heard of my reputation?"

She made a scoffing noise. "It may come as a surprise to you, Lord Amberley, but what I've heard of you was nothing but the highest regards."

He straightened at this, an odd sensation tingling along his spine. "Is that so?"

Clearly she had not spoken to his mother, and he looked around suddenly as though the Countess of Amberley were lurking, ready to pounce on her lamentable son.

She glanced briefly at him before turning her attention to the crowd. "I've heard you have nothing but the utmost respect for a woman's honor."

This was news to him. The only rumors he'd heard about himself were strictly about David.

He swallowed, pushing thoughts of his brother aside.

"And that doesn't speak well in favor of my suit?"

The glance she spared him could shred paper. "Hardly."

"Do you wish to receive the suit of a gentleman who would treat you poorly?"

She turned so quickly again, he had to step back once more.

"I wish to receive no one's suit. Can't you see that?"

Her voice had gone up enough that a few heads turned in their direction.

He plastered on a smile and laughed as though she were

telling a joke. It was enough to have those who might have been curious turning their tiring attentions back to the spectacle of the dance floor.

He recalled what Hawk had said about the spinster aunt.

He drew in a measured breath. "Lady D'Arcy, I would ask for a favor."

"Haven't you asked for enough?" Her tone was back to normal levels.

He ignored that. "I would like a single, uninterrupted conversation with you in which you may help me to understand why it is you will not accept my courtship. In that time, if you convince me of the merits of your argument, I shall leave you alone."

He wasn't sure what he had expected from her at this offering, but it wasn't the furtive glance or the way her teeth nibbled nervously at her lip. He may take such gestures to suggest she didn't wish for him to leave her alone.

"One conversation and you'll let me be?"

"If you can convince me." He whispered the words close to her ear, and he was rewarded when her shoulder trembled with a slight shiver.

"Very well," she said after a time. "Where are we to conduct this conversation? I should think the cloakroom would be rather stifling. Perhaps you would prefer the terrace in the moonlight. Isn't that how the novels portray it?"

"I was thinking we could find a bedroom."

He had meant the statement in terms of the practicality of it. No one should be wandering about the bedchambers of a home during a ball, and he thought they would have the best chance of being undisturbed, and more for Lady D'Arcy's reputation, undiscovered. But based on her reaction, one might have thought he had invited her directly to bed.

She made a choking noise and bent slightly forward, her hand pressed to her chest.

"I beg your pardon—"

"I meant a bedchamber for its privacy, Lady D'Arcy," he spoke calmly, resting a hand slightly on the arm that hung at her side closest to him.

The touch was brief, and he doubted anyone would have taken it for more than an accidental brush caused by their forced proximity.

Lady D'Arcy quieted. "I suppose you're right."

"We could find an unoccupied drawing room along this floor if that's more agreeable to you, but what you've heard of me is true." He considered her face, the way her eyes remained wide as she refused to look away. "I do have the utmost care for a lady's reputation, and I would not wish yours to be ruined because I wish to speak with you."

He watched her swallow, but she didn't look away.

"I've never snuck away from a ball before," she whispered.

He smiled slowly. "Have you not? It's a right adventure."

He wasn't sure what happened, but suddenly there was a light in her eyes that had nothing to do with her contemplating his imminent demise. Something he had said had triggered a change in her, much as he had seen previously in her, and he wondered what it could be.

Was it the prospect of daring to sneak away? He eyed her more closely. Was that her terrible secret? Did the quiet, plain Lady D'Arcy wish for a chance to escape the mundane? To do what wasn't expected of her?

He pondered this even as she seemed to be sorting through what he had said.

What if she did yearn for something different? What if she weren't at all inclined to marriage and what that might entail? For the first time, he felt his assurance slipping. He was usually so adept at convincing a woman to bend to his will, but he thought he would not be so cunning with Lady D'Arcy. He wasn't sure if he were thrilled at the prospect of a challenge or something else. Something that harkened back to old wounds he resolutely ignored.

Lady D'Arcy seemed to finish her study of his offer, and she raised her chin to meet his gaze.

"What do you propose, Lord Amberley?"

He took a sudden interest in the dancers assembling on the floor, peering through the many heads that obscured his view.

"I shall take my leave of you in a moment and wander over to the refreshment tables. You shall slip off as if going to the lady's retiring room. I shall then meet you in the corridor."

"Isn't the corridor filled with guests coming?"

He returned his gaze to her, unable to stop a grin. "Not at this late hour. Everyone is in the ballroom by now."

"The corridor will be empty then," she said as she moved her gaze back and forth across the crowd as if they weren't planning their escape.

"Precisely." He tugged at the lapels of his jacket. "Lady D'Arcy, it has been a pleasure." He made to leave but she stopped him with a hand to his arm, the gesture subtle and likely unnoticed.

"You promise to leave me be if I tell you the truth. You swear to it?"

He met her eyes directly, struggling to maintain his wits when he wanted nothing more than to sink in the warm depths of her gaze. One conversation. Could he do it? Could he let her go if she told him the truth?

Something inside of him sang with a note that sounded like nothing more than pure survival. In his mind flashed a hundred instances that argued against what he was about to do. That warned he was stepping too close to something that could hurt him all over again.

But mustn't he try? Didn't circumstances call for him to take the risk?

Because if he didn't, he would be alone, and that was far worse than anything else.

He nodded. "Yes. You have my word."

Her eyes passed over his face as if she were deciding whether or not to believe him, and she must have been pleased with what she saw because she stepped back and gave a slight nod of her head.

"It was a pleasure, Lord Amberley. I do hope you enjoy the rest of the evening." She turned and slipped through the crowd before he could say anything else.

He stood there for several minutes, the beats of the waltz echoing around him as guests jostled for space along the dance floor. He heard and felt the ball around him, but he could only think of her. Would she show up in the corridor or would she prove the coward?

For one sudden moment, doubt gripped him. Who was he to pursue a lady like her? She was obviously different from the flighty debutantes that were his normal preference. He knew even if he couldn't admit it that he preferred the debutantes because there was no risk involved. They were usually simply pleased to have an earl's attention, no matter the earl.

He knew that wasn't the case with Lady D'Arcy, and if he

should get her to accept his suit, it would require a great deal more from him.

As if sensing his thoughts, his mother stepped from the crowd as he made his way to the refreshment table.

They had arrived together, and her appearance shouldn't have startled him, but as he spent as much time as possible avoiding her company, having her suddenly appear was unsettling.

"Mother."

The Countess of Amberley was small in proportions, and her features were sharp. She raised her pointed chin now.

"Dashiell, I should hope you are spending your time wisely this evening. You are not growing younger, and the title is at risk so long as you remain unwed." Her tone was gravelly with age, and she held a champagne flute in one hand like a scepter.

"Of course, Mother," he said, eyeing her cautiously.

"David would never have allowed such risk, but I suppose I couldn't expect the same care and attention from you."

He felt the stab to his chest as his mother had intended, but oddly, the image of Lady D'Arcy floated across his mind, and the pain receded more quickly than usual.

"If you will excuse me, Mother," he said, and he didn't wait for her answer.

6

It was far too easy to slip from the ballroom.

She wondered if any lady could have removed herself with such ease or if it was because no one noticed a wallflower.

She thought it to be the latter.

She decided to slip into the gaming rooms first. She figured if she were caught she could say she was simply looking for Gavin.

But caught by whom?

It wasn't as though her mother was looking for her.

She moved through the tables, their occupants' attention fixed on the game before them, and soon she eased into the corridor without anyone glancing in her direction.

She peered over her shoulder as she made her escape, sure someone would catch her, and that was why she collided with her brother.

Just not the one she had been expecting.

"Ethan." She might as well have confessed her guilt on the spot for all she gave it away in the high pitch of her voice.

His gaze narrowed. "Audrey." He peered around them. "Where are you going? Where's Caroline?"

The rapid-fire questions were typical of him, and it was only practice with such scrutiny that kept her from betraying her objective.

"Caroline is with Mother. I'm just attending to a—" She dropped her voice and her gaze conspiratorially. "To a womanly matter."

"Are you ill?" She'd forgotten how unfazed Ethan was by mention of womanly matters. "I will take you home at once. I'm sure the carriage—"

She held up her hands to stop the deluge. "Ethan, I'm just going to the retiring room."

She had to raise her voice to speak over him, and now several heads from the doorway of the gaming rooms turned in their direction. She smiled and avoided making eye contact.

Ethan was not so tactful.

"Is there a problem, gentlemen?" His tone suggested that for the sake of the gentlemen, there had better not be one.

The men turned their attention back to the games.

"Excuse me, dear brother," Audrey said and picked up her skirts to indicate the conversation was over.

"Audrey?"

She stopped at the questioning note in her brother's voice, at the soft tone of inquisition.

"Have you seen Lady Atwood?" he asked, his tone just as soft and wondering, his eyes flitting about her without settling.

Atwood was a name not spoken in the D'Arcy household for some time. Not since Ethan and Gavin had returned from Waterloo.

Audrey shook her head. "I hadn't noticed her here this evening."

She didn't miss how her brother flexed his hands into fists and relaxed them. He strode away from her without reply.

She was so absorbed in the oddity of her brother both being in attendance at a ball, speaking the name of his dead best friend, and asking after the whereabouts of the man's widow, she almost forgot she was on an adventure of her own. She took several long strides down the corridor, her thoughts still muddled with her brother's sudden appearance.

What on earth would he want with Lady Atwood?

Lord Amberley was correct. The corridor was deserted at this point, and she found a spot in the shadow of the staircase that led up to the family's quarters.

She had a pleasant view of the ballroom door and was able to watch the earl emerge minutes later, looking as if he were doing nothing more than going for a stroll. Had she known about this trick with the corridors, she would have employed it much earlier in her wallflower days. But then hadn't she witnessed as much when she'd gone to retrieve Grandmother Regina's handkerchief at that fateful ball the week before?

She knew Lord Amberley wouldn't notice her immediately the way she was hidden in shadow, and she took the opportunity to enjoy the sight of him. He was a devastatingly handsome man, and it seemed impossible that she should have shared such an intimate embrace with him. She felt the flare of attraction even now as she observed him and wanted nothing more than to step into the fire and let it consume her. She knew he was more than willing to explore it with her, but something held her back.

The prospect of freedom held her back.

She was almost there, and she couldn't give up now. Not for a handsome face.

Could she?

"Tell me, Lady D'Arcy, do you make a habit of skulking in dark corners?"

Her smile was slow. "Only about as much of a habit as wandering off with earls."

He raised an eyebrow as he drew in front of her.

"I'm not the first earl to lure you away from the safety of the pack?"

"A lady never tells." She had never spoken so boldly in all her life. Perhaps it was something about the shadows, the sounds of the ballroom only feet away and knowing discovery could happen so swiftly and fatally.

Perhaps it was just him, Lord Amberley, who awakened something inside of her. Something with a scandalous beat that called to her.

She hoped it wasn't him because what would that mean for her careful plans?

"Then I suppose our adventure tonight is safe in your care."

She didn't miss how her heart thudded at the word *adventure.*

"I'm not likely to tell anyone, am I?" She had meant it in jest, referring to her solitary wallflower status, but the words spoke too closely to the peril of what they were about to do.

If they were discovered, her reputation would be ruined, and Lord Amberley would be forced to marry her.

She didn't like how her stomach clenched in anticipation at the thought.

This wasn't how it was supposed to be. She was to age

out of the social wheel and be free to pursue her own life without facing criticism and failure at every turn.

But she'd never had a man look at her the way Lord Amberley did, his eyes so intent and bright in the shadows as if she were the only thing in the world. She tried to tell herself it was only because he was a charmer. He was used to this sort of thing, knew exactly how to ply his skills to make a woman melt in his arms.

But he hadn't even touched her. He hadn't spoken a single word in her favor. He'd only accused her of lurking in shadows, and yet she was ready to give up her plan for him. This was utterly ridiculous. She would not fall victim to his charms. She just couldn't.

"I would hope not." His tone had dropped, low and dangerous, and she couldn't help but lick her lips when he peered at her like that.

When he took her hand, her toes curled in her slippers involuntarily.

Perhaps it wasn't her fault. Maybe this man had inordinate control over a woman's physiology. Audrey couldn't be blamed for something that occurred naturally.

He didn't speak again. He tugged on her hand, pulling her into the darkness along the corridor. The sconces that lined the upper part of the walls were not lit as they moved deeper into the house. She knew this was to discourage people from wandering, but it seemed not to hamper his movements at all.

She wondered suddenly if he'd done this before, here in this house. Had he led another lady into the darkness? She gave herself a mental shake. He didn't do that, surely. His reputation had never been something so dastardly.

But who was she to believe? Miss Holloway? She'd only just met the woman after all.

She wasn't sure how far they had gone before he suddenly stopped and pulled her into one of the rooms off the hallway. The darkness here wasn't as complete. Large windows filled one wall, and moonlight flooded the room. She could make out the ghostly shapes of chairs and sofas and accent tables and even what looked to be a harp.

They were in some sort of music room.

He had let go of her hand as soon as they entered, and she heard him rustling behind her. A warm light flooded the space behind her, and she turned to see him lighting a spray of candles set on the table by the door.

Her stomach clenched, not at all in anticipation this time.

"You've done this before."

His glance was questioning. "Done what?"

She backed away, trepidation crawling up her arms. She'd fallen for it. Her. She was the most sensible person she knew, and she'd fallen for his charms. It was really the perfect game. He had convinced everyone he would never harm a lady's reputation, and yet...

She pointed a finger at the candelabra in his hand, hating how much it shook. "You've done this before." She repeated the same words ineffectually.

He eyed the candles. "Lit a candle? Yes, I have done so before."

His glib tone undid something inside of her, and she curled the shaking finger into a fist.

"Excuse me," she said, heading for the door, but he caught her arm as she passed him.

"Are you asking how I would know where to find a light and candles in this room, Lady D'Arcy?"

She hated how she thrilled at his low tone. Damn her

body for responding to his charm even when she was trying desperately to be mad at him.

She poked him in the chest. "You've done this before. That's how you know."

He let go of her arm and walked away, leaving her to stand in front of the door. She eyed it, escape almost tangible, and yet her gaze turned back to him.

"You're right, Lady D'Arcy, I have done this before. Lady Hubert, your hostess this evening. Have you met her?"

Audrey swallowed. Had he seduced the kind, elderly Lady Hubert?

"Briefly, yes."

He set the candelabra on the sideboard under a painting of spaniels in the hunt. When he turned, his smile was broad.

"Lady Hubert is my aunt. I play cards with her on Sundays."

Audrey deflated, the air escaping from her lungs so quickly, she was unable to respond.

"Aunt Mae prefers this room because the light is good. Her eyesight isn't what it used to be, poor dear." He shook his head as he wandered to the other side of the room, found more candles, and lit them, filling the space with a warm, welcoming light. When he was finished, he turned to her. "Do you play cards, Lady D'Arcy?"

He was trying to make her feel comfortable, and the damn man was rather good at it.

She marched over to him and poked him in the chest. She enjoyed doing that, poking him, and she hated herself for finding pleasure in such a childish act.

"I won't be seduced by you."

His mouth tilted up on one side. "Who said anything about seduction, Lady D'Arcy?"

"And stop calling me that."

Both eyebrows went up at this. "Call you what? Your name?"

"My name is Audrey. I've never had anyone call me lady something with such regularity. It's rather—"

"Audrey. Splendid. I'm Dash. I'm glad we can be comfortable using our given names."

She swallowed the urge to rail at him. He had neatly boxed her into that corner, and she couldn't fault him for such skill.

She poked him again as it seemed to be the last thing she held in her arsenal—childish demonstration of frustration.

"I do not wish to court you, Lord Amberley—"

"Dash."

Why did he have to be so handsome when he contradicted her?

"Dash, I do not wish to court you."

"You keep saying as much, but you haven't told me why."

He spoke so calmly, it was infuriating.

"I am going to be a spinster." The words rang through the sudden silence in the room, and for the first time, such a pronouncement seemed ridiculous.

"That might be the case if you do not wish to accept my courtship."

"It will be the case because I plan to not accept any courtship. I wish to be a spinster."

His brow wrinkled, but his tone never changed. "Whatever for?"

She rolled back her shoulders, realizing with a jolt she was enjoying this. She'd never before told anyone of her plan. Not anyone besides Caroline, and she felt a flare of pride at finally telling someone.

"When I'm a spinster, I shall be free of the social obligations expected of me, and I can do as I please." She gave a small nod as if to emphasize her point.

"You'll be free?" He crossed his arms over his chest and seemed to settle in as if he actually cared about what she'd had to say. But then he said, "What will you do with your freedom, Audrey?"

She opened her mouth to tell him exactly what she'd do when she froze. He didn't try to cajole her into speaking. He didn't prompt her to tell him. He merely stood in front of her while her brain scrambled.

Finally she admitted defeat. "I haven't gotten that far actually. I thought I might figure it out when I became a spinster."

He dropped his arms. "You value this freedom so much, and yet you haven't figured out what you might do with it?"

She hated him most when he was being reasonable.

He watched as a myriad of emotions passed through her and found himself once more stunned by her captivating face. Only now he realized what a boon it was.

He could plainly read what she was thinking just by the movement of her face.

The soft candlelight played over her features, highlighting the already mesmerizing effect it had on him, and he wanted nothing more than to stand there, in the quiet, and watch her face. He knew exactly why she was a wallflower, could only imagine what it was that drove her to the illusory freedom of the spinster, but he knew it for the lie it was.

If society only took the time to watch her face like he had, they would understand what a jewel she was.

But that made it all the better, didn't it? No one else knew of her beauty, and he could keep it for himself. But the thought saddened him. Beauty such as hers shouldn't be kept for one. Everyone should see it.

She still hadn't spoken for several seconds, and he took pity on her.

"Your mother is a lovely woman," he said, and while he made to turn away from her and pace across the room, he waited long enough to watch her face transform at the mention of her mother.

He had been standing there in the ballroom long enough to overhear exactly what the Countess of Dartford thought of her daughter, and another piece of the puzzle had clicked into place. Hawk had been right about the woman's disdain for her daughter. He just wanted to see how Audrey felt about it.

She looked about her as if gathering her thoughts before raising her gaze to his. He'd made his way to the other side of the small room, putting a set of sofas between them. It was as though they had drawn battle lines and were forming their fronts.

She pivoted to face him, her hands coming to rest on the back of the sofa before her.

"My mother is a shallow woman, but I trust from your statement you already knew that."

"I did." He settled against his own sofa. "I was merely hoping you'd tell me how you felt about her."

She shrugged. "I feel about her as much as any young woman would feel about her mother when their priorities do not align."

"Priorities?" An interesting choice of words.

"My mother is only interested in what is aesthetically pleasing. I'm afraid I shall never meet her standards, and thus I'm a source of constant disappointment for her."

"Surely not constant." He turned to pace down the length of the room, stopping only long enough to say, "I assume at some point she must sleep. Surely you don't plague her then?"

Audrey gave a small shrug. "Who am I to know? I probably haunt her nightmares."

"You give yourself a great deal of credit. I wouldn't have pegged you for such pride."

She crossed her arms and eyed him. "I do not believe you asked me here to discuss my mother."

He stopped and leaned on the chair he had made his way behind. "No, I didn't. But understanding your relationship with your mother will help me to better understand you."

Even in the candlelight, he could see the flush creep up her face.

"My mother has nothing to do with me."

"She has everything to do with you."

She placed both hands on the sofa and leaned forward. "And I suppose your mother has everything to do with you."

He felt the fatal blow to his heart and sucked in a breath only after he had straightened and turned away from her. He was not the one under scrutiny here, and he had no intention of speaking about his mother. And yet he did.

"Victoria Evers, the Countess of Amberley, excels at being disappointed in her son." He smiled, but the effort he gave it was minimal.

Audrey eyed him. "Your mother too? Perhaps it's something in the water."

He couldn't help but truly smile then. He took a seat on

the sofa opposite her and leaned forward, elbows to knees. "I suppose your mother has critical things to say about your appearance, and you believe that as a spinster you will be free from such criticism."

She blinked. "How do you know that?"

"You said as much yourself."

"I said nothing about—" She licked her lips. "I said nothing about criticisms."

"If you weren't attempting to escape the critical nature of your mother, then why should you seek the supposed freedom of spinsterhood?"

She came around her sofa now and sank down, her eyes intent. "The freedom is not supposed. It is, and I intend to embrace it fully."

He held out his hands. "And yet you know not what to do with it."

"I—" She snapped her lips shut. "I will figure out what to do with it when the time comes."

"That hardly seems like a plan. I took you as being more sensible than that."

"I took you to be more charming."

He raised an eyebrow. "You find me charming?"

She made a noise then and surged to her feet, plodding her way across the room until she took advantage of the whole of it, putting as much space as possible between them it seemed.

He got to his feet and followed her.

"Frustrating and irritating is more like," she muttered when he came up behind her.

"That's not what you said in the cloakroom."

She jumped, and he knew she hadn't heard him approach.

When she spun about, she inadvertently tipped into his

arms. It wasn't fair. He was more skilled at this than she was, but he was suddenly gripped by the urge to hold her, to feel her once more in his arms.

He had believed he'd inflated the incident in the cloakroom, had allowed his memories to be tainted with the attraction he had felt for her subsequently. But he hadn't doctored his memories. She was exactly as he'd remembered. Fire and steel and softness and silk all in one.

Her eyes were mad with defiance while at the same time they bore into him with intensity and passion. Instead of pushing him away, her hands had made their way to the lapels of his jacket where they curled into fists around the fabric, holding him against her just as he held her.

And her legs. Her legs had somehow become entwined with his. She could have taken a step back. He held her loosely enough that she held all the freedom which she claimed to covet, and yet she had planted her feet firmly between his.

"Only because I hadn't had time to get to know you," she said right before she pulled down his head to kiss him.

He wasn't sure who was more startled. He could taste the surprise in the curiousness of her kiss, but it was several seconds before even he understood what was happening. But when he did, he leaned into it, wrapping his arms around her and lifting her slightly against him to deepen the kiss.

He plundered as she gave, and soon he was so caught up in the feel of her, he couldn't remember at all how to be charming, how to make this good for her. He only could think to respond, to feel, to consume more of her.

Because that was what he wanted.

He wanted all of her. For the rest of their lives.

The thought should have been frightening simply from

its enormity, but he felt no fear. This was what he wanted. This was what he had always wanted. This sort of connection with another person. Someone with whom he could forge a future, together.

He had only to convince her she wished for the same.

He shuffled them backward until he felt the arm of a sofa strike the back of his legs, and he let himself fall, keeping his arms fast around her as he controlled their tumble onto the cushions.

She gave a small, startled cry, but he captured it as he reclaimed their kiss, his fingers finding their way into her hair, sending hairpins flying. Her fingers tugged at his cravat, pulling the fabric until his neck and collarbones were exposed, and then the minx slipped her hand inside.

She still wore her glove, and the silk skimmed over his skin. He moaned against her lips, his body aching with the desire to feel her touch him with no barrier between them. But somehow the feel of silk was even more exotic, and his hands traveled down her back until they fit nicely against her buttocks, pulling her more snuggly against him.

She moaned and slipped a leg between his so her knee met the sofa, allowing her to leverage herself above him and take control of the kiss.

Sensation, pure and hot, shot through him at her boldness. For someone so inexperienced, she was not afraid to explore his body and to let him explore hers. The thought thrilled him and terrified him all at once. It was like the mesmerizing allure of fire. Something so life-changing and yet so dangerous if misused.

He'd been burned once before, and he knew to be careful. But he shoved those thoughts aside and buried himself in Audrey. In her kiss, in her touch, in her body.

She came up on him now, and it left him trailing after

her kiss as she nibbled at his lips. Her hands traced the outline of his collarbones exposed by his open shirt and swept up until she cradled his face, drawing him into her kiss.

God, she could end up ruined so swiftly. If only she knew the power she held over him.

She seemed as consumed as he was, her kiss ravenous and her hands imploring. He wanted to give her so much. He wanted to give her everything. If only she'd let him.

He wrenched his lips from her, holding her apart as her eyes slowly refocused. Her lips were swollen, and her riotous hair fell around her beautiful face like a curtain. He wanted to thread his hands through it. He wanted to kiss those sleepy eyelids and those ruddy cheeks. He wanted—

"Audrey, we must stop. I will not damage a lady's reputation."

Those expressive eyes were wide open now and peered around them. "Isn't that what we've already done?"

He sat up, pulling her onto his lap as he did so, pushing the hair from her face. God, it was so soft and thick. He could wrap his hands around it and bury his face in her scent. Not now. Not *yet*.

He settled with simply pressing his forehead against hers.

"Nearly. I swear your honor is quite intact, but it won't be if we stay here much longer."

He eased her from his lap and with the last of his strength, he pushed her away, setting her carefully on the opposite end of the sofa from him.

"Audrey," he said when he'd regained his breath. "I understand your desire for spinsterhood. I really do. But I worry that you've not thought it through entirely. What should happen if you make it firmly on the shelf only to find it's not the carefree life you had imagined?"

Her face settled into serious lines as he spoke, and he knew she was considering his words.

"But what if it is?" she finally whispered.

He scrubbed his face with his hands and took in the quiet room around him while he tried to find a way out of this. Breedlove's cruel laugh trespassed through his mind, and he shoved it aside, determined to focus.

But as soon as he did, an idea came to him. He picked up her hand and held it between both of his.

"I'll make a bargain with you, Lady D'Arcy. Allow me to help you figure out what it is that you plan to do with your freedom, and I will not pursue a courtship with you."

She wrinkled her nose. "But wouldn't I be forced to spend time in your company either way?"

He couldn't stop the grin. "Yes, but in the end, you'll have your plan, and you'll be that much closer to achieving it. In the meantime, I get to spend more time with you."

He knew the perilous edge he walked. She could discover spinsterhood was all she had ever wanted. The freedom from societal demands. The freedom from her mother's criticism.

But he could also make her fall in love with him.

And that was a chance he was willing to take.

She gave a short nod. "You have yourself a bargain, Lord Amberley."

7

It had been easy to escape after that. With her skirts rumpled and her hair in complete disarray, Dash had insisted on getting her to the closest retiring room. Once there, she determined it would be impossible to set herself to rights without someone knowing she had done something more vigorous than dancing.

It was only luck that she collided with Ethan once more in the corridor on her way back to the ballroom. He'd taken one look at her and determined something was wrong. She'd feigned a headache, and while he went along with it, she knew he didn't completely believe her.

She, however, eyed his disgruntled expression and agitated stride and an understanding came between them that they both had secrets they wished the other not to know about. So it was that they spent the carriage ride back to Dartford House in silence.

She'd lain awake that night, her body aflame with the memory of Dash's kiss, of his touch, of his embrace. But her mind—her mind would not settle for the anticipation of what she'd agreed to.

It was only when she'd entered the quiet of her bedchamber that she realized her mistake. She'd agreed to a plan with society's most skilled charmer that contained no perimeters.

He was to help her discover what she wanted from being a spinster but in agreeing to it, she'd failed to set boundaries for what he might show her. Had she done that accidentally or had it been unconsciously intentional?

She had shivered at the thought.

Was she not so unlike the debutantes that flitted around the edges of a ballroom hoping for just a brush of attention from society's eligible bachelors? Was she not so unlike her mother, wishing for a gentleman's attention and appreciation of her physical assets?

She'd shoved that comparison completely out of her mind. She was nothing like her mother. Audrey was sensible and logical and practical. It mattered not what she looked like; it only mattered...

What did matter?

This was the thought that plagued her as she sat across from Caroline at the breakfast table the following morning. Caroline had a tendency of showing up at Dartford House for breakfast some mornings, unannounced, and usually in a whirlwind of discussion as though she and Audrey were already engaged in conversation before Caroline had even arrived.

This morning's topic of conversation was, of course, Hawkins Savage, the Earl of Stonegate.

"He danced with her. Twice." She spoke the last word as though it were a knife, and she was somehow suddenly endowed with an incredible throwing arm.

Audrey blinked. "Perhaps he was being kind. You know what Lady Spencer has been through this season, and it's only been a handful of weeks. There's months ahead of her."

Caroline did not appear appeased. For one, Audrey worried the woman's grip on her fork would snap the implement in two, but worse, Audrey feared should anyone enter the breakfast room then, their death would be perpetrated with a simple look from Caroline.

"He should not have danced with her at all. Lady Spencer is a delight, and she should not be subjected to such pandering."

Audrey paused in the act of pouring herself more tea. "Was it an act of pandering?"

"Who is pandering?" Ethan's words were gruffer than his footsteps as he stomped into the room.

Audrey slid him a glance, her mind casting back to how she had seen him the previous night as he marched in much the same bearish manner from Lady Hubert's ballroom. Her brother seemed much as he always was, taciturn and guarded, and it was as though nothing at all had occurred the night before.

And perhaps nothing had.

Just because Audrey had engaged in an illicit rendezvous with a renowned charmer did not mean her brother had also indulged in risky behavior. She eyed him once more as he poured a measure of coffee into his cup. He added neither sugar nor milk. She couldn't believe her brother could indulge in anything.

"Stonegate," Caroline said the word as though she were addressing something unpleasant like cold turnip soup.

"What's he done now?" This from Gavin as he sailed into the room.

Audrey was surprised to see he was four seconds behind Ethan instead of three.

"He danced with Lady Spencer last night. Twice." Again, she spit the word.

Gavin plopped a heaping serving of eggs onto his plate at the sideboard. "For someone you dislike so much, you talk about him an awful lot."

Caroline turned a nearly mad eye on her cousin. "Of course I do. People must know of his dastardly ways."

Ethan, who had not spoken since Gavin entered the room, considered his cousin with a frown before turning to Audrey. "I trust you are feeling better this morning."

Gavin and Caroline turned inquisitive glances in her direction. She fumbled with her cup of tea.

"Much better. Thank you," she murmured around the edge of her teacup.

Ethan made a gruff noise of confirmation and dug into his eggs.

Caroline set down the fork she had so recently attempted to mutilate. "Were you unwell last night? I didn't see you again after you went off to dance with Lord Amberley."

Ethan abandoned his eggs faster than her mother would have abandoned an invitation from anyone lower than a countess.

"You danced with Lord Amberley last night?"

Audrey wondered not for the first time if this was the look Ethan had given the soldiers in his command on the continent.

She was happy to reply, "No, I did not dance with him."

Caroline's brow wrinkled, and Audrey smiled with immense satisfaction that she was not forced to lie to her brother.

"I did not dance with him," she repeated directly to her cousin before turning with an explanation to Ethan.

"Mother suggested that I should, but I knew it would be unwise, so I refused. Politely, of course."

Ethan considered her for a moment and went back to his eggs without comment.

Caroline continued to watch her, however, and Audrey shifted under her scrutiny.

"I, for one, don't see what's so bad about the chap. Miss Holloway says his reputation is impeccable," Gavin said.

"Miss Holloway?" Caroline perked up at the mention of Lady Spader's companion.

"Did you speak with her again last night?"

Gavin gave a casual shrug that Audrey saw for the guise it was. "Only when our paths crossed."

"They crossed more than once in that crowded ballroom?" Audrey asked as Gavin settled into a chair at the table.

He took a mouthful of eggs before he could respond, but Ethan grumbled from the head of the table, "Bloody hard to cross paths with anyone in a ballroom even when you're intent on finding someone."

Once more Audrey wondered why Ethan would be seeking out Lord Atwood's widow.

Gavin looked as though he might comment, but his attention was pulled to the doorway as Philip sauntered into the room.

"There you are," he said as he took in his sister. "You weren't in the breakfast room at home, and I thought I might find you here."

He went to the sideboard and helped himself as if he lived there, which given how much the cousins were at the other set of cousins' house it might seem as though they all lived under the same roof.

"Oh, Philip, dear, you're late as usual," Caroline said over her shoulder in her brother's direction. "Do you remember Miss Holloway from the other night?"

"The companion?" he asked, shoveling sausages onto his plate.

"She's more than just a companion," Gavin muttered at a forkful of tomato.

"Do you remember what she had to say about Lord Amberley?" Caroline asked, ignoring Gavin's grumblings.

"Lord Amberley? You mean Dash?"

Caroline turned in her seat to face her brother as Audrey's attention flew to her cousin.

"You call him Dash? I didn't realize you were so familiar with him. You didn't say so the other night." Caroline's gaze narrowed.

Philip shrugged and eyed the kippers with a wrinkled nose. "It didn't come up. Miss Holloway seemed to have the matter in hand." He passed on the kippers and speared a length of bacon. "Dash was at school with us."

Caroline's eyes narrowed. "Would that us include Lord Stonegate?"

Philip plopped the bacon on his plate. "It would," he said, oblivious to his sister's growing ire.

Audrey had not been aware of this either.

"You were at Cambridge with Lord Amberley then? What is your impression of him?" Gavin asked.

Ethan stabbed a sausage, pretending to ignore the conversation, but Audrey didn't miss how his eyes slid to the right to take in Philip approaching the table.

"Dash is a fine bloke. He's considerate and genuinely honorable. No matter what is said about that business with Lady Wilson a few years back."

Ethan gave up all pretense of ignoring the conversation as he dropped his fork and speared his cousin with a glare.

Audrey hid behind her teacup, her eyes watchful and intent.

"What business with Lady Wilson?" Ethan growled.

Philip held a forkful of egg in front of his lips but set it down when he glanced in Ethan's direction.

"He was engaged to Lady Nicole Wilson a few years ago. We were just out of school at the time, if I remember. She broke off the betrothal though."

"Do you have any idea why?" Caroline asked.

Philip shook his head and chewed his eggs thoughtfully. After swallowing, he said, "Dash never really said. He's rather private about that sort of thing."

"What sort of thing?" Ethan again.

"His family. Dash has had a rather hard go of it at home. He likes to keep quiet about it."

Gavin sipped at his coffee. "Why so quiet? Surely we all have a hard go of it with our families. That's what family is all about, isn't it?"

Audrey didn't miss the glance he sent in Ethan's direction, and her heart squeezed, wondering not for the first time nor the millionth what exactly happened that day at Waterloo. The day Ethan received the scars that now marked his face like a map.

But Philip shook his head at this. "It wasn't like that, I'm afraid. Much darker stuff." He pointed down the table with his fork. "Dash holds honor above all else. Of that, you can be certain."

Ethan did not appear convinced, a deep divot forming between his brows. "A man who is not free to speak of his family does not seem honorable to me."

Philip took a sip of coffee. "But that's just it. Honor keeps him from speaking of it."

Audrey didn't know what Ethan might do with this, but

then her brother settled back in his chair, crossing his arms over his chest in silent rumination.

"What sort of dark stuff? Surely there have been rumors?" Audrey was grateful for Caroline's forthrightness just then, because she desperately wanted to know what could be so terrible that Dash wouldn't speak of it.

Her mind conjured the image of him, his dashing smile and dangerous good looks. How could a man brimming with such happiness be plagued by something so terrible?

And why would this Lady Wilson break off their engagement? Had Dash loved her? Lud, why was she even thinking it?

She was already so terribly confused about the man, and now she was inexplicably tethered to him because of her outrageous bargain.

Philip shook his head again. "It's only what's been surmised. You know how society can draw conclusions based on what's only seen from the outside."

Audrey set down her cup, painfully aware of the truth of Philip's words, but she returned her gaze to him immediately, her heart pounding to know what else he might say.

Philip took another bite of eggs and chewed thoroughly before continuing. "You know Dash was never meant to be the earl. He had an older brother, David. He died."

"Oh, that's terrible," Caroline whispered.

"That's not so unusual," Gavin said, turning his head ever so slightly to take in Ethan. "Even if it is heartbreaking."

Philip gestured with his fork before stabbing another bit of sausage. "It's not his brother's death that's the dark part. He died in his bed of scarlet fever. As you say, those things do happen. It's what his parents did that caused the rumors to start."

"What did his parents do?" Try as she might to appear

uninterested, Audrey was unable to resist interjecting as Philip seemed to be taking his time in relating the story.

Philip turned his gaze on her, and not for the first time she was struck by how unaffected her cousin always seemed. Even when he was relating a story that could so severely affect her future.

His tone was flat as he said, "They had Dash."

Audrey blinked. "I beg your pardon?"

She wasn't sure what she had been expecting, but it was surely something more prosaic than that.

Philip nodded and took another bite of eggs. "They had Dash. They were older at the time. David was eighteen when he died after all. It couldn't have been more obvious that Dash was meant as some kind of replacement for his dead brother."

Audrey felt her stomach fall, and she regretted that last cup of tea. "Replacement?" She could hardly force the word between her lips.

Philip nodded. "For the whole of his life, the poor man's been compared to a dead man he's never even met."

WHAT WAS on the stage didn't hold his interest the way what was off the stage did, and Dash found himself willing intermission to come more quickly, so he could make his way to Lady Hodge's box. He could just make out the dowager marchioness from where he was sitting. Her white crown of hair glinted in the harsh light from the stage, and he thought he could see the profile of the obscure and dearly beloved Aunt Verity.

Not for the first time did Dash wonder what sort of strange hold the woman had over Audrey. Did she see her aunt Verity's life as glamorous simply because the woman existed out from under the critical eye of the Countess of Dartford? Or was it something else? Was it the idea that a woman required a husband to lead a fulfilled life?

There were two problems with this.

The first being that he feared Lady Verity Hodge did not have a fulfilled life. The few times he'd seen her she appeared careworn and gray as though she were simply moving through the tasks of the day and eschewing from all things that may pertain to an actual life.

The second problem was that should Audrey find a fulfilling life on her own it would preclude him, and just the idea of it made him sad. It was all terribly selfish, but he found when it came to Audrey, he wanted to be selfish. He wanted to keep all of her for himself. Her wit, her intelligence, her own special kind of charm.

He couldn't though. She was too much of a delight to keep squandered away, and though it pained him, he knew he would share her. Perhaps when she was the Countess of Amberley more people would notice her. This was the saddest thought of all, and for a moment, he understood what Audrey might face every day she stepped into society. How cruel to be judged before one even got a chance to prove oneself.

He swallowed an uncomfortable lump in his throat and turned back to the stage, hoping the entertainment for the evening had grown more interesting. It had not, but he was relieved when the curtain went down only minutes later, and after a delicate round of applause for the performers, the patrons began to rise and shuffle about their seats, some switching boxes to visit with friends and filtering out into the lobby for refreshment.

Dash rose. "Shall I mention to the youngest Lady Hodge that you are in attendance tonight?"

Hawk raised his eyes from where he'd been exchanging glances with a petite blonde across the way. "Oh, please do. I could use a little stimulation to get me through the next act."

"What's that, dear?" Hawk's grandmother, Lady Sherrill, said over her shoulder from her perch in the front row of the box.

Hawk leaned forward to pat her shoulder reassuringly. "It's nothing, Grandmama." He leaned back and flashed a grin in Dash's direction.

Dash felt almost guilty ruining his friend's good mood. "I'm afraid it's a five-act play tonight."

Hawk's expression fell. "Dear God. Perhaps I shall partake of some refreshment then."

He got up and followed Dash from the box.

Dash was rather surprised to find a line streaming out of the box that belonged to the Earl of Dartford, but as he drew near, he discovered the line consisted mainly of young men wet about the ears or worse, still at school in Oxbridge. He marched up to the clog at the door and cleared his throat.

"Excuse me, gentlemen."

The one closest to him turned a scathing glance in his direction. "We were here first, chum."

Dash raised an eyebrow. Is that how they were teaching young men to address their elders these days?

The man turned about and resumed struggling to peer over the shoulder of the man in front of him. Dash looked heavenward before reaching up and grabbing the collar of the young man who had so readily snubbed him. The man let out a squeak of surprise, drawing the attention of the other men crowded at the door.

Dash drew the young man's ear closer to his lips so he could whisper, "And you should learn to mind your manners." He set the young man aside, and the other gentlemen still in the doorway backed up on scrambling feet.

Dash pressed his way inside only to find the box as crowded as the corridor. Lady Hodge sat in the foremost row, slumped in her chair, and Dash suspected, likely napping. The esteemed Aunt Verity sat next to her, her gaze unflinchingly set on the stage as if she were attempting to avoid the debacle behind her.

Lady Caroline Hodge was swarmed with young men attempting to get her attention. It was ridiculous to watch the grown men bandy about her, but it wasn't what forced him into action. It was the sight of Audrey sitting quietly beside her cousin, her gaze on her hands folded in her lap. Not a single young man spoke to her.

His heart twisted at the injustice, but at the same time, he thrilled at the sight of it. She was his for the taking, and no one would even know what they had missed. He strode forward, shoving aside another dandy sporting an outrageous outfit entirely designed of pink and bent to greet the youngest Lady Hodge with a grin.

"His lordship, the Earl of Stonegate, sends his regards. He says you look particularly lovely this evening."

He felt more than saw Audrey's head turn at this, and his smile grew more wicked.

Lady Hodge surged to her feet with a noise he swore he'd heard a barnyard animal produce and flew from the box, taking her crowd of swooning dandies with her.

Dash watched them go with mild satisfaction before turning back to the remaining occupants of the box. He bowed to Lady Verity Hodge and the dowager, who was indeed sound asleep in her chair.

"Lady Hodge," he said to the spinster aunt. "You look lovely this evening."

She gained her feet almost immediately, a tight smile on her lips. "I must thank you properly sometime for ridding our box of those men, but for now, I must excuse myself." She cast a glance in Audrey's direction. "Grandmother Regina will be an adequate chaperone for you."

All three of them cast a dubious eye in Grandmother Regina's direction, but Lady Hodge seemed satisfied and left the box at a modest clip.

Dash turned an inquisitive eye on Audrey.

"I think it's the only time she'll have to see to her own needs," Audrey said, her attention slipping to her grandmother who let out a soft snore.

That worked well for him, and he dropped into the seat Audrey's cousin had just vacated.

"Good evening, Lady D'Arcy. You look lovely this evening. How are you finding the theater?"

"Oh, come off it. What do you want?"

He leaned back in the chair, making himself comfortable. "I'm visiting you in your theater box. Have you ever had a gentleman visit you before?"

Her eyes narrowed. "No."

He gestured with a hand. "There you have it. I am already expanding your horizons as I promised to do."

She wrinkled her nose. "Is this your attempt to help me determine what it is I shall do with my freedom?"

He smiled. "I think I'm proving rather good at it."

"You've proven nothing at all." She shook her head. "I don't plan on gentlemen visiting my box should I be a spinster."

"Well, that would be a terrible shame. And rather lonely if you think of it." He passed a casual glance over the crowd, keenly aware of Audrey at his shoulder.

Her gaze never left the side of his face as she seemed to consider his words.

"I don't think it shall be lonely." The words came out as hardly more than a whisper, her tone soft and wondering.

He turned and met her gaze, and he could feel the thing that existed between them as if it were real. He had promised not to court her, but he had never promised to resist the attraction he felt for her.

"I think it should be terribly lonely." He held her gaze, knowing that a look could be far more seductive than a caress if done properly, and when several seconds later she looked away and licked her lips nervously, he knew she had felt it.

She had felt the truth of his words because for one moment he made her feel what it would be like to live the spinster life she craved. It would be a life without him. It had been a gamble considering it hadn't been a fortnight since they had met, but he knew the strength of the thing that existed between them.

"Have you thought any more about what you would like to try in order to figure out what you will do with your freedom, Lady D'Arcy?"

She blinked several times as if rearranging her thoughts.

"I haven't—" She stopped so abruptly her top teeth came to rest on her lower lip. And then strangely enough, she stood. It was just enough that she could lean forward and take in her sleeping grandmother's face. Seemingly satisfied by what she found, she resumed her seat and faced him directly.

"I didn't know about your brother. My cousin Philip told

me, and it's not my place to speak but—" She licked her lips, her tongue passing over her too large front teeth. "Well, I'm heartbroken for you. You have a brother that you will never know, who will never know you, and brothers can often be wonderful things." She gave a wobbly smile as if thinking of her own protective brothers. "And instead, you'll always live in his shadow, and that's not fair. It's rather cruel actually, and I just wanted to tell you that's how I felt." She stopped, but she looked as though she wished to say more. He waited, holding his breath, but finally, she looked away without speaking.

They sat in silence for several seconds, and he let the space around him settle like falling leaves. He felt upended and hollow at the same time, as though what he had expected had turned out not to be what happened at all. He was left directionless, sitting there beside her, and he couldn't remember any of the charming things he'd planned to say.

He was wasting precious time. Either of the ladies Hodge could return any minute. He had only this stolen moment in time in which to press his case, whatever that case was, but he couldn't remember right then, and instead, he found himself drifting as though he had been set free from something that had been holding him down.

Audrey studied the other patrons filtering in and out of boxes and mingling with the crowds on the floor below, so when he took her hand in his, she started, her lips parting but no sound emerging. She looked first down at where their hands met in the space between their seats and then back up at him before averting her gaze so no one would suspect what was happening out of sight.

He squeezed her hand once and released it.

By the time the senior Lady Hodge returned with a

small smile and a ducked head, he was already on his feet wishing Grandmother Regina a good evening even though the woman was still presumably asleep.

Audrey smiled and gave a nod as he made to leave, but he could see the way her features stumbled, and the expression didn't quite stick.

He was several feet down the corridor on his way back to Hawk's box when he stopped and pressed a hand to the wall, sucking in a much-needed breath. He turned back to look at the curtain that marked the entrance to the Dartford box, but he still couldn't quite make out what had just happened to him.

8

"I can't believe he would even think of it!"

Audrey had a difficult time focusing on Caroline as her cousin paced across the drawing room and back again, her skirts a mad flutter of indignation.

Audrey found it difficult to concentrate because her mind kept wandering to the night at the theater when Dash had taken her hand in his and squeezed it gently, an understanding so acute and yet so deep passing between them.

She'd never felt closer to another human being than in that moment.

Was this what all of those flighty debutantes sought? This heady, intoxicating connection with another person?

She was not naive enough to believe it. The stark reality was many debutantes were forced to find a match deemed advantageous by their father or one that brought wealth into the family. Love was a luxury few could afford, but that did not make it any less addictive.

Because that was what had happened to her. Audrey. Quiet, mousy Audrey had become addicted to the way her heart raced when she was near him, the way her body seemed to tingle when it merely sensed he was within close proximity.

The way he kissed her was one thing. His kisses tended to consume her until she wasn't sure where she ended and he began, but that was only part of her growing addiction.

He seemed to know exactly how to get her ire up, where to press and needle, and it should have made her angry, but it didn't. No one had ever known her well enough to have such an effect on her, but now there was.

Someone *knew* her.

She wasn't the Countess of Dartford's unfortunate daughter any longer. She was a person. A person the Earl of Amberley appeared to find appealing.

He had promised to give up his pursuit of courtship should she agree to his bargain, but after that night at the theater, she suddenly wondered if she'd made the wrong choice.

Should she have chosen courtship all along?

No, that would never do.

She had plans, and they didn't include a husband. Her freedom was within reach, and she couldn't allow anything to deter her. Not even sweet, secret kisses and dangerous rendezvous.

Would he try to kiss her again now that she'd dissuaded him from his courtship?

And if not, why did she feel such pain low in her stomach at the thought of never feeling his touch again?

It was all nonsense. She needn't be without the touch of a man if she should choose so. After all, that was what freedom was all about. She could make the decisions.

Then why did the idea of an existence without Dash in it suddenly frighten her?

Caroline swung about, her nostrils flaring. "I thought we

had put all of this behind us. I thought once they were no longer thrown together in the confines of Cambridge, Philip would see reason." She stopped so quickly her skirts swooshed about her legs. She pinned Audrey with a glare Audrey knew was not meant for her. "We must stop him from going." Caroline's laugh was brittle. "Of course. Why didn't I think of it sooner?" She took a truncated step forward. "Of course we must stop him."

Audrey plucked herself from the whirlpool of her thoughts at her cousin's dangerous stare.

"We care to stop your brother—a grown man I should add—from attending a house party thrown by his best friend's *grandmother*?" She emphasized the grandmotherly bit.

Surely Caroline couldn't object to what may occur under the nose of a matronly old woman.

Caroline stuck her fisted hands against her hips. "That is precisely why we must stop him. That old bird wouldn't know if a turkey landed in her lap. It's the perfect opportunity for Stonegate to lure Philip into more trouble." Her face suddenly folded, losing the stark quality her anger had fueled. "I can't let it happen, Audrey." Her voice had grown quiet too. "Not after what happened before..."

She needn't finish the sentence. They had both been present when Philip's future had seemed on the brink of utter disaster.

Audrey stood and went to her cousin, tugging her fists away and prying her hands open until they relaxed into hers.

"We will not let anything happen to Philip ever again. You know that. But don't you think we should give Philip a little more credit now that he's older and wiser?"

Caroline's brow furrowed in obvious objection. "I think I

should be even stricter now that Philip is older. He's had too much experience, and experience can only lead to poor decisions."

Audrey blinked as she tried to work out her cousin's reasoning. "Do you plan to follow Philip around for the whole of his life then to ensure he won't commit to a poor decision in future?"

Caroline's mouth opened, and Audrey readied herself for the retort she knew to be coming. But then her cousin shut her mouth even as her eyes widened, and her lips tipped into a smile.

Apprehension gripped Audrey as she understood only too well what that look meant.

Caroline had just gotten an idea, and somehow it was going to be inconvenient for Audrey. She just knew it.

Caroline turned her hands over as they were still in Audrey's grip, and she squeezed Audrey's hands reassuringly. At least, it was supposed to be, Audrey was certain, but she felt anything but assured.

"Of course!" Caroline said with more enthusiasm than Audrey had heard her summon in the entire season. "I'll follow Philip!" Her laugh now bordered on manic. "Of course, how could I have been so stupid?" She let go of Audrey's hands to press her own to her forehead. "If I can't stop him from going, I can follow him so as to prevent him from making a very dumb mistake." She seized Audrey by the shoulders. "You are rather brilliant, you know?"

Audrey had been too dumbfounded to speak up until this point, her lips parted with no sound emerging. But then Caroline squeezed her hands once more and let go, striding toward the door. She was nearly gone before Audrey got her wits about her to respond.

"No. Caroline. Wait." She picked up her skirts and went after her retreating cousin.

Hodge House was often quiet during the late morning. Caroline's mother hardly rose before noon, and Uncle Reginald often left the house early to attend to business, as he said. Audrey thought he was just escaping to his club. Regardless, it left the cousins freedom to visit, and Audrey often found her way over to Caroline's before long, and that morning had been much like any other. Except she'd arrived to find Caroline in such a state.

Audrey chased after her now down the quiet corridors as her cousin wove her way to the back of the house. When she disappeared through the study door, Audrey was not surprised.

She was only two steps behind her when she stopped fully in the doorway to watch the tableau unfold before her. Caroline, fists at the hips. Hawk, reclined in a chair in front of the desk. Said desk occupied by Philip. The gentlemen had obviously been in some sort of discussion over a pile of correspondence they had clearly been passing back and forth and had stopped midreach when Caroline entered.

"Philip," Caroline spoke clearly, her firm voice echoing in the quiet of the study. "I shall allow you to attend the house party at Stonegate."

Hawk blinked sleepily. "Well, that's rather good of you," he muttered.

Caroline glared at him before turning a soft smile upon her brother. "I will allow you to attend," she repeated, sliding a glance at Hawk to see if he might interrupt. He didn't. Wisely, Audrey thought. "Because I shall be accompanying you to the party."

Philip set down the correspondence in his hand with a

thump. "You will not. A house party is no place for a debutante."

Caroline's glare turned thunderous. "I'm not a debutante, Philip. This is my second season. I'm practically on the shelf."

Caroline wasn't even near the shelf, but Audrey refrained from rolling her eyes at her cousin's dramatics.

Philip stood. "Semantics, Caroline. I will not allow you to attend a house party."

Caroline raised her chin. "So, you're admitting that house parties are filled with debauchery and mischief?"

Hawk scoffed. "Of course they are. Otherwise, why would anyone attend?"

Caroline's eyes grew so wide, Audrey feared for what was to come and stepped into the melee, placing a calming hand on her cousin's arm.

"I'm sure we can reach a mutual understanding here. Philip, perhaps you can promise Caroline that you shall refrain from anything improper?"

Hawk traced the arm of his chair with a single finger. "I find the word *improper* to be so subjective. Don't you, pet?" The glance he flicked in Caroline's direction was volatile.

Audrey sent a prayer to any and all gods who might be listening that there not be bloodshed that day.

"Philip?" Audrey interjected before Caroline could raise to Hawk's bait.

Philip pinched the bridge of his nose with two fingers. "I have already promised as much. Caroline, you must believe me—"

"No," Caroline snapped. "I will not allow your future to hang on mere trust."

Hawk dropped his feet to the floor and stood, his face suddenly tight. "Mere trust? You're one to talk. You spout nonsense about trust and yet you demand Philip trust you." He leaned down, his face only inches from Caroline's. "Why should he trust you and your judgment when you don't reciprocate? Pet." He spat the last word as if it were a final nail being driven into a coffin.

Audrey pulled Caroline forcibly away. "Please. The both of you. You are both adults now, and you can try to behave as such." She spoke over them to Philip. "How many days is this house party? Perhaps Caroline will agree to accompany you for part of it?"

"All of it," Caroline ground out between clenched teeth, her eyes still locked on Hawk.

Hawk straightened and crossed his arms over his chest. "Fine. I'll have Grandmother arrange an invitation for you as well."

"What?" Audrey blurted out the word before she knew she would, and Caroline seemed to deflate under her arm.

"What did you say?" Caroline asked, the incredulity apparently catching.

"I said I'll arrange to have an invitation for you. I'm sure Grandmother won't mind. She likes having young people in the house."

Caroline passed her gaze over Hawk and Philip. "Are you agreeing to my request?"

Hawk scoffed again. "Hardly. I'm forging a compromise so my friend may have some quiet time spent in the country."

Caroline's eyes narrowed. "Quiet time. Is that how you refer to it?"

"Refer to what?" The edge had returned to Hawk's voice.

Audrey tugged on Caroline's arm. "Wouldn't it be wise to leave it at that, Caroline? At least you'll be there, which is what you wished for."

Caroline didn't reply straight away; her eyes merely narrowed farther until Audrey couldn't be sure if the woman saw anything at all.

Finally, she straightened and tugged her arm free from Audrey's grasp.

"Fine then. I shall look forward to your invitation." She nodded once as she ran her palms along her skirt as if to resemble some sort of calm. "Be sure one is sent round for Audrey too."

Audrey had been watching Philip's reaction to the two most important people in his life determining his fate for him and almost missed this last bit.

"I'm sorry. What?"

"You would like an invitation for Audrey as well?" Hawk's gaze was penetrating, but Caroline didn't back down.

"Yes, of course. You don't expect me to attend a house party unchaperoned, do you?"

"I expect your mother can serve as chaperone," Audrey muttered, but Caroline only gave her a look that suggested how ineffectual her mother would be at protecting her daughter's reputation. But then she retuned her gaze to Hawk and neither of them was listening. They had entered some kind of duel that consisted of threatening eye movements.

She cast a baleful gaze in Philip's direction, but he merely shrugged. Of course he would be helpless. Just as much as Audrey was.

~

HE HAD THOUGHT about giving up entirely.

Even now as he stood at the edge of another ball, he

thought about it. He had tried to understand what had overcome him at Audrey's words that night at the theater. Had it been only her words? Had it been her tone? Had it been the way she so unequivocally stated the things he had felt for so long?

It wasn't fair living in the shadow of someone long dead, someone he would never meet. Never have the chance to understand and know. It wasn't fair that his entire existence predicated on his mother's desire to bring her son back from the dead.

Dash could never succeed at such a desire, but he could only imagine the pain that fueled it. He would understand it if his mother ever let him in. From the moment he had been born, he had been passed off to someone else. First it was the nannies and then the tutors and then onto schools.

A few times a year he was brought round to whatever house his mother was currently inhabiting to be presented to her as if for inspection. He recalled very few of them for it was always the same. Her eyes so wide and expecting only to pinch once they lay upon his face as if the expectation hadn't met her ideal and the pain of memory had robbed her of further sight.

He claimed that it didn't bother him, and he would even go so far as to say he wouldn't let it bother him. For why should it? The circumstances were wholly unfair, and how could he cast blame at his feet when he'd never been given a chance at the start?

Because it was easy to cast blame. It was easy to want a mother's love. It was easy to blame oneself when the love wasn't forthcoming.

Even as a sound adult, he understood that. He had always lacked a mother's love no matter how he refuted it.

Only now...

His mind scrambled whenever he tried to set his thoughts to some kind of order. He thought it all so simple. He had only to marry someone who captured his interest, start a family of his own, and then he would be...what? Fulfilled? That seemed a rather strange choice of words for the hollowness left by his mother's disregard. But somehow, he had made that determination.

The only change he'd made since coming to that conclusion was that the woman had to be someone who didn't know about David and didn't know him when he was alive. He had learned that lesson with Nicole.

But he had felt such a strong flash of certainty with Audrey. He had been so sure. But after that night at the theater, after the way she had so carefully spoken the words —she had said brother instead of speaking the man's name —he worried now. He worried that she would indulge him in pity, but even as he thought it, he knew that not to be true. Her tone had been one of absolute fact, not heart-wrenching pity.

Why then did he feel so unsure of himself now?

Why then had he thought about giving it all up?

He had thought himself so clever when he devised the scheme to lure her into his presence. He had appealed to her adventurous side, her thirst for freedom, and he knew if only she were to get to know him, he could charm her into liking him.

But now he wondered.

What would it mean if he did charm her? Would their relationship be built on the skill he had crafted over years in society? Would it mean what he needed it to mean if it were based on something so flimsy?

He couldn't even use the proper word for it.

Love.

Would it really be love if he convinced her it was?

He watched the couples swirling before him on the dance floor. He couldn't recall how many times he had witnessed a similar scene, and he found the boredom settle deep inside of him.

He was never bored when he was with Audrey. Perhaps that meant something.

Her face suddenly appeared through the crowd, and for a moment, he wondered if he had conjured her with his thoughts. Her face—God, that captivating face. Would he ever grow immune to it? Now it was pinched, her eyes darting back and forth as if she were searching for something. For some*one*. He realized with a start she was looking for him.

He turned, facing her fully so she may have a better chance of spotting him. It would be unseemly for him to approach her as she was unchaperoned, and they were not that well acquainted. Yet. He waited, willing her to see him, and finally she did.

His smile came easily as she threaded her way through the crowd only to vanish when she stopped in front of him.

"We need to talk," she whispered, her eyes darting to the people crowded around them.

She had changed her mind about the bargain then. He wasn't sure why the thought, so negative and harsh, came so quickly, and he looked away from her face as if to clear his thoughts.

"Lady D'Arcy, would you permit me a turn about the room?" He held his arm aloft. A promenade about the room was not the same as a dance, and he thought she might not balk at the suggestion. He wondered why she worried about them being seen together so much. His reputation should have shielded her from any serious connotations, but perhaps any connotation was too much.

She slipped her hand onto his arm, and he turned to lead them about the room. She didn't speak until they were in a less crowded part of the ballroom.

"I must leave London for a short time, and I'm not entirely certain when I shall return."

"Leave London? Are you unwell?" He wasn't sure why a spike of concern sprouted inside of him at the thought of her sudden departure from town.

She shook her head softly, her mouth pinched. "It isn't anything like that. I must accompany my cousin to a house party."

He raised an eyebrow. "You're attending a house party? I'm sure your mother will be going with you."

Audrey's mouth pinched harder. "I haven't mentioned it to her yet actually."

He tried to swallow his laughter. "You think you're going to a house party, and you haven't mentioned it to your mother yet?"

She slid him a weighty glance. "I should think she'll be pleased to hear I've received an invitation at all."

"How did you receive this invitation?" Now that the initial shock had worn off, concern had begun to replace it, and he wondered who it was that may be preying on the sensibilities of young women.

Regardless of the aspirations Audrey had for the shelf, she was still an unattached young woman, and someone had to look out for her reputation if her mother failed to do the job.

"I'm to chaperone my cousin, Caroline."

He stopped so suddenly, she tugged on his arm. When she turned to look at him, an eyebrow raised in question, he only shook his head and took her hand in his, slipping it firmly through the crook of his elbow before pulling her in the direction of the terrace doors.

He wasn't surprised when she pulled, rather frantically, back against his arm.

"Dash," she whispered, the sound so small no one could have heard her use of his given name, but he didn't stop.

He didn't stop when he pulled her out onto the terrace, their shoes ringing against the stones, and he didn't stop when they reached the stairs leading down into the garden. It wasn't until they were surrounded by the shadows of the hedges that he stopped and turned her to face him, keeping his hands on her shoulders.

"You're going to chaperone your cousin," he repeated, trying his best to keep his tone neutral. "Audrey, *you* require a chaperone. You're hardly in a position to provide such care to another."

She stiffened beneath his hands. "I do not. After this season, I shall be—"

"Firmly on the shelf. Yes, I've heard as much. But none of that matters at a house party. A house party is the very place to hang all of society's rules. Your mother surely cannot approve of this."

She tugged her shoulders out from under his hands and crossed her arms under her bosom. "I'm sure she will be delighted to hear—"

"Then she is a terrible mother."

Her wide eyes grew even wider, and her lip drew up over her overbite. "My mother..." She seemed to come to some kind of conclusion and shook her head, starting over. "My mother *is* a terrible mother, but that's beside the point. I'm perfectly capable of—"

"You are not—"

"Will you cease interrupting me?"

They both stopped speaking then as the realization that their tones had grown rather loud came over them. They both stood perfectly still and listened to see if they had been found out. When no one burst through the hedges to discover them, he continued.

"You are not capable of protecting yourself or your cousin at a house party. House parties are known to be the utmost in debauchery, and I shan't allow you to attend."

She scoffed. "Oh, you shan't allow me to attend? Well, all right then. I was really thinking of going, but now that you've *forbidden* it, I guess I won't. I'm so glad I have you to deny me things." She poked him solidly in the chest. "And this is exactly why I long for the shelf. I will not have a man telling me what to do. I've already withstood my mother's directives. I shall not continue to be the subject of another's whims."

He drew a deep breath and held up his hands. "Audrey, I'm sorry. I didn't mean that. I was simply overcome at the idea of..." But his voice just trailed away.

The moon shifted just then, and a sliver of light fell across her face, and once more, he was discovering it anew. Would he ever know it fully? He thought not, and he thrilled at the idea.

"Overcome at the idea of what?" she whispered after several seconds of silence, but he noticed she watched him as carefully as he watched her.

Finally, he only shook his head. "It's nothing. You're right. I have no say in what you choose to do, and I can only hope that you will keep your wits about you."

"I have every intention of doing so," she said, but her eyes wandered about his face as if she were thinking of something else.

"What is it?" he finally asked.

She shook her head but said, "I think I finally understand how my cousin Philip felt. Caroline won't allow him to make his own decisions, so she insisted on attending the house party he'd received an invitation to. I realize now this is what it must feel like to have someone so concerned for your reasoning."

"Lady Hodge intends to nanny Philip at a house party? Whatever for?"

Audrey shook her head. "Philip got into some difficulties a few years ago, and I think Caroline has the odd notion she can prevent him from making further poor choices."

Dash laughed, unable to stop it. "Difficulties? I would wager nuns are more apt to find themselves in difficulties than Philip Hodge."

Audrey's brow wrinkled. "What do you mean? How can you know that about Philip? It's such a personal matter."

"I went to school with Philip," he said with a shrug. "One tends to learn much about their mates in such close proximities."

Her features dimmed. "Then you must have learned a great deal about the Earl of Stonegate as well."

"I know Hawk very well. Why?"

Audrey shrugged. "Caroline blames him for the trouble Philip got into, and it's his grandmother's house party we are to attend."

The idea formed without his bidding, and he dismissed it immediately. But maybe...

"Perhaps I'll come too."

Audrey's eyes flashed to his.

"You'll come too? To the house party, you mean?"

He nodded, the idea taking shape. "Of course. We'll be

able to continue our bargain there. House parties are ripe with the opportunity to stretch your freedom."

Her stare could have frozen champagne. "You just said house parties were no place for a young woman like me."

"That was before I knew I would be there to protect you." He wondered at the tightening in his stomach at the idea. Protecting Lady D'Arcy? He wouldn't hesitate to do so.

"How can you be so sure you'll be able to gain an invitation?"

He couldn't stop his smile from tipping into a grin. "Hawk's grandmother loves me."

Audrey's captivating face fell into an expression of utter annoyance. "I bet she does."

9

She shouldn't have been able to ruminate on anything during the short ride to Hawk's grandmother's estate in Surrey. With Caroline and Philip curating a stream of constant bickering and Aunt Phyllida staring morosely out the window, her cold, empty stare somewhat unnerving, Audrey shouldn't have been capable of getting lost in her own thoughts.

But she did.

She was coming to understand just how easy it was for Lord Amberley to infiltrate her thoughts and how easy it was to then ruminate on them.

He had lured her into a dark garden, and she hadn't even noticed.

To be fair, he didn't exactly lure her. She had been the one to approach him, and it was she who needed to speak to him so urgently. By such accounts, it had been her fault, ending up in the secluded garden with him in the dark no less. But she couldn't help the niggling suspicion that it was entirely his doing.

He hadn't acted in the least improper though. He'd

touched her shoulders now and then and sometimes took her arm as he led her through the darkness, but there was nothing untoward about it. He was the perfect gentleman.

Curse him.

Maybe Miss Holloway was right. He never did endanger a lady's reputation. He was merely charming.

So why did Audrey want him to be more...improper?

At least with her.

The thought sent her resolve cartwheeling, and she resolutely stared out the window, trying to focus on the passing trees.

She mustn't let herself get distracted by him. They had a bargain, and that was all. She determined to discover exactly what it was she wished to do with her freedom just as soon as she achieved it.

In the meantime, she wouldn't let herself ruminate over the existence of Lady Wilson.

"Audrey agrees with me."

She was wrenched from her frustrating reverie at the sound of her name and turned to take in her cousin's expression. Caroline's face was set in grim lines as was to be expected, and she turned to find a similar expression on Philip's face.

"What is it that I agree with?"

"You agree that Philip would never have had cause to worry if he'd never formed a friendship with Stonegate."

Audrey slid a glance at Philip, remembering Dash's words from that night in the garden. He had seemed surprised to hear Philip had even been embroiled in any kind of difficulty before. They had left school by the time the incident occurred, so perhaps Dash wouldn't have heard of it.

But still, it seemed strange. Dash claimed to know him well, so wouldn't he be a fair judge of character?

Audrey folded her hands in her lap and met Philip's gaze. "Lord Amberley told me he was quite close with you and Stonegate at Cambridge."

Philip blinked. "That's right. I think he was a year ahead of us, but we were still quite good friends at the time."

At the time.

What an innocuous phrase that could mean so much.

"He also said you weren't one inclined to find yourself in trouble. I thought that an odd statement given your history. Do you care to elaborate?"

It was rather a forward question, but she'd practically grown up with Philip and Caroline. She would have asked the same question of either Ethan or Gavin, and she waited now for Philip's response.

She was surprised to see spots of color come to his cheeks as he swallowed.

"I do not care to elaborate. It was a long time ago, and I've learned memories can be faulty." He spoke quietly and assuredly, his gaze never wavering, and Audrey had the odd sense Philip was attempting to tell her something his words did not convey.

She turned to Caroline. "I may find I agree with Philip on this point. I'm terribly sorry."

Caroline's mouth dropped open. "You would argue in defense of that...that..." she spluttered for several seconds, unable to come up with a vile enough name to describe Stonegate.

"I argue in defense of the truth, and the truth is we were not there, and we cannot pass judgment on events to which we were not privy." Audrey laid a land on Caroline's shaking one. "I think it might be helpful if you let it go, Caroline. It was a long time ago, and if you persist on constantly bringing the matter to the fore, Philip will never be able to move past it."

Caroline's glare was lethal, but more surprising, Aunt Phyllida stirred from her stupor at the window.

"Audrey is right, dear. You must give up this witch hunt you find so compelling. Philip was just a boy. He did the right thing in the end, even if the conclusion was not to your liking."

Audrey had not heard her aunt speak in such complete sentences for quite some time, and it was several seconds while she gathered the woman's meaning.

"Mother," Caroline hissed, but that was apparently the entirety of her rebuttal because she fell silent then.

The tension in the carriage did not have long to build as they soon crunched over the drive at Stonegate Manor. The house was simple in design with the clean lines of Georgian architecture, accented by a reserved frieze at the top of the main house. But it sat at the precipice of a small hill, and Audrey knew the views from the house must be breathtaking.

Several other guests had arrived at the same time, and the front stairs were a confusion of ladies, maids, and footmen as drivers were directed to deliver trunks to the rear while maids helped their ladies to ascend the steps and asked after their well-being. Gentlemen were interspersed through the crowd, their ducked heads and unflinching strides showing their obvious determination to find a stiff drink inside.

Despite the chaos, Audrey located Dash immediately.

He stood at the top of the sweeping stone staircase, his poise casual. But his gaze—his gaze was directed entirely at her.

She warmed under the attention, her heart fluttering, and she cursed herself for such weakness. How had she let this man get to her? How could she have been so susceptible to his charms?

"Lady Hodge. Lady D'Arcy. Lord Greylock." Dash greeted each of them in turn as they mounted the steps before turning to Aunt Phyllida. "I do not believe we've had the pleasure, madam, but I can only assume you're Caroline's sister."

Audrey didn't miss his use of the same ploy he'd used on Aunt Verity.

Aunt Phyllida turned a dry eye on the earl, but once more she surprised them all by smiling ever so slightly.

"You're a cheeky young man, aren't you? You know perfectly well I'm their mother. Does that bit of pandering work on others?"

"This is the first it has failed me," Dash said with a grin of his own.

"I'm the Marchioness of Mattingly. Philip and Caroline's mother." She assessed Dash with an unflinching eye. "But I look forward to what else you might come up with." She continued into the house without further comment.

Audrey wished it weren't impolite to roll her eyes.

Philip went after his mother, muttering about manners, which meant Caroline went after him, obviously unwilling to let him out of her sight. This left Audrey standing on the stairs with Dash.

He immediately extended his arm.

"Permit me to escort you into the house, Lady D'Arcy."

She didn't like how her body leaned into him, how it had grown used to his heat and the feel of his arm under her hand.

"I trust you had a pleasant journey," he said as they

stepped into the foyer, which was crowded and noisy much as the stairs had been.

She scanned the crowd before leaning closer to Dash. "What did you mean when you said Philip wasn't inclined to trouble?"

Dash raised an eyebrow. "Are we to skip the pleasantries then?"

She met his gaze directly. "The drive down was intolerable as you might expect. Caroline is determined to control Philip's life, and it's rather terrible. If you know the truth of the matter, it might help stop Caroline's crusade."

Something like a shadow passed over Dash's eyes, and his mouth firmed. "It's not my story to tell," he nearly whispered.

She hated this most about him. His respectability. His honesty. His empathy.

It would be one thing if the man were simply constructed of charm, but he had the audacity to be a good person as well.

"I understand," she murmured. "But should you find yourself in a position to speak to Caroline while we're here, might you tell her what you've told me?"

"I'm not sure it will do much good, but I will try."

Audrey frowned. "I'm afraid you might be right."

They were pushed more than anything in the direction of a drawing room that had been set up to receive the guests. As they entered, Audrey spotted Caroline almost immediately as she stood nearly on tiptoe arguing with Stonegate in one corner while Philip looked on woefully.

A smallish, older woman held court in the center of the room, her white hair piled neatly atop her head, silver spectacles glinting in the sunshine. She spoke with her hands as guests made their way to her in greeting, and Audrey noticed both the flash of a wedding band and the way the woman's fingers curled in age. But the smile she gave each guest was genuine, and somehow Audrey knew she was going to like Stonegate's grandmother.

Dash pressed a glass of lemonade into her hands and led her to the side of the room to avoid the crush that was entering. She eyed him over the rim of her glass, and he raised an eyebrow in question.

"You're rather good at this," she whispered.

He tugged on the lapels of his coat with exaggerated pride. "Thank you, my lady. I endeavor to please."

She snorted into her lemonade. "You endeavor to charm."

"Isn't that the same thing?"

"Hardly."

They were prevented from speaking further when Stonegate's grandmother raised her hands and called to the room. The woman had incredible fortitude for such a tiny thing.

"Thank you all for coming," she said, her head shaking slightly as she spoke.

The slight tremor reminded Audrey of Grandmother Regina, and she felt a sudden pang of homesickness. Audrey had not been away from home much, but it wasn't as if there was much to miss while she was away. Her mother's criticism and her father's neglect. The bright spots were few and Grandmother Regina was one of them. Surely a house party in the home of a woman she'd never met must be better.

"I'm Lady Augusta Sherrill for those whom I have not had the pleasure of an introduction. I know my Hawk has invited quite a few of his friends, and I cannot wait to meet all of you." Her smile was genuine and encompassed the entirety of the room. "So many young faces here. Hawk, darling, I didn't know you had such lovely friends."

Hawk emerged from the crowd behind his grandmother and came to stand next to her, his arm going around the small woman's shoulders. The poor lady was made to appear even smaller next to Hawk's large frame, but it was evident how much she loved her grandson by the way her eyes took on a sparkle as she peered up at him.

Not for the first time, Audrey was beginning to wonder about Stonegate and his influence on Philip. Her gaze drifted to Caroline who still stood firmly between Philip and Stonegate, her face like stone.

Audrey released a sigh and before she realized what she was doing, she found herself leaning ever so slightly into Dash beside her.

When his hand touched the small of her back, she was too distracted by her own body's betrayal to startle. Instead, she leaned into him farther. They were pressed against the wall of the drawing room, a veritable barricade of guests in front of them, and she knew no one could know what transpired there, and this sent a delicious thrill of danger through her.

His hand flattened against the small of her back, and she felt the sigh rising in her throat. It took all of her concentration not to make a noise, not to give away what was happening.

But it needn't have mattered because at that moment, Lady Sherrill made an announcement.

"Hawk, darling, I think we shall have an assembly at the end of the week."

~

"I CAN ONLY ASSUME you wrangled an invitation to this madness because of Lady D'Arcy."

Dash was not surprised Hawk had sought him out. He was only surprised that he'd done it so quickly.

Dash found no point in lying to his friend. "Yes," he said simply.

Hawk crossed his arms over his chest as he took a position on the stone terrace overlooking the gardens where Hawk's grandmother was giving some of the guests a tour of her roses.

"I thought you said you had honorable intentions in regard to Lady D'Arcy."

"I do," Dash said, his eyes picking out the woman in question with little trouble. She lagged behind the others, her arm linked with Lady Hodge's as she attempted to propel the woman forward and not dash off to find Philip.

The man had disappeared some hours ago, and Dash wondered if he were hiding in his rooms.

Slowly he turned his gaze to Hawk. "I'm here to look after her if you must know. Her mother doesn't seem inclined to the task."

Hawk's features loosened, and he dropped his arms, moving to perch against the stone balustrade of the terrace.

"The Countess of Dartford has never been overly interested in her daughter's life, I'm afraid." Hawk looked out to the gardens at the meandering guests. "Do you honestly think you can protect her though?"

Dash raised both eyebrows. "Do you think I can't?"

Hawk's gaze turned pensive. "I saw you earlier in the drawing room when Grandmother was making introductions. You two seem...close."

Dash remained silent, waiting for his friend to say what it was he suggested.

Hawk leaned on the balustrade now with his hands flat against the stones.

"One would almost say the rumors are correct. You plan to wed Lady D'Arcy."

Dash turned his back on the guests to face Hawk as he shifted back against the stone wall.

"Are you suggesting I shouldn't ask Lady D'Arcy to marry me?"

Hawk met his eyes directly. "How long have you known Audrey?"

Dash recalled that first encounter in the cloakroom, his blood thrumming in his veins at the thought. Could it have been nearly a month since that night? How had time passed so quickly?

"Long enough I should think." He couldn't stop the way his tone hardened. He had never before felt defensive when engaging in a debate with Hawk, and he wondered now what drove the emotion. He felt the tangled web of his past tightening around him.

Hawk must have sensed it because he relented, straightening away from the balustrade. "I'm not trying to suggest you're being rash because of what happened with Lady Wilson. I know these circumstances are a great deal different. It's just—"

But his friend stopped, his gaze moving out over the gardens. The guests had wandered farther onto the grounds, and the hedges immediately below the terrace were now empty. Only the wind passing through their branches made any noise.

After a length of time, Hawk looked back at him. "It's just I hope you are seeking Lady D'Arcy's hand for the right reason. Your own reason, Dash, and not because you feel some kind of vendetta against what has happened to you in this world."

"Why would I do that? Lady D'Arcy is—"

"Goddamnit, Dash." The sudden curse was not unexpected, but the harsh tone was. Hawk pinned him with a steely glare. "Don't live your life to get back at your mother. Live it to be happy."

He straightened, feeling the muscles along his neck tighten. "I'm surprised you haven't noticed. I am living my life to be happy."

Hawk scoffed and looked away. "Society's charmer? Is that what makes you happy? It sounds to me like your life is based on an illusion." His friend's stark expression more than the words themselves stopped whatever retort had been on Dash's lips.

Because he knew his friend's words were true.

Dash's life was an illusion. One he had carefully constructed from the ashes of his childhood. If his mother would not deign to give him affection and good will, he would find it elsewhere, and he would be damn sure he earned it.

But Hawk was right. Flattery was little more than a passing summer breeze. Warm while it caressed his skin but sooner rather than later it would only leave him chilled.

Dash turned and looked out over the garden even though he couldn't have said what it was he was looking at. He could only feel the rage boiling inside of him. The rage that had festered for so long. The turmoil he felt when he thought of David, his dearly departed brother whom Dash had never met but who had controlled the outcome of Dash's life from beyond the grave.

The anger and frustration he felt for his mother. How could she have thought to replace David with another child?

And now that she had, why couldn't she love Dash the way she had loved David? Why wasn't Dash enough?

Dash didn't bother to answer his friend. Hawk would already know his answer. Instead, they stood there in silence for several minutes longer, the wind buffeting them on the unprotected terrace. The drawing room where they had gathered earlier opened onto the terrace where they now stood, and vaguely, Dash heard the noises of servants clearing the refreshments that had been served. The sounds melded together to lull him into an odd sense of detachment.

Eventually Hawk straightened and nudged him with a playful elbow.

"Fancy a walk in the garden? We could visit the old pond. God, it's been years since we've been there."

Dash had visited Hawk at Stonegate Manor many times over the years. It was easier to stay with friends on school holidays rather than face the dour silence of his home.

But Dash didn't feel like visiting old memories.

He smiled and moved toward the house. "I think another time actually."

Hawk's expression turned somber. "Dash—"

But he was interrupted by the arrival of Philip or rather, Philip's head as it peered around the edge of the door from the drawing room.

"Is she gone?" he asked.

Dash stopped and took in Philip's furtive nature.

"Greylock." Dash hadn't seen Philip in quite some time. While he had been friends with both men, he had tended to spend more time in Hawk's company. Philip was always called home on school holidays for one thing or another and quite honestly, Philip had spent a great deal more time in female company when they'd been at school. "Why on earth has your sister got it in her mind to follow you about?"

Philip emerged from the drawing room. His cravat was loosened as though he'd been relaxing somewhere beyond his sister's keen eye, and his hair was slightly disheveled.

"I'm afraid Caroline has insurmountable good will. It is only in her application of it that she goes astray."

"I've heard it said that she's attempting to keep you from making poor choices. Again, it would seem. Why would she think you had made them in the first place?"

Philip's gaze narrowed before it moved to Hawk standing behind Dash. "Has he been speaking to Audrey again?"

Dash looked between the two men. "You two have been talking about me?"

"We've been talking about you talking with Audrey. It's all very circular."

Philip made his way over to them while scanning the area as if expecting his sister to reappear at any moment.

Dash ignored Philip's attempt to escape the question. "This doesn't have anything to do with that business with Lady Lowe, does it? That was years ago now. Surely she can't still hold you accountable for that. Even so, you were the injured party."

Dash didn't miss the look Hawk and Philip exchanged.

"Lady Hodge doesn't know the truth of the matter, does she?"

Philip met his gaze directly. "It wasn't my place to tell Lady Lowe's secrets."

Dash couldn't fault the man that, but then his gaze narrowed, and Dash knew the conversation had turned back to him.

"What are your intentions with my cousin? I had always heard you had a respectable reputation when it came to women, but it's been years now since we've been at school." Philip stopped in front of him, his gaze assessing. "What have you been up to, Dash?"

Dash felt his frown deepen. "Apparently, I've been being scrutinized without my knowledge."

Hawk waved the accusation away without much effort. "Studied, not scrutinized. You know it's up to us to protect Audrey. Her brothers may be more attentive to her than her own parents, but you know how distracted Grays has been since he's returned from Waterloo."

Dash noticed the way Philip winced at the mention of the great battle. He knew Hawk had enlisted as soon as it became apparent men were needed on the continent, but he wasn't sure what Philip had done during the war. Dash's decision whether or not to fight had, like everything else in his life, been decided for him.

As he was the only heir to the title at the time, he had been commanded to remain home. His father had died shortly after, and Dash had assumed the title, but he hadn't enlisted then either. For some pitiful reason, he thought it would please his mother. It had not.

"Which one is Grays?" Dash asked.

While he had gone to school with Philip and Hawk, he was fairly certain the D'Arcy brothers had attended Oxford.

"The elder brother, Ethan," Philip replied.

Now Dash couldn't prevent the wince he felt at the mention of Audrey's brother with the scarred face.

"Did it happen at Waterloo?" He didn't need to specify what he meant. The entire left side of the man's face was a field of pits and scars where once a cheek might have been.

Hawk nodded. "He got too close to a canister shot."

Dash cringed. He had heard of what a canister shot

consisted, iron balls and sawdust, and he couldn't imagine taking one to his face.

"Christ, the man's lucky to be alive."

Philip nodded. "Gavin was there and pulled him out of the battle to get him to the field hospital."

Dash's chest tightened at the image of one brother hauling the other from death's door.

"Does Audrey know this?"

Philip nodded again. "She's quite close with her brothers. More so before the war, but I think she understands the enormity of what they endured. But I would say their relationship has changed since the brothers returned. Gavin has always been protective of Ethan, but after Waterloo..." His voice trailed off, but Dash could fill in the rest.

"Did Audrey's mother agree to allow her daughter to attend this house party?"

Philip rubbed the back of his neck, his expression chagrinned. "Aunt Eugenia was delighted Audrey had received an invitation, and when she heard my mother would be present to serve as chaperone, she was all too happy to let Audrey attend."

"Will the woman do whatever it takes to see her daughter wed no matter how it puts her reputation in danger?"

Dash's resolve to protect the young Lady D'Arcy hardened, and he glanced back over his shoulder to the place where they had disappeared in the gardens. Perhaps he should take a stroll in the flower beds.

He turned to tell his companions just that when something else caught his attention.

Great gray billowing clouds rolled across the horizon growing ever nearer. A real storm appeared to be brewing.

He motioned at the clouds with a nod. "It looks like

rain." He cast his gaze meaningfully back at the gardens. "Shouldn't the guests be returning?"

Hawk shook his head, his shoulders slumping, giving the effect that this was not the first time he had to chase after his grandmother in the gardens.

"Grandmother will not be paying attention to such things. We should attempt to locate the guests before the rain comes."

Philip had already made it to the top of the terrace stairs when a gust of wind pushed against them.

"We'd better hurry," he said, but his voice was lost in the wind as he descended the steps.

Hawk was right behind him, but Dash lingered back.

There was only one person he would be looking for in those gardens.

10

She was lost.

It wasn't as though she'd known where she was before the rain started. Or before Caroline had gotten it in her head to turn away from the other guests and go back to the house to find Philip.

They had vaguely kept Lady Sherrill within earshot as she traipsed through her gardens, a trail of guests meandering behind her. But when the house had dropped from view and the hedges around them had grown taller, Audrey watched as Caroline's nerves wound tighter and tighter.

At first, she had merely looked over her shoulder several times a minute in the direction the house should have been. But then she'd started gnashing her teeth against her lower lip and trying to shred fistfuls of her skirts between her hands.

When the first of the drizzle started, she had announced she was returning to the house immediately.

The only problem being at that point they had no idea where the house was.

Audrey couldn't help it if guests often found themselves

lost in the gardens at house parties. She'd heard any number of stories from the maids at Dartford House, but she had thought such wanderings only occurred to the servants.

It would seem this was not the case.

They had taken shelter in a rose arbor, and within seconds, Audrey knew the application of the term shelter was more than a little overdone. Perhaps had the rain stayed mild, it would have provided better respite, but when the rain turned into a downpour, all hope was lost.

As if driven by the urgency of the rain, Caroline had declared her intent to find the house no matter what it might do to her person. When Audrey had cautioned against this, Caroline had struck out into the rain. It was several seconds before Audrey had registered what her cousin had done, and it was this lag that had allowed them to become separated.

By the time Audrey had gathered her skirts to charge after her wayward cousin, several yards separated them, and Audrey felt compelled to run after the woman to keep from getting further separated. The ground, however, declared its intent to stop her pursuit at all costs, and with a single slip of her slipper in the burgeoning mud, she had landed in a flower bed with a spectacular splash.

By the time she had recovered herself, Caroline was gone.

At first Audrey determined to return to the house. Hopefully Caroline would be there already, warming herself by the fire, and it wasn't as though Audrey would face anything worse than what she already had. Her gown was ruined, her slippers irreparable. It was best to get on with it.

That was nearly a quarter of an hour ago, and she was no better off. The hedges all seemed to look the same, and she was certain she'd passed that bed of lavender several times already. The wind stabbed its way through her pelisse, and her sodden skirts snagged at her legs.

She tumbled through yet another hedgerow, caring not for her gown, driven only by the need to get out from this awful rain when she found herself kneeling beside a pond. At first, the sight of the small body of water confused her as she had not found a pond yet in her journey, but water features were quite common in gardens. Dartford House itself sported four of them.

She raised her gaze to take in the breadth of it when her eyes spotted something through the curtain of rain. She couldn't be sure what it was, but she could just make out the sure lines of stone and towering columns. She must have stumbled upon a folly or a grotto. The wind had been toying with her hair until that moment when it decided to unleash itself, ripping the coiled mane from its pins until it slapped her in the face.

She shoved the clinging strands away even as she gained her feet, stumbling in the direction of the stone structure. She stumbled more than once, slipping yet again in the mud, and once nearly into the pond itself. She didn't know how long it took her to reach the other side of the pond, but as she drew closer, the stone structure began to take shape, and she could make out some detail.

Four Ionic columns marched along the front of the small, stone structure, and it was topped by a dome made of some other material, perhaps copper, but it was hard to tell in the gray onslaught. The cold of the stone steps pierced what was left of her slippers as she grabbed hold of one of the columns to propel her upward.

She nearly made it to the top when she slipped again, coming down hard on her knees at the top of the stairs. Pain radiated through her, robbing her of breath, but she could see a heavy door wrapped in iron brackets just feet in front of her, and her bruised and battered body yearned for it.

She was out of the worst of the rain now as the columns supported a small overhang by which the door was reached. She pushed forward, fully expecting the door to the structure to be locked, but when it unexpectedly turned under her hand, she tripped forward.

The first thing she noticed was the quiet. The walls must have been thick with stone because once inside the torment of rain was nothing more than a quiet patter against the roof and walls. Two narrow, rectangular windows composed of stained glass dissected the walls on either side of the open space before her, but in the dim light of the storm, she could make out little more than the shapes of what might be before her.

She turned back toward the door when she spotted the first of several standing candelabras. She made her way carefully over to it as her eyes were still adjusting to the dimness of the small space. She found the sheath of long matches hanging from its side and struck one, lighting the candles on the multiple arms of the stand. Warm, yellow light flooded the space around her, and she began to gain a better sense of where she was. By the time she had lit the other four candelabras, she realized what surrounded her.

It was some sort of temple, complete with a raised dais at the front that held a small stone table upon which a brazier and several thick candles waited as if a ritual were imminent. The main space where she stood was covered in a thick carpet that had revealed itself foot by foot as she lit the candles until finally, she could see the rest of the temple.

She stopped when the room came into focus, and she was aware only of the dripping water from her skirts as it struck the stone of the floor from where she stood at the edge of the room.

"It's a temple to Artemis."

She was lucky she didn't knock over the candelabra behind her as she turned at the sudden sound of a voice in the doorway. She was not in the least surprised to see Dash, nor was she surprised to see that he looked like he'd done nothing more than take a stroll in a light drizzle.

She turned to face him. "What are you doing here?"

His face changed then, folding into lines of concern. Shutting the door solidly behind him, he strode over to her, taking her shoulders in his hands.

"Are you all right? What's happened? Where's Caroline? Are you hurt?"

She shoved against his chest as she shook her head. "One question at a time please, and I'm perfectly fine. Why are you so concerned?"

He raised an eyebrow and peered down the length of her. She followed the direction of his gaze, and for the first time took in the state of her dress. Mud caked the bottom of her skirts, and there was a tear at one knee where she must have fallen on the stone stairs. She looked back up at Dash.

"Well, I suppose that's rather concerning, but I assure you I'm fine." She nodded toward the wall and the gardens beyond. "We weren't expecting such a deluge, and it rather caught us by surprise."

"Yes, about that. May I ask after Caroline's whereabouts now?"

He still held her shoulders in his hands, and she rather liked the warmth they spread through her. She shivered, realizing for the first time how cold she was.

"I don't know. She grew agitated being away from Philip and disappeared into the rain. I tried to follow her and fell into a flower bed." She refused to look away at this admission, and Dash was kind enough not to grin at her mishap.

"Are you sure you're all right?"

She looked down at herself once more, plucking at her sodden skirts. "I'm right as I can be in this situation."

He squeezed her shoulders and moved away. She had lit the rest of the candles in the small temple, so she was surprised when he gained the dais and began rummaging amongst the candles there. Surely the ones on the stands about the center space of the temple were enough. With a little more rummaging, he lit a small straw taper from a match and holding the taper aloft and cupped in one hand, he made his way behind the stone table.

She stepped closer, entranced by his sure movements, and slowly from the shadows, she made out the shape of a stone hearth carved into the far wall. It sat on a small shelf nearly waist high with a flue cut into the stone above it. Dash touched the lit taper of straw to the bundle of wood already set on the stone hearth, and the dry fuel lit immediately.

Warmth. Blessed warmth flooded the small space almost immediately, and Audrey quivered as it reached her soaked body. Without hesitating, she gained the dais and made her way around the table to where Dash added small sticks to the fire from a basket on the floor. Soon a proper fire burned on the hearth, and she held her hands out to it.

"How did you know about this place?"

He prodded the flames higher with a shaft of wood as he answered, "I would visit Hawk on school holidays. There wasn't much to do in winter except explore the grounds. There are eight of these temples on the grounds and three follies." He raised a single eyebrow as he looked at her, and she couldn't help but laugh.

"That seems rather much."

"The previous earl enjoyed the Greek myths and traveled to the Greek peninsula several times in his life. I suppose when it was time to erect a temple on the grounds he had a hard time choosing just one god to honor."

She looked about them. "How is it that you know this one was for Artemis?"

He nodded over his shoulder in the direction of the closest stained-glass window. "She's rendered in the windows."

Audrey looked quickly, hoping to make out her shape, but the windows were dark in the gray light. She would need to come back when the weather was fair and see Artemis for herself.

"Lady Sherrill, she's Hawk's paternal grandmother?" Audrey asked the question that had been niggling her since the woman had introduced herself.

Dash brushed off his hands and faced her. "Lady Augusta Savage, the dowager Countess of Stonegate married the Earl of Sherrill three years after her first husband, Hawk's grandfather, passed away. When her second husband died, his children didn't approve of her living in the houses they inherited. They turned her out. Hawk has taken care of her since."

Audrey felt something fall inside of her, and when it landed it made a hollow ringing sound.

"Caroline's wrong about Hawk, isn't she?"

Dash rubbed the back of his neck. "I'm afraid she is, but I'm not going to be the one to convince her otherwise. I think that's something they will need to work out between the two of them."

She became aware of the chill receding as the warmth spread through her, and she bent to ring out the water from the folds of her pelisse. Her hair fell about her shoulders like a curtain though, and soon water dripped from her chin. It was all rather hopeless.

She straightened, allowing the water to run down her skirts and drip on the floor. She followed the direction of Dash's gaze as he looked out at the temple space behind them. She could see it more clearly now between the candles and the fire.

"Hawk's grandfather enjoyed traveling, didn't he?"

Dash nodded. "He died when Hawk was quite young, but there were some stories he managed to pass on to his grandson. Why do you ask?"

She gestured with her chin in the direction of the wall by the door. "If I am not mistaken, that is a divan, is it not?"

The low mattress sat along one wall with cushions piled at it's back to keep anyone sitting atop it from feeling the cold stones at their back.

Dash nodded slowly. "Indeed, it is, Lady D'Arcy."

She squeezed another round of water from her skirts before facing him squarely and raising her chin. "And don't think I didn't notice that once again you have managed to get me alone with you."

THAT HAD NOT BEEN his intention when he'd gone in search of her. It was rather more of a happy coincidence, but Hawk's words echoed through him, and he thought it better not to mention it.

Instead, he said, "I'm afraid we're only victims of circumstance." He held up his hands to indicate the world beyond the temple, and soon the soft patter of rain on the roof filled the space around them.

Her eyes narrowed. "I think you are skilled at taking advantage of circumstances."

He couldn't stop a grin. "What kind of charmer would I be if I didn't?"

He was surprised when she laughed, the sound warm and full in the small space. He felt his grin sliding as he absorbed the light in her expression. She looked terrible. Her gown was soaked through with both rain and mud. If she had been wearing a hat, it had long since vanished, and her slippers were bound for the rubbish bin. Her sodden hair fell about her shoulders in a tangled mess, but he couldn't help notice how it framed her face, accentuating the features he found so appealing.

He was gripped by the sudden urge to kiss her, and he swallowed, turning away in the hopes if he didn't look at her the feeling would fade.

"Hawk and I would come here in the cold of winter to get out of the house," he found himself saying as he made his way to the door. "We would light the fire in the hearth and sprawl on the floor, talking about what we were going to do when we were men." He laughed softly at the childhood memory and turned back to face her, hoping that by putting some distance between them he could better control his urge to touch her, taste her. It didn't. "Life after Cambridge was much different than we had imagined."

She watched him with almost a guarded expression, and he wondered what she might be thinking. He wondered again of Hawk's words and what damage the Countess of Dartford might have done to her daughter. He knew only too well how fatal words could be.

"I somehow understand that," she said finally, her voice stilted as though she were reluctant to agree with him on anything, even something so abstract as one's musings for one's future.

She picked up her skirts and slowly made her way around the table, pausing to run a finger along the brass edge of the brazier on the table.

"Did Hawk's grandfather make sacrifices to Artemis?"

Dash shook his head. "That, I'm afraid, was once used to light an Easter candle. One year Hawk's grandmother wanted to hold a vigil. We were forced to sit on the stone floor all night to remember Christ's sacrifice and subsequent rising."

Audrey wrinkled her nose. "Lady Sherrill suggested that? I wouldn't think her the religious type."

"Religious? No. Spiritual? Most assuredly. I think she was attracted to the ritual of it rather than the execution of it. She never suggested it again."

Her face changed again until he couldn't be certain of her expression in the shifting candlelight.

"You speak a great deal of Hawk and his grandmother, but I've never heard you mention your own family."

Something hard thudded in his chest, and he turned away from her, moving to the door as if to check on the storm.

"I wasn't prying, Dash. I know what it is to have difficulties with one's family members."

He stopped just inside the door and looked back at her. She'd stepped down off the dais now, her fingers plying her hair on one side as she tried to detangle it.

"I try very hard not to speak to my mother, but you already know that. Ethan and Gavin are wonderful brothers though. I'm very lucky to have them."

His conversation with Philip and Hawk earlier flashed through his mind. "Your brothers were at Waterloo."

She looked up from where she wound her hair into a kind of braid. "Yes, they were. The war changed them as could be expected, but I think what I miss the most is Ethan's smile. He used to smile a great deal before the war. Not so much now."

"I would think he hasn't much reason to smile."

She raised only her eyes to him. "Do you mean because of his face?" She shook her head even before he could answer. "Physical scars are nothing compared to what he must feel inside. His best friend was standing next to him when the canister shot exploded. Ethan woke up alive in a field hospital three weeks later, and his best friend's body was never recovered." Her eyes pinched as she went back to twisting her hair. "I sometimes wonder if he resents Gavin for saving his life. If he doesn't wish he had died on that battlefield with his friend."

Time seemed to slow around them. In the years that he had been perfecting his charming craft, he'd never once had a conversation of such depth, and he found a rush of exhilaration passing through him. This was connection. This was what he'd been seeking all along. He had to tread carefully, now more than ever. If he scared her away...

"It must be hard. Your brothers carry the burden of the war with them, and that leaves you all alone, without the brothers you grew up with."

She stopped twisting her hair and looked up at him. "How do you know that?"

He recalled that night of the dinner party, the extreme closeness of the brothers to the detriment of all else. It was as if they existed in their own world and no other was invited into it.

He shrugged. "I have no siblings with which to make the comparison, but isn't it said that our brothers and sisters are our first friends? It would be hard to lose such closeness I imagine."

She studied him for an uncomfortable length of time, and he wondered if he'd blundered it. He had only the ghost of David with which to compare, and that didn't exactly make him the expert on sibling relationships.

But finally, she blinked, and her fingers resumed their work on her hair. "Yes, I guess it's a lot like that. It's not as if I can tell them Mummy is being mean to me again and the gentlemen won't ask me to dance. It hardly seems right after what they've been through."

"To be fair I did ask you to dance. On more than one occasion if I recall."

The look she gave him was unlike any she had given him before, and he thought she was almost humored by his charm.

Something shifted inside of him, and he wondered if it might be hope. He knew she was attracted to him physically, but that wasn't enough. He wanted more. He wanted all of her.

He wanted her light and her wit. He wanted her unerring sense of adventure. He wanted her to smile at him the way she did when she spoke with her cousins and brothers. Her smile spoke of something shared, and he'd never shared anything with anyone like that.

He felt something give inside of him and before he knew what was happening, he spoke of his mother when he had never spoken of her before to anyone but Hawk.

"My mother will not let me change the Amberley residences. She wishes to keep things exactly as they were when David was alive."

Her fingers stilled on her plait. "Oh God, Dash, that's..."

"Heartbreaking really," he said, running a hand through

his hair. "The stables are rotting into the ground at Evers Park, but she won't let me do anything about it. I've had the plans drawn up and everything, and they sit unused."

"I see why you don't like to speak of your family," she said, her voice soft.

She finished plaiting her hair and left it hanging over one shoulder as she likely had nothing with which to secure it. It transformed her already mercurial face, and he took several breaths to admire it. With her hair in a loose plait and soft about her, it framed her face as if highlighting those captivating features he had come to love.

"You're so beautiful," he whispered.

Her eyes widened almost as if she were a rabbit in front of a hound, but no, that wasn't quite it. Her eyes spoke of being startled, not afraid.

"Has anyone told you how beautiful you are?" His voice grew rough, and it took all his concentration to get the words out. But once out, it was as though a weight was lifted from his chest, as though he simply had to tell her how he felt.

Her eyes were still wide as she shook her head softly. "No." The word trembled, and she licked her lips before speaking again. "No, I've never been told that."

She didn't refute his claim as he would suspect a wallflower to do, and he wondered at that. Nor did she look away or blush. It was as though she had known the truth all along and was surprised to find someone who finally saw it too.

They stood there in the stone temple, the rain falling around them in a soft patter on the roof and windows. It was warmer now, the small fire from the stone hearth flooding the space with much needed heat, and he noticed she no longer shivered.

He curled his fingers into fists, the urge to touch her, to

hold her against him, to warm her so strong it caused a physical reaction in him. But he couldn't touch her. He had made a promise to her, and he would keep his promise.

She was the first to blink and look away, her eyes traveling to the ceiling. "Perhaps the rain will stop soon, and we can make our way to the house."

As if Artemis herself were listening, a crack of thunder split the quiet then, and a gust of wind rattled the precious stained glass of the windows.

"Or not," Audrey said, her gaze turning to the windows.

"We'll be safe here," he said. "Would you care to sit?"

He gestured to the divan she had pointed out earlier, unable to stop a playful grin. The traditional davenport was low to the ground and would be awkward to sit on even if one was not soaked from the rain.

She pressed her hands to her stomach. "I shouldn't wish to soil the fabric."

He waved her worries away. "It's no bother. Lady Sherrill's already had it reupholstered several times. She changes the fabric of it as her whims change."

Audrey put her head to one side. "Truly? I would think she'd wish to keep the authentic fabric on it."

"The previous earl might have, but Lady Sherrill enjoys a certain aesthetic."

She seemed to consider this and must have come to a favorable conclusion because she gave a nod and began to approach the divan. Only she gave a wince within two steps, and now he did touch her.

He was in front of her in two strides, his hands going to her shoulders.

"Are you unwell? Did you hurt yourself in the gardens?" He dropped his hands and turned for the door. "I'll fetch a doctor. Don't move. And whatever you do don't attempt to find your way back to the house in this rain. I'll—"

"Dash!"

He realized she had been trying to get his attention for the whole of his diatribe, and now only turned back as he felt her hand on his arm.

Her face was soft, and he didn't miss the smile that played at the corners of her lips.

"I'm fine. I slipped on the steps coming up to the temple, and I must have hurt my knee is all. I'm perfectly well." She held out her skirts as if to assure him of this, but when she unfolded the gown, he saw the tear across where her knees might have been.

She gave a soft noise, and when he met her gaze, he said without room for argument, "Sit down."

He was somewhat surprised she did as she was told, and he followed her to the divan where he knelt in front of her.

"Is it both knees or just the one?"

She indicated her left knee. "Just this one. I think I might have come down harder on this one than the other."

He took her leg in his hands and gingerly felt around the left knee. She didn't react, and he pressed harder.

"Does it hurt to touch or only when you walk on it?"

She shook her head again. "It didn't hurt at all when I first did it. It was just that one time there. I must have moved it wrong is all. I'm sure it's fine."

He was not in the least satisfied.

"Do you permit me to conduct a more thorough exam?" He looked at her, and he wondered if she knew how his heart raced to touch her.

When she looked up, her eyelashes fluttering as she lifted her gaze to his, he felt it. This thing between them, whatever it was, had shifted, grown deeper and wider until he was no longer sure it was something he could grasp.

But then she spoke a single word, and he knew he was helpless.

"Yes."

11

She didn't know to what she was agreeing. Couldn't have understood the fathoms to which her desire had grown.

Why was it that she kept finding herself alone with this man? It was probably because deep inside she wished to be alone with him. The part of her that yearned for adventure, that yearned for excitement, that yearned for *more* wanted to be there with him. So it shouldn't have been a surprise that he was touching her again, here, in this sacred space isolated by nature and happenstance.

He held her leg between his hands, and while his intentions were honest, she didn't miss how his fingers lingered at the softness at the back of her knee, at the way he held her gaze, the lines of his face tense, his eyes afire. Her heart thumped in her chest, anticipation singing through her veins.

Finally his hand slid down her leg, cupped her calf through her skirts before moving lower. Carefully, so painstakingly carefully, he lifted the hem of her gown, his fingers sliding over the fine bones of her ankle. He kept his gaze locked on hers through all of it, and she wanted to look away, the desire thrumming inside of her, the agony of anticipation building to unbearable levels.

But she didn't look away and neither did he as he raised his hand under her gown, sliding it back up her calf.

A slow grin crept along his face, breaking the hypnotic trance he held over her.

"Wool stockings." He shook his head slightly. "I wouldn't have taken you for a wool stockings kind of lady."

"They're practical." Her voice was flat as her heart continued to pound, as his fingers continued to climb.

His smile softened, and he closed his eyes as if thinking of a private joke.

"Of course they are."

He found her knee, but he didn't move her skirts. They draped piously over her leg still, and she felt a ridiculous surge of innocence she knew not to be true.

As if reading her thoughts, he peeled back her skirts, exposing the wool stockings, her ankle, and finally her knee. It was the same knee she had seen this morning, clad in serviceable gray wool, but it wasn't her knee anymore. Now it was something dark and forbidden because he touched it, he held it, he *saw* it. No one except her maid had ever seen her knees, and now he held it as if he had every right to it.

He tapped the kneecap with one blunt finger. "I can't very well make a proper assessment without seeing it though, can I?"

This time he didn't wait for her to speak. He only met her gaze, and the heat she saw there had her licking her lips. She wanted this, but she didn't know how to speak the words. So instead, she leaned back on the divan, her hands going to the fabric at her sides, effectively offering herself to him.

It was bold and wanton and dangerous, and she loved every second of it. He didn't hesitate. He pushed her skirts higher until he discovered the plain gray ribbon that held her stockings up. He touched the tiny bow there with the same blunt finger he'd put against her knee cap.

"Audrey, I can't—"

Panic seized her, and she shoved his hand away, grasping the delicate end of the gray bow herself and tugging it loose. The ribbon unraveled, and her stocking went slack around her thigh.

They both stared at the pale skin the relaxed stocking exposed, and she suddenly became aware of their breathing. The sound was harsh in the quiet of the temple, and she realized he was as aroused as she was.

When he had called her beautiful, she had believed him. There had been no doubt refuting his words, no insecurity welling up inside of her. She listened for her mother's voice, her mother's ridicule and disdain, but it hadn't been there. It was only Dash, and the words he spoke had been true.

With a single finger, he reached out and traced the pale, soft skin. She felt it like a lightning bolt directly to her soul.

"Audrey." His voice was filled with longing, and her heart stuttered at the depth of emotion it held.

For her.

She had done that to him. She had made his voice growl with desire, and a surge of power tore through her.

"Audrey." Two fingers now. Then three. His touch so light she almost wasn't sure it was actually there. But then he looked at her, and the fire in his eyes told her everything. "Are you sure?" The desperation in his voice undid her. If she said no now, it just might end him.

But she didn't want to say no. Not now and not ever. She wanted all of this, whatever it was, whatever he was giving her. She wanted it all. No matter the cost she might have to pay.

She reached out and touched his face. His eyes were watchful, his lips slightly parted as if he were afraid of what he was about to do. Her fingers found the stubble at his chin, the hard line of his jaw.

"You made me a promise, Lord Amberley," she said, trying for a playful note in her voice, but her desire made her sound sultry instead, which she supposed wasn't terrible. But she was trying to reassure him, and sultry was not how she had planned to do it. "You promised to show me what I could do with my freedom." She tapped his chin with her finger. "And I'm afraid you haven't shown me much."

The stark look in his eyes faded to something warm and predatory, and her stomach clenched in anticipation.

"I haven't, have I?"

She shook her head, biting her lower lip. She wasn't sure what he might do. Was he used to women baiting him like that? Had she done a proper job of it?

But then he leaned forward on his knees and kissed her, and she forgot everything else.

It was as though the planets themselves had been knocked out of alignment only to find their way back now that he held her in his arms, and she glowed with a freeness she had never felt before in her life.

This was what she had been waiting for—surely, this must be it. She had never felt so at peace with the universe as when Dash kissed her, and now she reveled in it. It was as though she had found a place where she was enough, and the thought should have scared her, but it didn't. Nothing could scare her when she was with Dash.

He eased her back on the divan and suddenly she was wrapped around him, his hand still cupping her thigh, drawing her body fully against his. She felt every inch of him through her thin gown, and her skin prickled, wanting to feel his touch everywhere.

He kissed her softly at first, his lips tracing hers, nibbling and taking in the smallest way as if he were easing her into it. She yearned forward, her body remembering what it had been like in the cloakroom, in the music room, remembering everything.

But he didn't give her that. He gave her something else instead, and her body rocked with the newness of it.

He left her lips to trail kisses along her jaw, biting lightly only to soothe her skin with his tongue, and her body coiled against the onslaught, tightening and heating until she thought it impossible for him to stoke her desire more. But that was exactly what he did.

His lips found the sensitive place behind her ear, his hand caught in her hair heedless of the plait she had constructed, and quite frankly, she didn't care. His fingers massaged the back of her head at the base of her skull, and she wanted to purr, settling for throwing her head back against the divan and giving him full access.

His lips followed the column of her throat, sucking and biting and licking, and her skin tingled where he had touched it. She grew aware of the mounting heat low in her stomach, the clenching in places she didn't know could clench.

"Dash," she whimpered, unable to put into words the turmoil she felt.

He didn't answer her. He only moved his head lower, and she wanted so to look down, to see what he was doing, but it was impossible at this angle. All she could do was feel.

So when his lips touched the soft skin exposed above the bodice of her gown, she bucked against the sensation, startled and thrilled all at once. Her hands pierced his hair as she held him in place, urging him to keep touching her there, keep pressing his warm lips to delicate skin.

But he stopped all too suddenly, leaning on one elbow above her as he finally released her thigh to bring his hand to her collar, tracing the fine bones there.

"God, Audrey, do you have any idea how perfect you are?"

His words shattered something inside of her, and the earnestness in his eyes made it whole again. He spoke the truth. This wasn't charm or flattery. He meant what he said, and it rocked her. She wasn't perfect; she knew that. But maybe to him…

He dipped his head, kissed her lightly, softly.

"Audrey, tell me what you want."

She didn't know what she wanted. Wasn't that the very problem?

"Show me," she whispered against his lips. "Show me what I want."

He made a sound like a growl and more than anything this stoked the fire inside of her.

The hand that had been tracing her collarbones suddenly swooped down her body, pausing to cup her breast, her hip, her buttocks so briefly she wondered if she imagined it, but her body pressed into him, wanting more. His hand had already made its way back to her bare thigh, and it toyed with the soft skin there.

He seemed to hesitate, and she pressed her lips more firmly against his before taking his head in her hands and drawing his ear to her lips.

"Show me, Dash," she whispered. "You promised me."

She could feel his resolve snap as if it were a physical thing, and his hand began to move, higher and higher up her thigh. The urgency within her spun into a frenzy, and she clenched, her body preparing for something she knew not.

And then his hand found her.

He touched her softly at first, the very center of her. His touch was gentle, exploring deeper only when her body relaxed for him. But though her muscles seemed to know what to do, she did not, swamped by a desire that was so complete she even lost the ability to form words.

But they didn't need words, not now. His fingers plied her with precision, and soon he slipped a finger between her folds.

He groaned against her lips, moving until he buried his face in her neck.

"You're so wet," he whispered.

She didn't know what it meant, and she couldn't tell if this were a good thing or not. He sounded so distressed by the fact. But he kept going, his fingers discovering.

Then he slipped a single finger inside of her, and her hips drove up off the divan into him. She thought she heard him laugh softly, but her mind was swamped with her own arousal, and all she could think was that she wanted more of this, more of him, more of them.

He slipped the finger out, and she felt its loss, whimpering her dislike of his withdrawal, but then the same finger found her sensitive nub and began to stroke it with quick, sure swipes. She grabbed his wrist, the pleasure so intense, so acute she didn't know if she wanted him to stop.

"Dash."

She wanted to see his eyes. She wanted to see the assurance there, but he didn't pick up his head. Instead, he pressed his lips to her ear.

"I promised you, remember?"

The sound of his voice cut through her desire with a sharpness that only served to drive her arousal to stunning new heights, and the hand wrapped around his wrist tightened as if to hold him in place.

"Please, Dash." She hated the pleading in her voice, but she wanted this. Whatever it was. She wanted it so much. "Please show me."

His finger pressed more firmly against her, and the pain grew almost blinding, the urgency building and building. He stroked her, again and again, and her body moved against his torturing finger as if it knew what to do.

When the pleasure came it took her breath away, seizing every bit of her until she exploded into a pool of pure light. When she finally opened her eyes, she didn't know how she was still on the divan, the rain still falling softly against the roof.

With Dash leaning over her, his face terribly serious.

"I told you house parties are no place for a young lady," he said.

WATCHING Audrey through the next several days of the house party and not being able to touch her was the most exquisite torture he'd ever suffered.

He hadn't planned to seduce her in the stone temple. In fact, he'd resolutely meant not to. He was a man of his word after all, and he had meant it when he said he would no longer pursue her. While he tried to convince himself of this, he felt guilt weighing on his shoulders as heavy as the stones that made up the temple itself.

Just because he had promised to not pursue her did not mean he would avoid fate when she decided to crook her finger in a positive direction.

Perhaps it was Artemis herself having a little fun, and he was not one to go against any goddess.

He suffered through endless meals, listening to her laugh, seeing her smile at the other blokes present. He was surprised he hadn't ground his teeth to useless stumps.

The worst though, were the activities. Lady Sherrill thrived on activities. There were the scavenger hunts and croquet. Walks in the morning and afternoon. Charades in the evening. He had heard every lady in attendance play a minuet, sing an aria, or read poetry. While he couldn't remember any of the rest, he had remembered Audrey.

She had read from that novel that had caused quite a stir when it was first printed anonymously several years ago. He couldn't have told anyone anything about it, but he could recall quite clearly the sound of Audrey's voice. He had always been enamored of her wit. The way she spoke with such forthrightness and never backed down from a seemingly awkward interlude. But when she read aloud, she transfixed him. It was as though the words on the page came alive, and he could see them dancing in the air. To think of it now seemed absurd, but he would never forget how he'd felt that night as she read.

And suddenly, he wished for her to read to him every night for the rest of his life.

The readings had been brief, however, as Lady Sherrill preferred dramatics and so it was they returned to charades and music.

Try as he might, he never seemed to be partnered with

Audrey. He was forced to watch her from afar, to remember their one illicit afternoon in the stone temple. He did sometimes manage to walk next to her on one of the regular outings, but Caroline was always present, and Caroline's mood since that afternoon of the rainstorm had deteriorated considerably. He had tried to speak with Audrey about it, but the cousins never seemed to leave each other's shadows.

And so three days later, he found himself craving the touch of her skin, her fresh clean scent, the way she curled against his body.

He nearly choked on his drink now at the memory. Tonight it was a tournament of whist. He was never one to play whist and had taken a chair to the side of the gaming tables to watch, just as he'd been doing for the past several days.

She wore her hair pulled back in a twist of braids, and he couldn't help but remember that afternoon. Her braid had not survived the encounter on the divan, and he smiled now at the memory. He drummed his fingers against the arm of his chair, the urge to touch her, to pull the pins from her hair nearly overpowering.

Hawk dropped into the seat beside him, shattering his daydream.

"Keeping a close eye on the players? Hoping to catch the cheaters in the bunch?" Hawk gyrated his eyebrows playfully.

"Lady Hodge has been quiet this week."

Hawk's eyebrows stopped, and his lips parted momentarily. The man coughed and looked away.

How interesting.

"And Lady D'Arcy appears quite animated," Hawk replied after several telling seconds.

Dash swirled the drink in his glass. "I'm afraid I can't take credit for it."

Hawk looked at him swiftly. "Bollocks," he said quietly.

Dash shook his head casually. "I'm afraid it's true." He gestured discreetly in Audrey's direction. "That is not the look of a woman in the first blush of love, I'm afraid."

While his tone was light, the truth of his words pierced him. For it was true. Something had lit a spark inside of her, and Audrey had gone off like a hay fire. He had watched her grow in confidence in the last several days. She smiled and laughed, certainly, but more, she engaged her fellow guests, even suggesting outings and activities.

He recalled too clearly the missish girl he had first seen on the side of the ballroom, hovering by her grandmother and spinster aunt. This was not that woman. He wished to take credit for it. Hell, if it were him that had caused such a light to spark inside of her, he would have taken full advantage of it and claimed her hand in marriage already.

But he knew deep down it wasn't him that had done it.

Audrey had discovered her own light somehow.

"Then what is it?" Hawk asked now.

Dash took a swallow of his drink, rolling it around on his tongue as he took the time to sort out the truth.

Finally, he swallowed and said, "I think it's because she's away from her mother."

Hawk was silent at this pronouncement, and the sounds of the gaming room echoed around them.

Hawk pinched the bridge of his nose and shook his head several minutes later. "Do you know I think you might be right?"

Dash raised his drink. "Of course I'm right. Am I correct in thinking this is her first time away from home without her mother?"

Hawk only looked at him, his eyes heavy and considering.

"And I haven't seen much of this Aunt Phyllida wherever she might be."

Hawk shook his head and swallowed the last of his drink. "Philip's mother enjoys acting in absentia. That is, in no way at all."

Dash's brow wrinkled. "I find it hard to believe Lady Hodge could come from such a woman."

Hawk grew quiet again, but Dash didn't miss the way he looked at Caroline.

It was in this lull that Philip took up the chair on the other side of Hawk.

"Gentlemen," he said. "I seem to have been bested by a pair of spinster sisters."

"Out already then?" Hawk questioned.

Philip raised his glass in salute. "May the better man—or women in this case—win."

Dash and Hawk raised their glasses as well.

Philip frowned. "And how is it that you've let your glasses go empty?"

Dash didn't answer but instead looked to the table where Audrey and Caroline where still engaged in their hand of whist.

"I see," Philip muttered at the same moment Dash realized Hawk studied Caroline.

Dash thought momentarily of Ethan D'Arcy, Baron Grays. He hadn't heard Audrey mention her father, but she spoke highly of her brother. While it was customary for a gentleman to seek the father's approval in the marriage contracts, he wondered.

"Is Lady D'Arcy very close with her father?"

Both men looked at him, eyebrows askance.

Dash slumped back in his seat. "I take it she's not."

Hawk shook his head and stood. "This is a conversation for another room."

Without inviting them to follow him, Hawk strode in the direction of the doors, and Philip and Dash rose silently to go after him. Eventually they made their way to a billiards room, and Dash felt his comfort level rise. Billiards, he knew, and perhaps here he could find respite from his lovesickness.

Was that what plagued him? Love? It couldn't be.

He merely found Audrey attractive, intelligent, likable, funny, and kind. He wanted to spend the rest of his life with her, but did that mean he loved her?

Hawk filled their glasses and pulled the cues from the table to set up the field.

"Lord Dartford is a bastard of the first order," Hawk said without preamble.

Dash perched on the other side of the table. "How is it that I've never heard of the man?"

Philip joined them. "He neglects his seat in the House of Parliament and squirrels himself away at one of his country estates."

"Why would he do that?"

Hawk looked up from where he was setting the balls on the green baize. "Lord Dartford has some particular tastes when it comes to his mistresses."

"Many gentlemen of the *ton* do, I'm afraid."

Philip pondered the drink in his glass as he said, "I haven't met any like Lord Dartford."

The skin at the back of Dash's neck tightened. He thought about Audrey growing up under her father's presence.

"What sort of particulars?" The question felt sour on his tongue.

Hawk finished his business with the table and now leaned against it, his hands flat against the polished wood.

"Lord Dartford holds orgies at his country estate."

He wasn't sure what he'd been expecting, but it wasn't this.

"I'm sorry?" he asked.

"Orgies." Philip repeated the word as if he were speaking in a foreign tongue. "He brings prostitutes from London to his country estate. I heard he pays well."

Dash's stomach turned over. "You must be jesting."

Hawk shook his head. "The man is vile."

He wasn't sure exactly where to start with this new information. Several of his friends at school had absent fathers. Dash himself wouldn't have said his relationship with his own father had been close, but it had been better than the relationship he had with his mother.

But this—

"Does Audrey know?"

Hawk raised an eyebrow, and Dash realized he'd used her given name.

"Audrey," Philip said with an edge of warning in his voice, "is aware her father conducts himself improperly at his estate, but I've never heard her ask questions of Caroline or her brothers."

Dash studied the two men opposite him. "If he pays these prostitutes well, he must be emptying the Dartford coffers."

Hawk shook his head slowly. "Baron Grays has wrested control of the accounts from his father in exchange for the younger man's silence. Lord Dartford goes on cavorting at his country estate while his family remains in London without raising a word in protest."

Dash shook his head. "That's disgusting."

"I thought you would agree." Hawk straightened away from the table and gathered the cues from where he had set them on a sideboard.

As he handed one to Philip, Hawk asked, "Why the sudden interest in Lord Dartford?"

Dash had set down his drink, ready to accept a cue from his friend, and so the question unsettled him.

What was he to say to this? Was he to tell them the truth? Hawk already knew most of it while Philip remained in the dark.

But what he really wanted to say suddenly bubbled up from somewhere deep inside of him.

He leaned against the table, bringing himself closer to the other men. "I've gotten to know Audrey over the past several days, and I've been struck by her charm, her humor, and her positive nature. She's like a warm breeze on a cold English afternoon, and I wonder how a creature like that could come from the Dartford line. It almost seems impossible."

Hawk and Philip studied him for several uncomfortable seconds before Philip blurted, "Are you in love, man?"

Dash laughed at the man's outburst, but something squeezed in his chest at the use of the word.

Dash shook his head. "I'm afraid I've never been in love before, so I couldn't say."

But he caught the knowing look on Hawk's face, and Dash's smile faded.

"Shall we play?" Dash gestured to the field in front of them, and it seemed to startle Hawk from whatever trance Dash's declaration had cast over him.

He handed Dash the other cue, and the men set to playing.

But even as Dash studied the field of balls and cushions, he couldn't help wondering for the first time if Audrey didn't need him as much as he needed her.

12

She watched Dash leave with Philip and Hawk and felt her stomach twist at his departure. It wasn't a longing. He had just left the room after all. It wasn't as though she may not see him for an extended length of time. It was only...

She wished she could be closer to him without propriety frowning upon it. She wished she could partner with him on the blessed interminable activities Lady Sherrill seemed keen to conjure for her house guests. She wished she could collaborate on charades and devise schemes in the card games.

But it would be untoward for an unmarried lady like her to spend so much time in Lord Amberley's presence, especially given his reputation as a charmer. They would think her just another of his conquests.

And what if she was?

Was she?

It was not the first time the thought had plagued her over the last several days. It was hard not to think of it. Dash's reputation was everywhere, especially at the house party. There were several other young ladies present who were out and enjoyed gossiping about things they had overheard whispered in ballrooms. Their favorite topic of conversation was the Earl of Amberley, of course.

How much of what they said was true?

Audrey couldn't fathom, but she did wonder.

She wondered if that afternoon in the stone temple had meant anything or if she, like so many other foolish young women, had simply allowed herself to be compromised.

She knew she wasn't ruined in the truest sense of the word, but she was no longer innocent. The things he had done to her were…extraordinary, but they were also scandalous.

What would her brothers do if they found out?

They would demand retribution from Dash, but knowing them, they would argue over which brother would have the honor of calling out the Earl of Amberley.

And through it all she still wondered about the mysterious Lady Wilson.

It was hard to concentrate on her cards then while her mind scrambled to think of what her brothers might do, which was entirely ridiculous, and what had happened to Dash's engagement. Her brothers would not find out, and if they did, she would not allow them to harm Dash. It was her idea after all. She had been a willing participant.

Hadn't she?

The cards in her hands bent as she forgot herself in her thoughts, in the memory of Dash's hand on the soft skin of her thigh, at the heat in his eyes that had transfixed her. Had she been wooed by his charm? Had she been unable to think clearly?

No, that wasn't it at all. Dash had offered, and she had taken. Boldly. Courageously. Without hesitation.

Even now days later, sitting at a table filled with cards, surrounded by other tables filled with players, she could recall the taste of him, the scent of him as he held her. She could remember it all, and it still had the power to heat her blood.

She'd enjoyed every second of it, and she knew she would seek more of it before their time here was through. She wouldn't let the opportunity be wasted because she didn't know when she might have it again.

If she were a spinster, she could take a lover.

The thought pierced all the others, and she nearly dropped her cards.

A lover.

She had never thought of the possibility, but now she couldn't do anything but think of it. That was what she could do with her freedom. She hadn't thought of it before now, and that meant—

Dash had fulfilled his promise. He was showing her what freedom meant. Her heart thudded loudly in her chest, and she wondered how the other players at the table didn't hear it.

She wasn't sure she had taken him seriously when he had offered to show her what freedom could win her, but here she was, suddenly filled with an idea of what her freedom would get her.

Although, if she were honest, marrying Dash would attain the same result.

She chewed her lower lip.

He had offered to court her, hadn't he? Courtship insinuated that he meant to ask for her hand in marriage at some point, didn't it?

She couldn't think like that.

Freedom lay the other way. Freedom came when she was firmly on the shelf, and then...

She would take Dash as her lover.

It suddenly seemed so simple. But would Dash want her as a lover? She recalled what Miss Holloway had said about him. Dash didn't ruin the reputations of young ladies, but perhaps she wouldn't count. She would be a spinster then, and spinsters had different rules.

But that wouldn't stop Dash from continuing his charming ways.

She nearly snapped the cards in half now, and she drew a steadying breath of air.

Dash was free to do as he pleased just as she would be.

Why did it leave her stomach so sour?

It was only when Caroline let out an exaggerated sigh that Audrey realized the hand was over. She glanced at her cousin, slumped in the chair beside her.

"Must I point out your glum attitude?" Audrey whispered as the other players at the table gathered their things and rose.

Caroline eyed her. "Glum? It isn't glum." She stood with a swiftness Audrey hadn't expected and tore off for the side of the room where refreshments had been set out.

Audrey followed more slowly and found a glass of lemonade for herself.

"Care to talk about why you are not glum?"

Caroline had been acting oddly since that rainy afternoon. When Audrey had finally made her way back to the house, she'd found Caroline in her rooms, which was the first clue something was amiss. The fact that Caroline had not glued herself to Philip's door was telling.

Instead, Caroline had been perched on the sofa in her sitting room, wrapped in a thick blanket and her dressing gown. This was something to note, but the expression on her face was something else entirely.

If Audrey had not known better, she would have said her cousin looked frightened. Audrey couldn't say what had happened after Caroline wandered off in the rain without her, but after her own experience that afternoon, Audrey was prepared to take some fairly wild guesses, and most of them had included Hawk.

Dash and Audrey had returned to the house separately to keep suspicions at bay, and it seemed to have worked for the most part. After all, she had found the temple herself, so when asked, she simply told the truth. She just failed to mention Dash's arrival or anything subsequent.

But now as she stood next to Caroline several days later, she noted how her cousin's frightened expression had turned pinched and sour.

"It's a lovely evening. How about a turn on the terrace?"

"I hope the terrace sinks into the abyss," Caroline muttered around the rim of her lemonade glass.

"Well, that seems terribly unfair. I think Lady Sherrill rather likes her terrace."

Caroline's expression could have sparked an inferno.

Audrey set down her glass. "If you don't tell me what's happened, I cannot make you feel better."

"I didn't ask you to make me feel better." Caroline set down her own glass with a much harder thunk. "Why is everyone always going on about feelings? What's so bloody wonderful about them?"

So, it did have to do with Hawk...

Audrey pretended an interest in the trays of biscuits and fruit pies. "You're absolutely right, I'm afraid. People are always going on about feelings. It's like people experience them with an alarming frequency." She turned back to her cousin. "Is there a particular person who is speaking of feelings?"

It seemed Caroline had given up glaring, her features going lax with a suddenness that was troubling.

"Audrey." She spoke as if she were addressing a small child. "Have you ever thought about someone a certain way only to find out that what you might have thought is rather far from the truth?"

While Audrey could suspect of whom Caroline spoke, she felt an odd uncomfortableness in her chest as Caroline's words could easily have applied to herself.

Hadn't she just considered the fact that she could have the same outcome had she allowed Dash to court her and eventually marry her? Instead, she had conjured some bargain that gave her everything and yet nothing at all. For what did any of it mean if he weren't truly hers?

Was that what she'd wanted all along? Did she truly wish to be wed?

She thought of the hundreds of balls she had attended in her four seasons in society. She thought of the endless hours of sitting next to Grandmother Regina and Aunt Verity. The gentlemen who stepped on her toes because they didn't see her. The ladies who elbowed her because they tried to ignore her.

She had always equated marriage to the tedium of being out in society, but that wasn't it at all. Marriage was entirely different. How could she have been so wrong?

Marriage wasn't a trap. It wasn't a way for her to become ensnared in the same drudgery year after year. It was an escape. A beautiful, adventurous escape.

If only she had it with Dash.

But doubt still niggled at her, gnawing at her certainty until she wasn't certain of anything. The only thing she did know was that she wanted more of Dash, and she wanted him now.

"It's rather late," she said, and she realized how sudden her words were when Caroline's expression turned questioning. "I think it best if we leave this for the morning. Try to get some sleep."

She didn't wait for Caroline's reply. She made her way from the game rooms to the floor above and down the wing where the guests were staying. Her room was a tastefully appointed affair in soft greens and golds, and she wondered not for the first time just how wealthy the Stonegate title was, and for an absurd moment, she thought how lucky Caroline would be should she...

Well, Audrey was getting ahead of herself.

Perhaps Caroline had simply realized she didn't wish to murder Hawk every time she laid eyes on him. It would be an improvement.

Once in her room though, Audrey wasn't sure what to do. Should she change into her nightdress and gown? Should she remain in her evening gown? She'd never attempted a middle-of-the-night assignation with a gentleman and did not in the least know how to dress. This would all be so much easier if Dash tried to seduce her.

The thought should have been concerning, but then an image of her mother's disapproving face floated into her mind, and Audrey was filled with a sense of urgency and pride.

She would seduce Dash and enjoy every minute of it.

She decided to change into her night garments. She would be far more comfortable, and it would be easier to... well, those thoughts made her cheeks turn red.

She waited in her rooms then, leaving only a single candle lit on the table by the chair where she perched, listening to the other guests retire for the night. It was nearly an hour later when Caroline's step could be heard in the hall. Audrey knew it was Caroline because the light step paused in front of her door for the smallest of moments, and Audrey worried Caroline might knock. But then the footsteps continued, and the house grew silent once more.

Still Audrey waited.

She waited until she heard the creaking of wood as the house settled into slumber and only the tick of the grandfather clock in the corridor permeated the solitude.

She knew Dash's rooms were in the opposite wing. She didn't believe such separation was done for propriety's sake as Audrey's wing housed several other male guests, but rather it was done out of necessity. There were a great many guests in attendance, and Audrey thought of the coming assembly. It was sure to be quite a spectacle, and her stomach knotted at the thought of it.

But then it cleared almost as quickly when she thought of Dash. Perhaps it would be different this time. Perhaps she would dance with him. Perhaps she would dance with other gentlemen. Perhaps for once she wouldn't stay at the edge of the ballroom.

Her emotions and thoughts were in a right whirlwind by the time she eased open her door. Only to swallow a scream as her eyes adjusted to the shape of a man looming before her.

She made to shut the door when she realized who it was.

Dash.

He had come to her. He stood there, his gaze traveling up and down her body, and she could only imagine what he thought. She didn't know how long they stood there, one eyeing the other as a waterfall of questions and conclusions spiraled between them unspoken.

They could be caught at any moment and yet they stood there. But what if she were caught? What would happen to her? She'd be packed into a carriage and sent home to her disapproving mother, ruined, her place on the shelf all but secured.

Something stole over her at the thought.

Was that the worst that would happen if she were caught? She would be finally on the shelf?

Without another thought, she reached out and grabbed Dash by the lapel and pulled him into her rooms.

SHE HAD BEEN LEAVING her rooms.

In the middle of the night.

In her nightdress.

He was not one to suffer from insecurity, but the sight of her standing there rocked him until he wasn't sure he would ever catch his breath again.

Where was she going?

Worse, who was she going to meet?

And then came the surge of protectiveness he felt whenever he was near her. What was she thinking venturing out in the middle of the night at a house party? She could have been—

Reality dawned on him as he stood there in her rooms. His back was to her as she'd gone to shut and bolt the door after she'd pulled him inside, but neither of them moved as they waited for the inevitable footsteps chasing down the corridor, the pounding on the door to demand who was there.

But none of that happened. The night was filled with the ticking of a clock and the harsh sounds of their own breaths.

Finally he turned and found her perched against the door, her hand still on the bolt, her face pensive as if she were still listening.

"Where were you going?" He was surprised by how level his voice was.

Her eyes widened before narrowing to dangerous slits. "I was coming to find you. Where did you think I was going?"

Something surged inside of him at her words. "You were coming to find me? Why?"

"I had planned to seduce you, but I don't like the accusation in your tone. Do you think I make a habit of wandering around in strange houses at night?"

She spoke as if she were referring to nothing more exciting than the weather and yet at her words, his entire body clenched.

"Seduce me?" He could hardly get the words out. He'd had his fair share of lovers, but it had always been discreet and respectful. He never took advantage of a young woman, and he never dallied with wives who didn't express an interest in his attentions first.

But this...

He didn't know what to make of this. He had had women wish to seduce him before, but then he knew it had everything to do with his charm and very little to do with him. And while he was sure a little of that charm had eked out, he had been more honest with Audrey than with any other woman he'd ever met.

So why did she wish to seduce him? Surely she couldn't have chosen him for him. Could she?

And why now?

He had wanted to court her. He wanted to do the right thing, but she had refused.

But all at once it suddenly made sense.

"You're exercising your freedom, aren't you?"

Perhaps it did have nothing to do with him.

She let go of the bolt and took a step toward him. Her face remained hard, and he wondered what she was about when she snatched hold of the lapels of his jacket again. He had come straight from the billiards room, and he was still dressed in his dinner jacket. He wasn't sure what it was that had driven him to her door. He hadn't even knocked when he'd gotten there, and then she'd opened it as if he'd summoned her with his thoughts.

He had simply been drowning in his need to see her, to touch her, to taste her.

And now here she was, right in front of him.

And she was alight with a fire he'd never seen in her before.

"I thought about it, yes," she said. "But then I realized it wasn't freedom I wanted just now. It was you."

Her mouth slammed into his before he fully processed her words, and then it hit him, all at once and completely. His arms went around her, locking her to him as the kiss turned into something hot and carnal.

She wanted him.

Just him and only him, and something light and visceral spread through him.

He wanted to take it slowly. Somewhere in the back of his mind he realized this was likely her first time, but something else drove an urgency in him that he could not ignore. He had wanted this for so long; he had wanted her. He had been patient and understanding. He had given her the space she had declared she wanted, and that made this moment all the sweeter.

To have her here now of her own choice meant more than if he had persuaded her with his charm.

He felt a flash of guilt at the thought. He wasn't entirely innocent in all this, but he had discarded the idea of a formal courtship at her insistence. If the rest of their relationship was murky, he would leave that at fate's door, not his.

Who was he to resist her when opportunity presented itself?

But this...this was something else entirely. While he burned with the memory of their afternoon in the stone temple, this was something different, sharper and more poignant. They were warm and safe, and there was a proper bed and all night in which to employ it. The thought had him reaching for the tie of her dressing gown.

He pushed the garment from her shoulders, letting it drop to the floor as he felt her fingers working the buttons of his waistcoat. The need to feel her bare skin against his was sudden and acute, and he helped her, shucking his jacket and then his waistcoat. Her hands were already on his cravat, his on the buttons of her nightdress. It was a race to see who could rid the other of their clothing faster, and all the while his lips explored hers, nibbled, tasted, and discovered.

Finally, the last of the small buttons marching down the front of her nightdress slipped free, and the enormity of it hit him. He wrenched his mouth from hers, and putting his hands to her shoulders, pushed her back, putting much needed space between them.

She blinked at him in the soft candlelight, and he knew he would never see anything more beautiful. Her nightdress parted down the front, and he caught a glimpse of precious pale skin.

"I must know that you're sure about this." The words were strained as he struggled to regain his breath.

She didn't answer him. Instead, she stepped out from under his hands and reaching up, pushed the nightdress from her shoulders. His breath caught at the sight of her, her delicate skin dappled by the soft yellow glow of the candles. He took in the curve of her shoulders, the sweep of her neck, but he wouldn't allow his gaze to drop lower. Instead, he met her eyes.

"Are you certain?" His voice was steadier now.

She didn't look away and when she spoke her voice was firm. "I've never been more certain in my life."

He wasted no more time. He swept her into his arms and carried her to the bed, depositing her softly on the bedclothes. She sank into the mattress, and he was atop her. He was still mostly clothed, down to his boots, but the need to touch her, kiss her was greater than his urge to shed the remainder of his garments.

He came atop her, kissing her so thoroughly he pressed her farther into the mattress. His hands explored, sweeping down her sides, noting every curve, caressing every valley. He had had only the most cursory idea of what her body was like from the afternoon in the temple, but then there were far too many clothes between them that prevented him from really learning her body. But now he let himself indulge.

He cupped her buttocks, lifting her into him, molding her body to his. He groaned against her mouth, his own body hardening in anticipation.

"Audrey," he murmured against her lips before pulling back, trailing kisses along her jaw. "You are going to be my undoing."

In response, she merely lifted her chin, exposing the gorgeous column of her neck to him.

"Minx," he muttered before employing more exquisite torture to the sweep of pale skin.

He dipped lower, following the path his hands had covered earlier. He grazed the fine bones of her collar before slipping lower over the pale mounds of her breasts. He didn't stop; he didn't savor. He just took.

He sucked one nipple into his mouth and then the other before moving lower still, stroking the sensitive skin under each breast with a flick of his tongue. She came up off the mattress, her hands fisted in his hair as a strangled cry slipped from her lips. He smiled against the softness of her belly and moved lower still.

He knew the silkiness of her thighs, but now he could see the way they curved so perfectly into the swell of her hips. He gripped them, holding her still in sensual agony as he moved lower.

"Dash." His name was a plea falling softly from her lips.

She shifted beneath him, raising her hips as if offering herself to him, and he groaned, unsure how much more he could bear. He wanted to be inside of her. He wanted to feel her tight sheath around him. He wanted to know her completely.

But there was still so much to explore.

Later.

He promised himself that later he could explore her fully. For now, he just needed to feel her more than he'd needed anything in his life. He rose from the bed and hastily shed the remainder of his clothes. She watched him, and he felt himself harden further at her bold perusal. He should have expected such boldness from her, but experiencing it was something altogether more potent.

He wanted to rejoin her on the bed, but there was something about her frank gaze that stopped him. He let her look her fill, and when she finally raised her eyes to his, he wasn't surprised to find a curious expression on her features.

"What is it?" he asked.

If she were feeling suddenly unsure, he wouldn't press her. He had to know with absolute certainty that she wished to proceed. Tonight would unerringly change her life, and he respected the enormity of his power to affect it. The decision had to be hers, fully and completely.

"I'm not certain I expected to enjoy the male body so much." Her words were as frank as her gaze, and he couldn't help but grin as he lowered himself on the bed, slipping between her legs.

"As long as you only enjoy this male body," he said before taking her lips once more.

Her hands went immediately to his back, holding him tightly against her. He reveled in the feel of her, holding him so assuredly, but then she shifted, spreading her thighs for him, and he was lost in the entirety of her.

This was everything. This was everything he had been searching for. It was so much more than the physical act. Something existed between them that was far stronger than any physical bond could produce, and he thought it should frighten him, but it only made him want her more.

He slipped a hand between them and found her wet and ready for him, the thought sending a surge of desire through him. He stroked her sensitive nub, sensing her body coiling for him, yearning toward his touch.

"Dash." She moaned, her head falling back against the pillows as she arched against him. "Dash, please."

He pushed inside of her slowly, painfully slowly, and felt her stretch around him. He kissed her, first her lips then her jaw then her neck. He stroked her as he pushed through the last of the resistance, and then he was fully inside of her.

And nothing could compare to that moment. Nothing before and nothing after. It simply couldn't.

Her eyes flew open then, and she met his gaze directly.

"Dash, I need…I need…" Her voice was no longer frank, her words saturated with her own desire.

"I know, darling," he said and began to move inside of her.

Her hips came up off the mattress to grind against him, and he felt his control slip.

"Audrey." He couldn't say anything else, the rest of his concentration focused on making this good for her before he let himself go.

But then she moved her hips again, grinding against him in a circle. She was finding her own pleasure and watching her drove him to the brink of orgasm.

He studied her, transfixed by the pure desire that had shone so perfectly on her captivating face, and he knew he could not last much longer.

"Audrey," he said again, but she was already there.

She came in an explosion of tightening muscle and muffled cries, and his body responded, unable to hold back at the sight of such pleasure. He came hard, emptying himself in her as the force of the orgasm rocked him.

As he collapsed beside her and drew her into his arms, he should have thought about how he had never experienced anything so powerful in his life, but that wasn't what he thought.

He could only think about how right it felt, all of it, and how he never wanted to let her go.

13

She must have dozed because when she opened her eyes again, she could feel her body start as if pulling itself from a dreamless sleep. His leg was over hers, pinning her to the mattress, and his arm was slung over her stomach.

Warm.

She felt incredibly warm and safe, and it was as if the room was impenetrable as long as they stayed right there like that, entwined in each other's arms.

Only that wasn't true.

She pulled on his arm, and she felt a modicum of guilt when his breathing changed from the deep, steady rhythm of sleep to the shallower cadence of wakefulness.

He muttered something against her neck that she took to mean he was fully awake.

"We can't be discovered like this," she whispered, although no one could possibly hear them.

The rooms were generous, and the closest occupant to her was Aunt Phyllida down the hall. It wasn't as if the woman were waiting for an opportunity to find Audrey in a compromising position.

His response was to nestle his nose deeper against her neck, and her body tingled in anticipation. How could she possibly be responding to him again so soon? Her body ached in places she hadn't known existed; the blood still poured through her as it tried to restore the energy she had exerted in their lovemaking.

His breathing relaxed again, and she feared he would fall asleep. She nudged him with an elbow in his abdomen.

"Ow," he muttered against her ear. He pulled back, resting his head on the pillow beside hers. "We won't get caught," he mumbled.

"How do you know?" she whispered. "I'm new at this, remember? I'm trusting you to be the wiser one here."

He opened a single eye. "That is where you've made a grievous mistake, my lady."

She couldn't help her smile. Even though he jested over a serious subject, she couldn't help but feel lightness filling her body. Did it truly matter if they were caught? She had no grand designs for a match now. She only longed for the shelf. Or at least, she thought she did.

Earlier that night she could not have sworn to as much. Otherwise, why would she have tried to find him? If she were on the shelf, she could take him as a lover whenever she pleased. But now, here in his arms, she wasn't so sure what she wanted.

"Be that as it may, you need to leave."

He opened both eyes now and studied her. She wanted to squirm under the scrutiny, so unused to having someone consider her with such appreciation, but it was impossible to feel uncomfortable just then. Everything about being in Dash's arms just felt right.

"No."

She thought she had misheard him. "Did you just say no?"

"I did just say no." He bent forward, nuzzled her ear.

She pulled her head away from his on the pillow and turned to face him. "You can't say no. We can't be caught like this. It would mean—"

"We won't be caught. I keep telling you that." He squirmed against her, his arms finding their way around her in this new position and pulling her solidly against his chest.

Her fingers curled into the dark mat of hair there, enjoying the way the roughness made her skin tingle in anticipation. How she could want him again she didn't know, but there were many things she didn't understand now, and this was just one of them.

"You can't know that for sure."

"Will you just trust me?" He mumbled the words against her cheek, her jaw, as he nibbled kisses along the sensitive spot behind her ear.

She pushed him away just enough to meet his eyes.

"I'm being serious. We can't be caught. I'm not on the shelf yet, and—"

He silenced her with a soft kiss, and she let him.

When he drew back, his eyes were pensive and sincere. "Can we not talk of shelves until we're back in London?" Another gentle kiss. "Please."

Her heart ached with a sudden intensity she feared might rob her of her breath. She felt it in that moment, all of the things that lay unspoken between them.

She wanted freedom, but she also wanted him, and she didn't know if she could have both. It wouldn't be fair to him. He deserved something better than being her lover. He deserved a wife.

She could be his wife.

She searched his eyes, hoping to find the answers there, but she only saw her own reflection.

She nodded, her hair crackling against the pillow. "All right. We won't talk of shelves until we're back in London. But that still leaves us with the problem of you being in my bed."

His grin was slow, and when he rolled her, she let him. He came up on top of her, leaning over her to kiss her again, gently as before, but lingering just a little bit longer. When he pulled back, his smile was genuine and wide. He reached up and traced the line of her brow, the bridge of her nose.

"I am not leaving, Audrey. Not tonight. I want to wake up next to you." He touched each of her cheeks, dipped along the curve of her chin. "I want to see you with the morning sun on your face." He bent his head, replacing his finger with his lips. "I want to kiss all of the places the sunshine touches."

She could see it, the image his words painted, and her body coiled, ready for his touch, his kiss, his attention.

"We can't," she whispered, but her words held no conviction.

He continued to kiss her along her jaw and down her neck. She wanted to touch him everywhere, her hands sliding along his shoulders and down his back, the muscles rippling under her touch.

He pulled away though, until he could see her face. A line had appeared between his brow, and she realized it was the first she had ever seen him so worried.

"What is it?" she whispered.

"It's just...well, I hope you'll dance with me at tonight's

assembly. I've been turned down so much, more rejection might—"

She pulled his head down to kiss him into silence even as she couldn't stop the smile that came to her lips.

After several long kisses, she released him to say, "I will see if there's room on my dance card for you, my lord."

Something shone in his eyes then. Something stark and revealing, and it sent a bolt of lightning straight through her.

Possession.

That was what was in his eyes. She felt a flash of fear, worried that his attention might be the end of her chances for freedom, but it wasn't like that. This wasn't the possession of a person. This was a possession of her heart. It was his no matter if she allowed him to court her or not, if she took him as a lover or not. There wasn't a choice in it for either of them. She understood that now only too well.

She studied his face, something inside of her urging her to speak now before it was too late, but she feared it already was too late.

His face shifted, his eyes softening as he leaned down and whispered against her lips, "Make room."

He kissed her then, and her heart thudded in anticipation.

She thought she'd known what to expect; thought she had experienced it all, but he proved her wrong.

He touched her in new places, found new ways to make her body thrill. She didn't know how much she could want the roughness of his hands against the soft curve of her thighs or the scrape of his chest hair against her sensitive nipples. She wanted all of it.

And not just tonight. She wanted it forever.

But could she give up her freedom to have it?

This time when he slid into her, her body relaxed around him as if it had always known his. The connection was real and deep, and she relaxed into the mattress, ready to be pleasured.

The first time had been frantic, and her body had responded in ways she couldn't fathom. But now, she let the pleasure come to her.

As if sensing the change, Dash seemed to take his time, torturing her with slow, deep thrusts until she was no longer sure she could wait for him. She wrapped her legs around his hips, opening herself up, taking him deeper.

"Dash," she moaned, her head going back as she arched into him, as her nipples scraped his chest.

Exquisite pleasure was everywhere, all along her body and inside of her too.

"Dash, please," she begged.

He must have felt it too, the growing urgency, the unbearable desire, because he picked up his pace, thrusting into her with smooth, deep strokes until she could feel her release just beyond her reach.

Again, he seemed to understand because he shifted, and when he thrust into her, he rubbed against her sensitive nub, and she exploded on a wave of sheer lust.

But it wasn't over.

He continued to thrust, rubbing against her with each stroke until the tension built again. She couldn't possibly. There was no way—

She came apart with him that time, his body shuddering above her, and she held him so tightly, never wanting to let him go.

She stirred several minutes later when she felt him get up and leave the bed. She reluctantly opened her eyes to see him pushing back the curtains. When he returned to bed, she rolled immediately into his arms.

"What was that about?" she murmured, sleep already pulling at her.

"I meant what I said about the sunshine," he said, pressing a kiss to her bare shoulder.

When morning came, she would learn something else about him.

Lord Amberley always did what he intended.

As promised, he snuck out of her rooms without issue. The house was still slumbering when he slipped from her bed. Not even the upstairs maids were about to start the morning fires and open the curtains. There would be no curtains to open in Lady D'Arcy's rooms. He had made certain of that.

When he finally made his way back to his rooms, it was with a much lighter step than he'd had in all of his life. It was strange this feeling. He wasn't sure if it was love, but he suspected it might be.

Not once in the past several days had he thought about Evers Park, had he thought about how the Amberley estate languished under his mother's enforced neglect. Not once had he thought about David.

He had plenty of time to think on why that might be as he got ready for the day, lingering for a long time in his rooms to not give fodder to any suspicions that he might not have spent the night there. The men were to engage in some pheasant hunting for the assembly dinner as Lady Sherrill wished for fresh game to serve her guests. Dash wasn't much of a sportsman as his father had never been one to teach his son the mechanics of it. But he had learned the rudimentaries from Hawk who had learned from his grandfather, and he got on well enough.

What he looked forward to most though was a chance to be outside in the fresh, crisp spring air, the sunshine on his face and the breeze blowing by him. It would give him a chance to think about what had happened last night.

There was the physical part of it, sure. Audrey could very well be pregnant with his child even now. He would marry her, of course, but that wasn't the difficult part. He knew only too well she would resist, and he couldn't blame her. He would only need to make her see reason.

But even more than that, he wouldn't allow a child of his to be raised under the nose of the Countess of Dartford. It was bad enough what she had done to her daughter; he wouldn't allow the woman to prey on another innocent. Audrey must marry him if only to get away from the woman.

But that was something to be worried over should the time come. He had more pressing things to mull over.

Like whether or not he was in love with her.

He suspected it. And if he were in love with her, what was he to do about it? The old fear gripped him, but as soon as it came, it fled and not once did he feel the ghost of Nicole. He wondered at that, but once again, he knew this was different, and because of its difference, the fear never gained a foothold.

Could he hope that he'd shown Audrey the truth about her idea of freedom? That spinsterhood was just another cage into which women were captured? That true freedom lay in a partnership with one's spouse? That the world opened up to possibility and adventure when one stood on the foundation of a marriage?

He hated to think that they lived in a world where

Audrey was denied the same freedoms as him simply because she was born a woman, but that was the reality of it.

But she could marry him. His name alone could provide protection far greater than spinsterhood. But would it be enough to convince her?

More, would it be enough to fulfill her?

He couldn't forget the moment she had opened that door though. She had been coming to find him. *Him*. She had planned to seduce *him*.

He warmed at the memory, and his hands flexed, wishing she were here now where he could touch her and hold her.

Later. He promised himself. Later at the assembly he would find her.

He made his way downstairs to the breakfast room only to encounter a melee in the foyer. When it was determined that an assembly would cap off the week, Lady Sherrill had dispatched more invitations to get the numbers up. Dash knew Hawk had tried to restrain her, but Lady Sherrill did as she pleased. It seemed the new guests were arriving in force.

It was much as it had been the first day when he'd arrived and waited for Audrey on the front steps. The front door was stuffed with incoming ladies and gentlemen, servants attempting to take parasols and hats while Lady Sherrill stood in the middle of all of it. Her lips were pinched even as she attempted to smile, and Dash thought she might not have planned to be caught in the middle of such chaos.

But she was a gracious host and did her best to direct the newly arrived guests to the various drawing rooms. Some even wandered in the direction of the breakfast room though the hour was late. As Dash was just now headed there himself, he couldn't fault the guests for expecting to find nourishment there.

He made his way down the remainder of the stairs, slipping past a beleaguered footman covered in scarves, pelisses, and gloves. He recognized a few of the new guests and nodded where appropriate, bowing when he encountered someone he knew better.

It was nearly a half hour later that he finally entered the breakfast room to find it just as packed as the corridor and foyer. Every seat at the table was occupied, and guests loitered on the fringes with cups of coffee and tea as they seemed engaged in animated conversation with fellow guests.

Dash slipped to the side and filled a plate with what remained of the breakfast stuffs before escaping the room through the terrace doors. It was quieter here, and the fresh air felt good after the closeness of the breakfast room. He wasn't surprised to find Hawk lurking at one of the small tables that had appeared seemingly overnight.

"May I join you in hiding?"

Hawk appeared distracted and even started when Dash approached. "Yes, of course," he mumbled, his gaze returning to whatever it was he'd been studying.

Dash sat and tried to look in the direction that seemed to so preoccupy his friend. He wasn't surprised to see Caroline seated at a table farther down the terrace. She was alone and appeared to be nursing a steaming cup of beverage.

"When are you going to admit you love her?" Dash asked, tucking into his breakfast.

"I don't love her," was Hawk's immediate reply, and Dash couldn't help a knowing smile. "I find her infuriating."

Dash swallowed his eggs and picked up his cup of coffee. "Some would say there's a fine line between love and hate."

Hawk eyed him. "I thought hate was the opposite of love."

Dash shook his head. "You're thinking of indifference."

"When did you become an expert on the matter?" Hawk asked with one eyebrow raised.

Dash thought of the hours of the night he'd spent in Audrey's arms, but instead, merely smiled.

Hawk shook his head and with a scoff returned his attention to Caroline.

"I noticed you didn't return to your rooms after our game of billiards last night," Hawk said after several seconds.

Dash was glad he'd finished his breakfast, or he might have choked on it.

He carefully picked up his coffee. "Is that so?"

"You must have required a...stroll before retiring for the evening?"

"Something like that," Dash said.

Hawk turned a stony glare on him. "You know I will not hesitate to protect her honor."

He didn't need to say her name. They both knew of whom he spoke.

Dash set down his cup and leaned forward, ensuring Hawk understood him. "And neither will I."

The men stared at one another for a length of time, and it was as if an understanding passed between them.

Hawk shook his head, breaking the trance. "She'll never agree to marry you."

Dash waited to reply as a footman approached and took away their empty plates. When they were once more alone, he said, "I'm wounded that you would underestimate my abilities."

Hawk laughed and shook his head. "It's not your abilities I underestimate. It's her fortitude that you have failed to consider properly."

"Must you work so hard to dampen my mood?"

Hawk's laugh was stronger now. "Whatever I can do to make you feel more welcomed in my home." He spread his hands as if to indicate the party around them.

Dash looked about. The terrace had even filled now.

"How many more guests did your grandmother invite?"

"I'm afraid she's invited the whole of Surrey. Maybe Essex too."

Dash finished his coffee and set down his cup. "Is the shoot still on then? With this many gentlemen it will be a difficult thing to separate the groups safely."

Hawk shook his head. "We'll still attempt it, but I might insist we take it in turns. The last thing I wish to deal with today is some idiot getting himself shot."

Dash stood and placed a hand on his friend's shoulder as his attention had once more returned to Caroline.

"Have you ever thought about telling her the truth?"

Hawk looked up to meet his gaze. "That's the problem, isn't it? It's not my truth to tell."

Dash glanced in Caroline's direction, feeling the weight of his friend's predicament. "I suppose you're right." He squeezed his friend's shoulder and let go. "I must collect my things before the hunt. Are we still meeting at eleven?"

Hawk made a non-committal noise Dash took to mean agreement and left his friend to his pining.

Audrey still hadn't come down when he made his way back through the breakfast room, and he wondered if she were feeling any ill effects from last night's endeavors. He scanned the breakfast room again just to be certain and thought perhaps he'd check the drawing rooms in case she might have been diverted by a newly arrived guest.

He slipped into the first room, prepared to have a simple look, but the room was fuller than he expected, and he was soon jostled several feet from the door. He nodded at acquaintances as he tried to make his way back to the corridor when someone stood abruptly, knocking him backward into the lady standing behind him.

He had to make a grab for her shoulders to keep her from falling, and he uttered an immediate apology, straightening and stepping politely away.

It was then that he finally took in her face.

A face so familiar it pulled the air instantly from his lungs.

It was several seconds before he uttered a single word.

"Nicole."

14

She had had an even more difficult time concentrating that day on what Caroline was saying as Lady Sherrill had gone about ensuring the newly arrived guests were comfortable. This involved a great deal of tea and confections, several rounds of piano experimentation by several young ladies, and of course an extended walk about the gardens.

By the time the ladies had retired to their rooms to dress for the assembly and dinner, Audrey could not have said much about what had occurred. Her thoughts had been entirely commandeered by Dash. Memories of their night together haunted her with delicious torture, and there were times when she swore she could still feel his hands on her body, his lips on hers. Was this what love was all about? This heady, intoxicating feeling that completely separated oneself from the trials of everyday? It was no wonder then that so many should fall victim to its siren call.

She had thought herself different. She had thought herself incapable of being seduced, but then, she hadn't met Dash yet.

As she dressed for the assembly, her thoughts kept vacillating between what she had thought she wanted and what she could have. She no longer understood which was the more desirable. Did she want her freedom and Dash as her lover? Or did she want the security of marriage?

Her stomach tightened at the thought of marriage. Even the mention of the word conjured images of society wives held to even more rigorous standards and complications. She couldn't possibly be any good at those either. Could she? She had already failed to live up to so much. She didn't wish to embark on a new set of obstacles over which to fail.

But what if she didn't?

Wives were not held to the standard of beauty that debutantes were, and while Audrey may lack in looks, she certainly held a degree of intelligence and good humor that would benefit a wife. Perhaps she might not entirely fail at the role.

But why was she even contemplating marriage? After this season she would be free to pursue the life of a spinster and do whatever she pleased.

Only so far, their bargain had produced very little to look forward to in her spinsterhood. In fact, the only thing on her list was making love to Dash, so that clearly hadn't worked in her favor.

But surely there was more to be gained from spinsterhood. She only need more time to discover it. In the meanwhile, she had to keep her heart intact. She mustn't let herself succumb to the wonders of love.

When she stepped into the ballroom that evening with Caroline at her side, she wondered momentarily if all of London hadn't arrived at Stonegate Manor. Lady Sherrill took her hosting duties rather seriously, it would seem. The room was filled with any manner of eligible young bachelors with whom the already present debutantes could mingle.

Audrey frowned, but it was Caroline who spoke. "I thought we left London to escape this."

"Perhaps it's better because it's referred to as an assembly rather than a ball."

Caroline gave her a sardonic look. "The label hardly matters."

"I would tend to agree."

They watched Aunt Phyllida disappear through the crowd in the direction of the refreshment table, and by unspoken agreement made their way in the opposite direction.

The ballroom at Stonegate Manor opened onto the stone terrace that ran along the length of this wing, and as it was now into May, spring was in full bloom, the night air heavy with the scent of fresh earth and blossoms. The breeze was refreshing when she caught it as the room was so very packed.

She eyed each of the guests as she passed, but somehow she managed to recognize no one. Maybe they had truly left London and the monotony of its society behind. How Lady Sherrill could have conjured this, she couldn't be sure, but suddenly she felt a lightness she had never before felt at a ball.

Was it because the people were different? Was it because her mother wasn't present, and there was no possibility of her appearing?

Or was it because Audrey had changed?

She had felt it coming, but admitting it was too frightening to consider. Since she had met Dash, she had felt her entire world shifting beneath her feet. The feeling had been like a specter at first, and she couldn't quite be sure it really was happening. Like a boat under her feet, rolling with the ripple of water, it didn't happen all at once, and unless she stopped and focused, she wouldn't have noticed it.

But she noticed it now. She could feel it in the way she moved, her shoulders back and her chin up. She no longer scanned the room from the edges of the dance floor for eligible men to fill her dance card to please her mother, but instead, listened to the sounds of the orchestra warming up, wondering if she would even wish to dance that evening. She found she did actually. She *did* enjoy dancing. It was just the task of attracting partners that vexed her.

She stopped in her stroll around the room, and Caroline looked back at her.

"Is everything all right?"

Audrey didn't look at her as she answered, her gaze fixed on the crowd around them. "Caroline, do you think balls would be more enjoyable if we simply...did as we wished?"

Caroline's brow wrinkled. "I don't think so." She stepped back and looked in the direction Audrey was looking. "What do you mean? Do as we wish?"

Audrey turned her attention to her cousin. "Do you like dancing?" Caroline immediately wrinkled her nose, but Audrey pressed on. "If you could choose whomever you wished to dance with instead of worrying over selecting the right dance partners, would you enjoy it?"

Audrey watched as Caroline's expression cleared. Finally, she met Audrey's gaze.

"Do you know I think I might? It's so exhausting wondering if you've selected enough earls or marquesses for the evening or perhaps you've ignored too many viscounts." She shook her head, her gaze traveling back to the dance floor. "Do you know I think I might enjoy the act of dancing rather than the rituals around it?"

Audrey nodded. "I've just come to the same conclusion myself."

Caroline looked at her once more. "Why now?"

Audrey shook her head, but her reply was forgotten as she spotted Dash coming through the crowd toward them.

He gave a small bow when he approached. "Ladies, how lovely you look this evening."

Audrey knew he was required to address both of them, but she didn't miss how his eyes lingered on hers. He had been absent most of the day with the hunting party that had left just after breakfast, and she realized how much she had missed him. Her conflicted feelings raged anew inside of her, and her stomach twisted oddly in...anticipation? Did she wish to see him again so soon?

He was smartly dressed in black evening attire, but suddenly in her mind she saw him as he had been when she'd opened her door to him the previous night, and her heart thudded with desire.

Yes, she did wish to see him again.

"Hello, Amberley," Caroline said, but Audrey noted her distracted tone.

She looked about them and discovered Philip had just entered with Hawk directly behind him.

"Please excuse me," Caroline said quickly and disappeared into the crowd.

Dash shook his head. "She will not leave him alone, will she?"

"I'm afraid not." She gave Dash a small smile, suddenly finding it awkward to converse with him as she wanted nothing more than to step into his arms again. "I trust you had a successful hunt."

"I successfully kept myself from getting shot by the

much less experienced members of our party. I consider that to be a day well spent."

She raised her eyebrows. "Then I congratulate you. I should think I would be rather distressed should you have suffered harm."

His grin was slow. "Would you have?"

She scrambled to find a pithy reply, but his look had turned heated, and she found she'd lost all track of the conversation. Heat spread within her, and her conflicted thoughts suddenly became crystal clear. She knew she couldn't trust them though. She was simply confused by Dash's nearness. She couldn't believe even herself when he was this close and this handsome.

"I was thinking..." His voice trailed off as he let his gaze move slowly over the crowd around them. "Are you and your family returning to London in two days?"

The house party was due to end on Sunday, and Aunt Phyllida had already told them to expect her departure promptly after breakfast on Sunday.

She nodded. "We are."

One side of his mouth lifted as he looked back at her. "Then perhaps you'd like to pay your respects to Artemis before you leave?"

Her stomach flipped over, both by his veiled invitation and the fire in his eyes.

"I think that would only be appropriate." How she managed the words with her suddenly dry throat, she couldn't say. She leaned closer. "And I suppose you might suggest how I am to sneak out this time?"

He smelled of soap and sandalwood, and her toes curled in her slippers.

"When the dancing starts, of course. The guests will

wish to see whom Hawk chooses to partner, and it would be all too easy to slip out for some fresh air."

She raised her chin. "I do like a spot of fresh air. It's good for one's constitution."

"I always suspected you of being a do-gooder."

She made to retort when she caught sight of someone coming up behind Dash and tapping him rather improperly on the shoulder.

"Dash, I wanted to—" the woman stopped, her icy blue eyes turned to Audrey. "Oh, I'm sorry. I didn't see you there."

Something old and heavy crashed inside of Audrey then, and the feeling of lightness she had so recently discovered fled at the sight of the beautiful woman who stood before her. The beautiful woman who had so casually tapped Dash on the shoulder. *Dash.* She had even used his given name.

"Nicole." Dash coughed, his smile faltering.

Nicole. Audrey watched him, this man she thought she loved, as he addressed this goddess by her given name, his voice strained, his face tensed.

He didn't want her to know about this Nicole.

She didn't know where the thought came from, but suddenly it was there, and she wished to be anywhere but where she was standing just then.

Because she knew.

She knew exactly who Nicole was.

"Lady Wilson," Dash tried again. "This is Lady D'Arcy, the daughter of the Earl of Dartford."

Lady Wilson. The name Philip had uttered at the breakfast table not more than a fortnight ago. The name that haunted her thoughts. Here she was, a living person come to destroy the happiness Audrey had just discovered. The thought was whole and dramatic, but somehow Audrey felt the truth of it.

Lady Wilson's smile was cool, her curtsy shallow. "Lady D'Arcy, a pleasure. I believe I know your mother."

Audrey wouldn't doubt it. "Lady Wilson," she said only in reply.

"Lady Wilson is, uh..."

Audrey looked quickly at Dash. Never before had she known him to be at a loss for words, but Lady Wilson seemed perfectly prepared to help him.

"I'm his betrothed," the woman said, and now the ice had spread to her eyes.

"Former betrothed," Dash finally managed.

It didn't matter which state the betrothal was in. The word was enough to have Audrey's stomach dropping again, her heart thudding as the blood pounded at her temples. Even though she'd already known it, hearing him say it made it that much worse.

"I see," Audrey said.

It took all her strength to maintain her composed smile. She wanted to flee, but something in her told her to stand her ground. It needn't matter though, because Caroline—blessed Caroline—returned at the moment, her face tight with restrained fury.

"Amberley, would you please excuse us? I have need of my cousin."

Audrey managed only a smile before Caroline tugged her away, but she looked back.

Oh God, why had she looked back?

And when she did, she saw Lady Wilson's gloved hand resting knowingly on Dash's chest.

And Dash.

Dash wasn't even watching her walk away.

~

It was strange when the brain ceased to work properly, and at that exact moment, in the ballroom of Stonegate Manor, Dash's brain had ceased to work. He thought if he didn't look at Audrey she would forget the encounter with Lady Wilson entirely.

He wasn't sure why he didn't want the two women to meet. It wasn't as though he could avoid it for the rest of his life, and as he planned to spend the rest of his life with Audrey, that seemed a very difficult task. It was just...

Nicole had known David.

She was five years Dash's senior, and there was something about the fact that she had been alive when David had been that made her somewhat difficult to place for Dash. There was no neat box in which to put her. She existed both before and after David. Something he, regrettably to some, lacked.

And this, he could think of nothing else, compelled him to keep her away from Audrey. He didn't want Audrey sullied by Nicole. It seemed strange, but then, as previously noted, his brain had ceased to work, and his only objective was to keep Nicole away from Audrey.

The first thing he did was step away from her, effectively putting space between him and her wandering hand.

"You can't touch me in public, Lady Wilson," he uttered softly.

Her hand hung suspended between them, and she looked at it as if it weren't her hand at all.

"Dash, I must speak with you. I must explain." Her brow was folded into an accordion of concern and almost despair, and Dash found it suddenly difficult to breathe.

She couldn't do this to him. Not now. Not here.

He wanted Audrey. He wanted Audrey for the rest of his life. The words played over and over again in his head like a prayer, but it didn't stop the power Nicole held over him, and he worried, horribly, if she would always have such control of him.

"Not here," he whispered.

He held up his arm as if to promenade her around the ballroom, and she placed her hand on it. Nicole had always been good at acting the proper lady, and she slipped into the role easily now as they made their way about the room. They nodded and smiled politely at people they knew while he steered them in the general direction of the terrace doors. His stomach was tight with nerves. Nicole hadn't wished to speak to him in the eight years since she'd broken off their engagement. Why would she be so eager to speak to him now? Was it only because he stumbled into her?

It had been a shock to see her that morning, standing so innocently in Lady Sherrill's drawing room. But even in the shock, he hadn't hesitated to flee. He'd hardly bid her good day and exited the drawing room to prepare for the day's hunt. He had resolutely shoved her from his mind for the day, preferring to think of Audrey. It wasn't until he returned to the manor house after the hunt that he realized what lay inside.

Everything had been going so well. Why had she turned up now? What could it possibly mean?

Dimly he was aware of the first dance starting as he stepped out onto the stone terrace. As soon as they slipped from the scrutinizing view of the guests, he dropped his arm and stepped to the side, putting much-needed space between them.

The night was cool but not terribly so, and a slight breeze blew in off the gardens. He couldn't have said if it smelled of spring or if the stars dotted the sky. He focused on the stairs, at hurrying to a secluded spot to get this conversation over with.

Even when his feet touched the flat grass of the park below he kept walking. He heard the rustle of Nicole's skirts behind him, but he didn't turn to check that she was keeping pace with him.

It was several minutes later that he realized where he was heading. He stopped so abruptly Nicole collided with him. He wasn't angry enough to overrule his gentlemanly instincts and turned in time to catch her from falling. He immediately released her though once he saw that she was steady on her feet.

The sounds of the orchestra and the ball were faint here, this deep into the gardens, but he could still make out the notes of the first dance. Everything inside of him tightened at once, and he looked about them. The garden suddenly looked unfamiliar, as if he had somehow stumbled into a foreign land, and he sucked in a deep breath, willing himself to calm. He had to concentrate.

He had told Audrey to slip away from the ball at the first dance. Would she still do it? Would she still meet him?

The night seemed to close in around him, and he saw the looming hedges as though they were beasts, hunting in the dark of the night. He looked behind him and the moon glinted off the pond in the distance.

He took Nicole by the elbow, ignoring her protest, and turned into the hedgerows. There was a folly here surrounded by the high hedges, and towering Ionic columns sent a dizzying spiral of shadows across the ground. He stopped abruptly in the center of it and released Nicole's arm.

"Dash, I—"

He stepped away, out of her reach. Her lips were parted,

her eyes round and wet as if with unshed tears, and her hand hung once more suspended between them.

He steeled himself against it.

Once very long ago, he would have given anything to see Nicole remorseful. He would have given it all to see her like this, her need for him written so clearly on her face. But now it only made him wary.

"Dash, I'm sorry," she said softly. "I'm sorry for everything. I didn't get to tell you then, and I—"

"You broke off the engagement. There wasn't much to tell."

She shook her head, and now he saw the glint of tears on her cheeks. "It wasn't like that. I wanted to—" She choked and swallowed, pressing a fist to her lips. "I didn't mean to hurt you."

"You were in love with another man."

It was the first time he had spoken the words aloud. He had known the reason she'd broken the engagement even though neither of them had said it aloud. She had married the Honorable Mr. Thurber Wilson not even a month after their broken engagement.

But she didn't look like a woman in love just then. She looked like a woman who very much regretted her choices.

But maybe she didn't. Maybe she just truly regretted hurting him.

He didn't believe it. He hadn't believed it then. Love then and now came with a mixture of emotions that he knew were flammable.

He watched her carefully.

"I didn't know how to tell you." Her voice was steadier now, the tears falling softly on her cheeks. "I couldn't marry you, but our parents...they wished..." her voice died away.

Something strange passed over him then, and it was as

though he was back there, to that time eight years ago when they had stood in the drawing room of her father's home, and she had told him that the wedding was off. But instead of seeing only red, instead of being consumed by the anger that had raged through him, he saw a young man, hardly more than a boy, and a woman not much more than a girl. He saw two people controlled by their parents, by the expectations set into motion from the death of another child.

"Our parents wanted us to marry because they always thought you'd marry David." He spoke the words in a flat tone, feeling the weight of what she must have felt then.

She didn't speak, her shoulders slumping, and her tears had stopped.

She shook her head softly. "I couldn't do it. I couldn't spend my life loving another to fulfill some idea our parents had about me and David. It wasn't fair to either of us."

Something broke inside of him then, and like a dam failing, he filled with a torrent of emotion and an overwhelming sense of remorse.

Nicole had stopped them from making a mistake when he'd been unable to. Hawk's warning was somehow overcome by Breedlove's grinding laugh, and Dash suddenly felt the fool. He would have walked into the loveless marriage with open arms because it would have meant he'd done something that David had been supposed to do.

"I was so stupid."

He didn't realize he had spoken aloud until Nicole surged forward, her brow wrinkled with empathy.

"No, you weren't stupid," she rushed. "We didn't know any better. David was so—"

"Alive," he supplied.

She nodded, her lips parted. "He haunted all of us, and

our parents the most. They wanted an alliance between our families, and when David died..."

"They expected me to fulfill his duty." It was so obvious now, but it hadn't been then. Then he had let down his father. He had disgraced his mother. And worst of all, he had thought Nicole didn't love him because he wasn't David.

Something rotten and sour churned in his stomach, and he stepped back until he felt the cold hard surface of stone against the backs of his knees, and he sank on one of the benches that littered the edge of the folly. He sat there unmoving for several moments, and eventually Nicole joined him.

"I'm sorry, Dash. I should have told you, but there wasn't time then, and it was so...sudden."

He nodded, her words washing over him, even as his thoughts were filled with so many other things.

Hawk had been right all along. He was chasing something that hadn't been his in the first place, and worse still, he had been trying to force someone into a duty she wasn't destined for. He just as guilty as his mother.

But it wasn't like that. He could feel it deep in his gut.

Marrying Audrey might have started out as a quest, but it was no longer.

He loved her. He knew it with a sudden clarity that only comes when one breaks through the mental barriers holding one back.

He loved her, and he was going to marry her.

And not because Breedlove had challenged him, and not because he thought to prove the ghost of his dead brother wrong. He was marrying her because he loved her.

Vaguely he became aware of the sounds of a waltz drifting over the night air, and he almost shook his head. It couldn't be a waltz. The waltz wasn't to be played until the third dance. How much time had passed? Audrey was waiting for him.

He tried to gain his feet, but Nicole laid a hand on his arm. When he looked at her, her eyes were pleading.

"I'm sorry you never got to meet David," she said now. "He really was a kind young man. He was always nice to me," she said with a shrug. "I'm sorry your impression of him is marked by your mother's cruelty to you."

Dash's image of David had always been formed by his mother's reverence for her dead son, and now that, too, shifted in his mind. He could picture the eighteen-year-old David, dashing and vibrant on the brink of life being kind to a five-year-old girl.

With a jolt, he realized David would have been a kind brother too.

Dash swallowed and patted Nicole's hand, the need to get to Audrey pushing at him.

But then Nicole was crying again, in earnest this time, and he felt a surge of concern.

"Nicole, what is it?" Awkwardly he patted her arm, but the tears came harder now. Finally he put his arm around her and drew her against his side, hoping to calm her.

"I should have married you," she finally managed through her tears.

Dash felt the night slip out of his grasp like a horse missing his footing over a jump. The slightest misstep, and the rest was over.

"Nicole, don't talk like that. Thurber—"

"Is a drunken sod!" She spoke with such sudden vehemence it took Dash by surprise.

He looked over in the direction of the stone temple. He could feel it there somewhere just beyond the hedgerows. Audrey was waiting for him. If she had still gone to meet him, she would have been waiting for some time. Nicole let out a gusty wail then, slapping her hands against her knees.

"I should have known. Do you know how many maids he's impregnated? Dash, are you listening? I don't have a lady's maid because my husband can't be trusted to keep his pants up."

Dash pried his eyes away from the hedgerow, let the inevitability of the night crash around him.

"I'm sorry, Nicole," he said and pulled her more tightly against him until she sobbed into his chest.

15

The stone was cold against her bottom. She didn't know how much time had passed while she waited for Dash to appear, but it was apparently long enough for her bottom to turn to ice from the hard stone of the temple stairs.

She shouldn't have been waiting out in the open like that. Anyone could see her, and as she had come to understand, house parties were rampant with couples wandering in dark gardens.

But right then, she couldn't have cared about her reputation. Too many questions burned inside of her and more than anything she wanted answers. She hated how much her insides twisted at the memory of Lady Wilson's hand on his chest.

Would it always be like that?

No matter which path she chose, as his wife or as his lover. Would women always think it was all right to take such liberties with him? His reputation as a charmer was vast and renowned, and that wouldn't change with a marriage license. Would it?

Was there too much to overcome? Had he spent too much time chasing the ghost of his brother, constructing a life of illusion for her to find something real with him?

This wouldn't happen if she were a spinster. She'd have her freedom without the heartache. But that was just it, wasn't it? Her heart couldn't ache if it were broken, and it would be broken if she didn't have him. She understood that. If it weren't the truth, she wouldn't be sitting on that cold stone step in the middle of the night while an assembly filled with laughter and dancing and refreshments carried on not yards away.

And yet she stayed where she was, watching the place in the hedge where the gardens opened onto the pond in front of the temple. Once she thought she heard movement there, but the night had fallen silent around her once more. She could hear the music from the orchestra from here, the echoes of a cadence like a ghost in the moonlight.

While she couldn't make out the distinct measures of the dance, she could hear the interruptions in it and marked the end of each dance. The violins started up on the sixth dance when she finally stood, accepting what she already knew.

He wasn't coming.

Audrey was no fool. She'd seen for herself how beautiful Lady Wilson was. Audrey had just been an arbitration in Dash's charming schemes. A happy accident, but she wasn't sure who was to be happy about it.

She took the path along the pond slowly. The darkness was almost complete at this hour, and the last thing she wished for was to find herself in the water. She walked with a hand pressed to her stomach. She thought it was to settle her nerves, but she knew the truth of that as well.

She could be pregnant.

She would think about the consequences of such a thing should it come to pass. She wasn't so naive as to think it couldn't happen from the one night they had spent together, but what was worse was the surge of happiness that flooded her at the thought of being pregnant.

Her fingers worried the embroidery at the waist of her gown. Was it the thought of a child itself that compelled such happiness, or was it the thought of having Dash's baby that thrilled it?

She couldn't be sure honestly. She was afraid to admit to either for if she did it would be as if she were forsaking her wish for spinsterhood.

But standing by the pond in the moonlight, spinsterhood didn't seem so glamorous. It seemed rather lonely, in fact. She thought of Aunt Verity, and for the first time, Audrey wondered what it was like to spend the whole of one's life at another's elbow. As much as they didn't wish to think it, Grandmother Regina wouldn't be here forever, and then what was Aunt Verity to do?

Audrey shuddered at the thought and continued her walk along the pond.

The first noises reached her as she slipped between the hedgerow to enter the path back to the manor house. At first it was just voices, and she easily attributed it to the wandering couples she imagined littered the whole of the garden. Until the wind shifted, she couldn't have been sure it was even Dash, but then it was unmistakable.

She stopped, frozen in the darkness, as her whole body keened forward. She had heard him; she was sure of it. She would recognize his voice anywhere now and for the rest of her life. But the night grew still around her once more, and she wondered if she had imagined the whole of it.

She began her trek back to the house, the hedgerows

towering over her, blocking out the moon and forcing her to move more slowly, carefully picking her path.

She only realized she had come to a break at the hedge when moonlight spilled onto the path in front of her, and she paused, turning to look at the moon only to find herself frozen once more.

The break in the hedge led into a folly, surrounded on all sides by Ionic columns and a circle of stone benches. On one of those benches sat Dash, and he held Lady Wilson in his arms.

She didn't think a heart could keep beating when faced with such a betrayal, and yet somehow hers kept going. She knew it because it thudded so loudly inside of her she worried it would break straight through her ribs.

She didn't fear that she may make a sound and give herself away because the sight of the man she loved holding another woman so tenderly had robbed her of all breath. Time passed, flowing around her like a tangible thing, and she let it, unable to pull her eyes free from this thing that once not so long ago she thought could never hurt her.

But now the pain was so real, so intense, she wondered if it would be the death of her.

At least then she wouldn't need to make a choice between love and spinsterhood, but then, if she were thinking properly, she would see she must not make the choice anyway.

Dash had decided for both of them.

She wasn't sure if it were a touch of the night breeze or a branch shifted in the darkness around her, but something finally broke her trance, and sweet, delicious air filled her lungs. And with that blast of life-sustaining air, energy rippled through her. Powerful, stark energy, and her legs were moving once more.

She didn't remember returning to the house. She didn't remember passing through the ballroom or gaining the stairs to the upper floors and the guest rooms. She didn't even remember entering her rooms.

She only seemed to rouse sometime in the early hours of the morning when the sky was just touched with gray as night began to melt into dawn, and the sounds below from the assembly had faded to the occasional burst of laughter. She had heard footsteps along the corridor at intervals through the night and with each footfall, her breath would catch, and she would freeze, wondering if it were him. And as each footfall passed her door, she wondered when she would cease to be a fool.

Her trunks were packed by the time the sun crested the horizon, and by the light of dawn, she scratched off a quick note to Caroline with her apologies. She had thought about staying for her cousin's sake, but Caroline didn't really need her. Aunt Phyllida served as chaperone, terrible at it as she might be, and Caroline had already proven more than capable of holding her own against Hawk and Philip. What need had she of Audrey?

London was only a couple of hours' drive, and she would send the carriage back for them. It was only a day until the house party was due to break up, but it was a day longer than she could bear to stay.

So when the sun broke over the trees surrounding Stonegate Manor, Audrey was already on her way back home.

~

It was several seconds before he realized the pounding wasn't only in his head.

He came fully awake with a start. The blinding pain in his neck was the first of many realizations. He was in a chair in a state of dishabille that included a missing jacket, waistcoat, and cravat. Thankfully his pants were still on. An empty whiskey bottle sat on the table beside his chair. A glass was not to be found.

The pounding continued as he took inventory of both where he was—his rooms, thank God—and if he had all of the necessary body parts still attached.

When he was sure he could stand without falling over, he gained his feet and went in search of the pounding. When he wrenched open the door to the hallway, he was not surprised when Lady Caroline Hodge charged into the room, a crumpled piece of paper clenched in her raised fist.

"What did you do to her?" The words were pushed through gritted teeth, and he backed up as she advanced. "What did you do to her, Amberley?" she asked again, shaking the paper at him.

He wasn't sure he would have been able to understand even if he had his wits about him, which judging by the empty bottle still on the table by the chair, he wasn't likely to have about him anytime soon.

He held up both hands as if to ward off the woman's attack. "Please. Lady Hodge." But the words hardly came out, and he realized now his mouth was made of dry cotton and kindling. He rubbed his tongue against the roof of his mouth, but that only seemed to make it worse.

He collapsed back into the chair from which he had awakened and closed his eyes, welcoming the blissful darkness.

"Do not think you can ignore me, Amberley. I—"

He wasn't sure what happened then, but Lady Hodge

made an abrupt noise of indignation followed by a great deal of rustling and scampering.

Then—"Leave off of him. Can't you see you're not going to get anywhere by hounding him when he's in that state?"

Hawk.

Dash let his eyes flutter open only to wince at the now bright light in the room.

He turned in the direction of the windows to find Philip opening the curtains. The man came toward him then, and Dash was surprised to find the empty bottle had been replaced by an urn and cup.

"Drink," Philip said, pouring thick black liquid into the cup and pressing it into Dash's hands.

Dash closed his eyes as he drank deeply, letting the hot, bitter coffee flood his body. He felt each of his limbs come back to life, even as his stomach teetered uneasily at the sudden onslaught of sustenance. It wasn't until the second cup that the cobwebs seemed to lift from his brain, and he could flex his tongue without wishing to vomit.

Finally, he raised his gaze to Lady Hodge. He was, again, not surprised to find her restrained by Hawk to one side of the room, her face tight, her hands still fisted, and that blasted piece of paper still held in her hand like a weapon.

"What are you doing here?" he finally managed.

Philip leaned against the back of the chair opposite his and said, "I couldn't stop her, so I thought I would at least protect her reputation." He gestured to the coffee urn. "And judging by the contents of that letter, I suspected you would need that."

Letter? What letter?

His eyes swam back and forth and finally settled on Hawk who only shrugged. "I'm here to keep her from physically harming you."

Dash eyed the slight woman in Hawk's grasp. "Do you believe her capable of it?"

She made a noise then not unlike a growling dog.

He sat up and sipped his coffee. "Point taken. What letter is this that you refer to?"

He had a feeling this might be the reason for the paper in her hand. He was rewarded with a shake of her fist in his direction, the paper rustling between her fingers.

"This letter!" Lady Hodge shook her fist enough to have Hawk tightening his grip on her shoulders. "What did you do to her?"

"What did I do to whom?" The muscles along the back of his neck had begun to tighten as the pieces of the tableau before him seemed to right themselves, falling into place to form a picture he did not like.

"Audrey." Caroline spoke the name as though it were sacred. "What did you do to Audrey?"

He held the cup between both hands now, his fingers tightening on the china. "I didn't do anything to Audrey." The words were a lie, but he wasn't about to tell the truth and ruin Audrey's reputation. For all he knew she still planned to be a spinster, and if he told the truth, she would not survive the scandal.

"That is a lie!" Lady Hodge surged in Hawk's arms, and only the man's quick maneuvering kept her from catapulting herself across the room at Dash. Hawk wrapped both arms around her now and lifted her bodily away, setting her down even farther across the room.

He held up a hand to stop her immediate advance at finding her feet once more on the floor.

"We will not get anywhere if you continue to hurl insults and accusations at him. Please, Caroline. Allow me to speak."

Dash doubted she would agree to this, but she surprised him by nodding shallowly, her eyes narrowed to dangerous slits.

Hawk tugged on the cuffs of his jacket and turned to face him. "It appears Lady D'Arcy has left. She's returned to London quite suddenly."

Hawk's words made no sense.

Dash shook his head. "Lady D'Arcy has left? Left where? Left Stonegate?"

"I'm afraid so," said Philip from his perch against the opposite chair.

Dash felt the need to stand but when he tried it, he swayed back into the chair. He set down the cup, pushing both hands through his hair.

"What do you mean she left? Is she alone? Did anyone go with her? How do we know if she's safe?"

He was aware that he was rambling, but he couldn't stop the torrent of thoughts as they cartwheeled through him. Why had she left? Why had she gone back to London when the party was due to end the next day? What was so terrible to make her leave one day sooner?

His mind was a gray mass of hazy memories, and he pushed through them like wading into a swamp, trying to find something concrete that he could recall from the night before.

Reality came back to him like an archer's arrow finding its mark.

"Oh no," he breathed.

"I knew this was your fault." Lady Hodge exploded again only to be caught in Hawk's ready arms.

He twirled her away and set her down again.

"Caroline, I will not have you attacking my guests—"

"I don't care what you'll have," she fired back, clawing at him to release her.

Dash stood, his legs suddenly sure beneath him. "I must go," he said, looking about his rooms as if he could figure out how to do so. "I need to return to London. I must explain—"

"Explain what?" Lady Hodge shook the letter at him. "Explain how you broke my best friend's heart?"

He straightened at this, meeting Lady Hodge's gaze. He held up a hand and gestured for Hawk to release her. His friend did so, although rather reluctantly.

She eyed Hawk with a narrowed gaze as she suspected him to trap her again at any moment. Only when she seemed satisfied did she move ahead.

She held up the letter as she spoke. "Audrey says she's returning to London to see to her duties. That she must fulfill the invitations her mother has accepted for her." She stopped mere inches from him, her nostrils flaring, her mouth a tight line. "You and I both know she wouldn't return to London for anything her mother asked of her, not even to meet the king himself." She held up the letter between two fingers now. "The only reason she would return to her mother any earlier than she had to was to run away from the thing she fears most." She stabbed him now with those two fingers and the letter directly in the chest. "A broken heart."

He considered her, this small woman with hair the color of spun gold, a cherubic face, and bright heavenly eyes. How could such a strange little creature contain so much fortitude?

"How do you know she fears a broken heart most?"

Finally she dropped her hand, the creases along her brow dissipating as if she were pleased to find she had his attention. "Audrey has spent her whole life being told she's not good enough. When you're told something for that long, you start to believe it. Why do you think she concocted that ridiculous idea to be a spinster?"

Dash shifted uncomfortably. "She wanted her freedom."

Lady Hodge shook her head sadly. "That's what she has told herself in order to avoid the truth." A line appeared between her brows, deep with concern. "I've spent three seasons standing next to her at the periphery of every ballroom, every social, every dinner, and do you think I didn't see the way her face pinched every time someone asked me to dance and not her? Every time her face closed when her mother approached? Do you know how many times I listened to her mother tell her how worthless she is?" Tears entered Lady Hodge's voice then, and Dash feared for his own composure. "I can't stand by and watch it happen any longer." She shook her head. "Stupidly I had hoped you had seen the truth. But I guess I was wrong."

She turned, her arms hanging useless at her sides as she made her way to the door.

He stopped her, reaching out to touch her shoulder and draw her back. "The truth about what?"

"The truth about Audrey," she whispered, her eyes incredulous. "I don't know how no one sees what an amazing person she is." She shook her head again, her eyes shiny with unshed tears.

"I saw." He was whispering too, his throat closing on the feeling welling up inside of him as the tumult of emotion of the last several days spilled over him all at once, forming into a perfect crystal realization.

Audrey.

He loved Audrey.

He wanted to spend the rest of his life with Audrey.

And he'd chased her away.

"I saw, and I intend to make this right," he said, his voice firmer. "I need only get her to listen to me."

Lady Hodge's eyes narrowed again. "Why would we need to get her to listen to you?"

He looked down at his feet to find he was wearing only one boot. "Something may have occurred that would require an explanation." He glanced both at Philip and Hawk. "But I'm afraid if I tell you, it would be grounds for calling me out."

Hawk crossed his arms over his chest leisurely. "It's not us you should be worried about, mate." He nodded at Lady Hodge. "It's that one that scares me."

He looked back at Lady Hodge to find the face of a warrior had once more descended over her features.

"We're going back to London, Lord Amberley, and on the way, you're going to tell me exactly what it is you've done to hurt my cousin."

He was surprised to find a smile coming to his lips, and softly he shook his head. "I'm afraid I can't do that, Lady Hodge."

Her fisted hands went to her hips. "And why not?"

"Because a carriage is much too slow. A horse will get me back to Audrey much faster."

16

She was not immune to the fact that she once more sat at the edge of the room, she on one side of Grandmother Regina, Aunt Verity on the other. Audrey snuck a glance at her aunt now, and for the first time, saw the pallor about her face, the grayness that seemed to envelope her visage.

Before Audrey had seen it as freedom, but now she knew better. She saw the prison in which Aunt Verity was trapped, and she hated it. Both for her aunt and for her. This was what society had done to women, given them only two choices, both of which were filled with unsavory possibilities.

Why were women not afforded the luxury of choosing their own path? Of forging a profession and making their own way in the world? Some women did, she knew, but it was often at the expense of their health or standing in society. Again, a choice that wasn't really a choice.

She straightened her shoulders as the musical number came to a vibrating conclusion and the audience politely clapped. It was a musicale this evening. Audrey couldn't remember the name of their hostess, but the night featured a quartet of young women of mediocre talent and extraordinary dowries. Audrey was only too happy to sit at the back of the room with Grandmother Regina and Aunt Verity.

The guests in front rose to pay their congratulations to the musicians while others wandered off to the refreshment rooms.

Audrey turned to Grandmother Regina. "May I get you some tea, Grandmother?"

Audrey's mother reached out a cold hand and laid it possessively on Audrey's arm.

"Verity will see to it. You mustn't waste your time on such matters. There are gentlemen I wish you to speak to." She rose then, and Audrey noticed her mother's practiced polite smile was already in place as she pushed her way into the throng.

Audrey could feel Aunt Verity's gaze on her, and she turned and met the woman's eyes, an understanding passing between them.

Grandmother Regina shook her head as if she'd missed the entire exchange. "I'm quite all right, dear." She peered about the room, her head shaking slightly with its ever-present tremor. "I had hoped to see that young man this evening though. Do you know if he's here, Verity?"

Audrey stilled. "What young man, Grandmother?"

Audrey had left Stonegate Manor three days previous, and she had not spoken a word to anyone about the reason for her hasty departure. She especially hadn't confided in her mother who would only use the information to secure a match with the Earl of Amberley. There was no reason Grandmother Regina would be speaking of Dash, and she forced herself to relax.

"He came round the other day. Didn't he, Verity?" Grandmother turned slightly to take in her youngest daughter who was busy folding Grandmother's shawl and didn't look up. "He wanted to know what invitations you had accepted this week. I think he wished to see you, but he was afraid you wouldn't receive him." Grandmother Regina's smile was filled with mischievous glee. "I think the young man fancies you, my dear."

Audrey swallowed. "What young man, Grandmother?"

Grandmother Regina turned again. "Verity, what was that nice young man's name? The earl. You spoke with him, didn't you?"

Aunt Verity set the shawl in her lap and finally looked up, her eyes searching as if she were dragging herself back to the present.

But she was saved from speaking when the young man in question arrived, stopping neatly in front of them with a sharp bow.

"Ladies," the Earl of Amberley intoned. "A pleasure to see you this evening."

She didn't want to look at him. She didn't want to remember the night she'd spent in his arms. She didn't want to remember the things he had done to her body, but she even more didn't want to remember what he had done to her heart.

She stood so abruptly she nearly knocked her chair over.

"Excuse me," she said, not meeting Dash's gaze, and made for the corridor.

She didn't know where she was going. She didn't even know whose house she was in. She simply had to walk. To get away from him. Her heart pounded in her chest, and her breath came in shallow pants. She walked to the end of the corridor, unknowingly searching for a retiring room, but had she had her wits about her, she would have known there would be no retiring rooms here. Few sconces on the walls were lit, and the dimness of the space around her should have clued her in that this was not a part of the house open to guests.

But she wasn't thinking. She was simply walking, and finally she settled on a door and opened it, slipping inside. She thought she had shut the door behind her, but she couldn't string one thought after another, so she couldn't be sure. She was in some kind of drawing room, the only light the moon that came from the curtains left open on the opposite end of the space. She wasn't sure how long she stood there, but she did know exactly when it was that he stepped through the door.

She could smell him, sandalwood and soap, and her heart ached anew.

"Audrey, I must speak with you. Please don't run away. There's been a misunderstanding." He spoke so quickly she couldn't object.

But even as she registered his words, the hurt inside of her overwhelmed all logic, and she spun on him.

"A misunderstanding? What misunderstanding would that be? The one where you failed to tell me you'd been previously engaged? Or the one where you planned to meet another woman in the gardens that night?"

He reared back, his eyes going wide, and she felt a surge of pleasure that she'd surprised him.

"You saw us," he said, his tone too calm for her liking.

She wanted him to be angry too. She couldn't explain why, but she wanted...*something* from him. She wanted to know he hurt as much as she did even though she knew that wasn't true.

"You must keep a busy schedule, Lord Amberley. I don't see how you can do it."

He stepped toward her, his hands raised as though he meant to touch her, and she took a sharp step back.

"Don't," she warned, wrapping her arms about her like a shield.

"Audrey, please. Let me explain."

She eyed him, wondering if she could bear to hear what he had to say. Wasn't it enough that he'd already broken her heart? Did she need to hear why he had done it?

He must have taken her silence for acquiescence because he went on. "Lady Wilson and I were engaged once. I don't know why I didn't tell you. I thought perhaps it was irrelevant. It was the past, and it didn't matter, and all I wanted was you. Lady Wilson wasn't even a thought in my mind."

She scoffed and took a step back. "She's a part of the past? That's rich coming from someone whose life is dictated by a ghost."

The words met their mark, and she instantly regretted speaking them when his eyes closed in obvious pain.

She opened her mouth to apologize, but the words were stuck on her lips. He had hurt her so much. Why did she want to apologize to him? He needed to apologize to her.

He opened eyes again, and even though she could see a new tension on his face, he kept going. "That night." He paused and licked his lips as if he were struggling, and something like guilt sliced through her. "That night Lady Wilson surprised me. I didn't know she was a guest until that day, and when she approached me at the assembly, I didn't wish to cause a scene. She wanted to speak to me, and I thought I could stop the situation from evolving if I let her talk."

"Is that what you were doing when she was wrapped in your arms in the garden? Talking?" She wasn't sure who was more surprised by the vehemence in her voice, and she swallowed and looked down at the floor as if to gather herself.

"I was trying to comfort her. Audrey, she told me something painful, and I was trying to be a decent gentleman."

"And does being a decent gentleman mean abandoning the woman you promised to meet in the middle of a dark, cold garden?" Her voice was no longer strained with anger; it was deadly calm and flat. She met his gaze, unable to look away now.

He held out his hands as if helpless. "I didn't want to upset Lady Wilson further. I didn't wish to hurt her."

"But you had no problem hurting me."

The words hung in the air between them and finally, he was silent. Something moved through her then, leaving her hollow and numb. She laughed, but the sound was brittle in the empty room, and she pressed a hand to her forehead.

"Do you know I've always wondered, why does no one choose me? Why does no one consider my feelings? It's always the Lady Wilsons of the world that men are so concerned about upsetting. What about me? Why is it so easy for me to be ignored?" There was no pity in her voice, no complaint because she wasn't complaining. Finally she was stating the simple truth, and suddenly it wasn't so difficult to keep her shoulders straight.

Dash didn't answer. He stared at her, the moonlight cutting over his face as if to highlight his surprise. His surprise and his inability to answer her.

It didn't matter. None of it mattered now.

She made to move around him, to go to the door, but he stopped her with his words.

"Lady Wilson was meant to marry David." His tone had lost what little life it had held, and she looked at him. "She's five years older than me. She knew David. When I reached my majority I offered for her because it was what was expected of us." His eyes changed then, and it looked as though he might be imploring her to understand.

And lud if she didn't feel herself sliding, weakening in her resolve. So much of his life had been determined by others just as hers had been, but right now she didn't want to feel this empathy for him. She wanted to stay angry with him. She wanted someone to blame for the hurt inside of her.

"She was the one strong enough to break it off." He shook his head. "I didn't understand it at the time, but I do now. We were never meant for each other, and it was just one more thing I was trying to do to overcome David's ghost." He held out his hands again in that helpless gesture. "My whole life I've tried to get out from under his shadow, but instead I keep running right into it. And when I found you, I thought I had finally escaped."

Something twisted inside of her. She wanted to believe him, but something didn't quite settle. Something was wrong.

She wanted him to love her. She didn't want to be a means of escaping his past.

She shook her head. "I'm sorry, Dash. I'm sorry."

She left the room without looking back or waiting for a response, her feet carrying her in the direction of the other guests. She'd almost made it to the main part of the house when someone stepped in front of her. She looked up to find a tall, thin balding man with a hooked nose standing before her. She didn't know him, and she leaned away, feeling him too close to her.

"I beg your pardon," she said and made to move around him, but he sidestepped, blocking her path. She looked up. Now was most certainly not the time to try her patience. "I said I beg your pardon, sir. Please move." Her tone was flat and unforgiving, but the man only smiled, showing over-large canines. Her body recoiled instinctively, but she held her ground.

"Breedlove."

She hadn't heard Dash come up behind her as she'd been too focused on the man in front of her. Dash stopped next to her, and she swore she could feel his hand hovering at her back as though he meant to protect her physically at a moment's notice.

"Amberley," the man called Breedlove said with a sneer. "Firming up plans with your betrothed, are you?"

Betrothed?

Audrey looked quickly at Dash to find a muscle in his cheek twitching.

"I'm sorry, Breedlove. We haven't the time to chat just now."

Breedlove laughed, the sound grating. "Oh, I know how it is with young people in love. Never the time for anything else."

Audrey felt her insides tumbling as though she were standing on the edge of a cliff about to slip over the side. She turned to Dash.

"What is he talking about? We are not betrothed."

"Oh?" Breedlove spoke again with a sneer. "I thought you were rather overconfident in your wager, Amberley, but even my expectations of your failure have been surpassed." Again, the grating laugh.

But Audrey spoke through it, her heart racing. "What wager?"

Breedlove's eyebrows went up. "He didn't tell you?" He glanced briefly at Dash as a satisfied smile came to his lips. "Lord Amberley wagered that he would marry you by the end of the season, but it looks as though it's not going well."

She turned to Dash to ask him if this were true, but just as before, his eyes closed in obvious pain, and she had her answer.

She didn't know what happened then, and later she would have no explanation for it. But if she had to come up with a reason for it, she would have said she was tired of talking. So instead, she raised both of her hands and shoved Breedlove, hard and fast, directly against his chest. It caught him off guard, and he stumbled backward, falling directly on his arse in the middle of the crowded corridor of the musicale.

The crowd around them fell into a buzzing silence, their eyes riveted to the spectacle, and Audrey calmly picked up her skirts and stepped over the prone man now squirming on the floor to regain his feet and likely, his pride. When her feet were firmly on the other side of him, she raised her chin and met the gazes of the astonished guests.

"I did ask him to move," she said and walked away.

Dash stepped into the foyer of his home a little after ten. He expected his mother to either be abed or at some ball or dinner or some such social nonsense. He didn't really care.

So he was surprised when he heard her voice as he was pouring the first of what he planned to be many drinks in his study ten minutes later.

"Dashiell, the maids were in the west wing again today.

I've told them time and again not to touch David's room, but they insist—"

All at once, he knew what Audrey had felt. In that moment standing before Breedlove, she must have been overcome with an urgency too great to harness in one's person. It was the kind of energy that propelled one forward, and now, at merely the sound of his mother's voice, he felt that urgency crawling within him.

"Dashiell, are you even listening to me?"

He set down his glass precisely on the corner of his desk. He didn't bother looking up. "No, Mother, I am not listening." Finally, he turned to face her, his grin mocking. "I haven't been listening for a long time, in fact."

Her lips pursed, accentuating the lines that stemmed from them. "Really, Dashiell, there's no cause for impertinence. If you simply hired capable maids, this wouldn't be a problem. I'll speak to Mrs. Christy in the morning and get this sorted out. I'll have her let those maids go without reference, of course. We cannot allow another family to fall victim to such terrible service."

His mother was almost to the door before he had thought he could speak without yelling.

"No, Mother, you will not speak to Mrs. Christy in the morning."

"Really, Dashiell, I must. You've clearly proven yourself incapable of taking care of such things—"

"Mother, you will not be speaking to Mrs. Christy in the morning because you're leaving tonight."

His mother finally shut her mouth only to blink several times and say, "I beg your pardon. I am not leaving. Do not be insolent with me."

Dash straightened away from his desk and faced her. "I haven't been insolent, Mother. I've been cowardly. And look where it's gotten me." He gestured to the dark room around them. "I'm having a spat with my mother in my empty house in the middle of the night." He laughed, the sound fragile and slightly on edge. "I've spent the whole of my adult life living an illusion because I wanted someone to accept me. I wanted women to accept me. I wanted women to fall at my feet." His laugh was edgier now, and he worried he might be losing what little control he had left of his anger. "There are rooms in this house that haven't been touched since David died. The stables at Evers Park are in dire need of repair, but they will fall into the ground before you will allow anything to be touched. And that's not the worst of it. The worst of it is the fact that I let you do it. You." He pointed at her as if the person at which he was directing his anger was in question. "I let you do it. You horrible, selfish woman."

Something unlocked inside of him as soon as the words were out, and it was as though someone had cast a spell over him, and the anger that had been boiling inside of him, the anger, the frustration, the despair, it simply evaporated.

"I will not be spoken to like this." His mother's sharp chin went up.

"You're right," he said. "You won't." He went to the corner and pulled the bell pull. "I will have Mrs. Christy help you pack your things. You're leaving."

"Don't be absurd."

Dash looked up as he settled at his desk, reaching for paper and pen. "I've been absurd my whole life. That stops now. Mrs. Christy will help you pack. I don't care where you go, but the Amberley residences are no longer available to you with the exception of the dowager cottage at Evers Park."

The sharp inhalation of breath had him looking up from

where he scratched out a note to his solicitors, and he was pleased to see his mother's nostrils flared, her eyes wide.

"Dashiell, whatever are you saying? Surely you can't mean to put me out."

"That's exactly what I plan to do, Mother. Just as you put me out the day I was born. I will provide you with an allowance fit for a dowager, and I will leave the dowager cottage to your disposal, and that is all. You don't deserve anything more."

He stood, folded the note, and sealed it just as Mrs. Christy hurried into the room, her cap slightly askew as though he had woken her, and she had rushed to dress. He felt a pang of guilt at that and promised to give her an additional sum in her next pay.

"Ah, Mrs. Christy. My mother is leaving. She will need help with packing, and I assume the coachman will need to be roused. Mother, where shall he take you?"

His mother's lips moved without sound, and Dash ignored her, coming round the desk to hand the note to Mrs. Christy.

"Please see that this is delivered as quickly as possible. I shall also need to see my man of affairs. Can you send someone round to fetch him?"

"My lord," Mrs. Christy breathed. "It's nearly midnight, and—"

"You're right. I should really review the plans for the stables before I see him. It can wait until morning then. Thank you, Mrs. Christy. Just the note to my solicitor then."

He turned away, and his mother made a choking noise, the rustle of skirts suggesting she was following him.

"Dashiell, darling, I think there's been a mistake."

He whirled so quickly she stumbled to a stop before

colliding with him. He pinned her gaze with his and bent close so she would not miss a word of what he had to say.

"The only mistake I have made was in thinking I could win your affection, but that was an impossibility, wasn't it?"

She blinked, but he caught the hardness in her eyes before she could hide it.

"I could never replace David, but then you shouldn't have expected me to. I'm done trying to be someone I'm not because as it turns out, I'm enough just being myself, and I don't need you to tell me so."

Vaguely he was aware of Mrs. Christy hovering by the door as she waited for instructions from his mother, and he could very well understand the awkward tableau they made just then.

After what seemed an age, his mother finally raised her chin. "Fine. If that is how you would like it to be. Putting your mother out into the night. Refusing to put a roof over her head. Refusing to give her the funds she needs to maintain the lifestyle that is expected of her. I hope you are pleased with yourself, Dashiell."

"I'm very pleased, Mother," he couldn't help replying.

Her eyes narrowed. "You have fulfilled every low expectation I've had of you. David was always the superior person to you, and I hope you realize it."

He couldn't stop the grin that spread over his features. "And you, Mother, have fulfilled every low expectation I've had of you. Now that we're even, I think nothing will be lost if we part ways here."

Her gasp was loud in the sudden quiet, and she leaned back, her eyes wide.

"How could you, Dashiell?"

He kept his voice level and said, "How could you not love your own son?"

The words were so carefully targeted, and he saw the moment the volley made impact. Pain crossed her eyes, real, sharp, and fatal pain. And there in the dim room, in the middle of the night, with his heart already splintered into a thousand pieces that only Audrey could heal, he knew the truth of it.

His mother could never love him. It just wasn't in her, and in the pain riddled across her face, he saw she knew it too.

What had come unlocked in him moments before now separated completely, and it was as though a part of him, a heavy, dark part of him that he'd carried for far too long, let go like a piece of an iceberg separating itself into the sea. It floated away from him, and suddenly he was lighter. It didn't matter that the thing that caused it was so painful or deep. It only mattered that they had both recognized it for what it was, and now they stood facing each other with no illusions between them.

His mother gave a short nod. "I'll see to my packing now."

When she was nearly to the door, he said, "Good night, Mother."

He thought she wouldn't answer but eventually she turned, her face composed and cold. "Good night, Dashiell," she said and left.

17

"I am sure it will all blow over in a week. There's nothing to worry about, Eugenia. These young ones these days. They're so very much more vibrant than we were."

Was Grandmother Regina's voice growing shakier these days or was Audrey imagining it?

"Oh, Mother, really. What Audrey did is unforgivable. If there had been any hope of her marrying before this, it's gone now." Her mother paced the drawing room in Dartford House, her skirts flying behind her as if propelled by the force of her anger.

This was not the first dressing down Audrey had received since that night at the musicale. When her mother had first heard of the incident, Audrey had been sent to her rooms as if she were still a child. Audrey had gone, of course, happy to get away from her mother and really everyone for that matter.

The events of the night had gotten mixed up in her mind until her thoughts swirled in a hideous, painful kaleidoscope of torment.

While she could almost understand why Dash had been so affected by Lady Wilson's sudden appearance, it did not act as an excuse for leaving her waiting for him. But the wager with that man Breedlove, that was unforgivable. Who was he to think he could bet on her future? Did she mean so little to him? It was so very easy to pick on the weaker ones, and as a wallflower in a society that prized beauty above all else, she was too easily a prime target.

Caroline squeezed her hand then, and Audrey looked over, forgetting her cousin sat next to her on the sofa. She had appeared only an hour before with Grandmother Regina and Aunt Verity, and Audrey's mother had received them in the drawing room as though Audrey's indiscretions were cause for some sort of family meeting.

Caroline leaned in to whisper as Audrey's mother swung about in her pacing to head to the other end of the room, her litany of despair never ceasing even as she kept her pace.

"Hawk says Dash didn't wager about your betrothal."

Audrey slid a glance at her cousin before moving her eyes back to her mother, sure she didn't hear correctly.

"When have you been speaking to Hawk?" she asked out of the side of her mouth as her mother stopped to regal Grandmother Regina with another recitation of Audrey's horrific actions.

If she only knew...

When Caroline was quiet, Audrey turned to study her cousin only to find her cheeks sported identical spots of color.

Audrey raised an eyebrow, and Caroline's frown was fierce.

"Hawk said Dash wagered to call Breedlove out *when* he

was betrothed to you and he had the right to avenge your honor," Caroline said, pointedly ignoring Audrey's question.

But it didn't matter because Audrey suddenly forget she'd asked a question.

Dash wished to avenge her honor?

"Whatever are you talking about?" Audrey hissed as her mother came dangerously close to them.

Caroline didn't answer until Eugenia had swept away again. "Hawk said this Breedlove chap is a real sod, and he said something unfavorable about you that Dash took affront to. He promised to call the man out when he was properly wed to you and had the right. That horrible Breedlove took it as a wager."

That hollow and numb feeling spread through her again, and she worried at how used to it she'd grown. But Caroline's words tumbled through her as though she truly were hollow inside.

"When did this happen?"

Caroline shook her head. "It must have been after the incident in the cloakroom. Hawk said it was several weeks ago when he first spoke to Dash about you."

Audrey straightened and pressed a hand to her chest as her heart rabbited there. Dash was swearing vengeance on her honor and Hawk was speaking to Dash about her?

"Why did Hawk ask Dash about me?"

"He heard about the wager and wanted to see that Dash's intentions were honorable."

Audrey must be in a dreamworld. That was the only explanation for what she was hearing. Never in her life had someone, let alone two someones, paid so much attention to her. Nor had they felt her worthy of such admirable action.

Would Dash really have called out Breedlove to protect her honor?

Without warning, her thoughts traveled back to that single night spent in Dash's arms, and the truth of it flooded through her.

Dash would protect her.

She just didn't know if he could love her.

The sight of Lady Wilson in his arms was burned into her memory, but it was what it meant that hurt her more. Dash would be forever trapped in a past not of his making, and she just didn't know if she'd ever fit in there.

It was several seconds before she realized her mother had stopped in front of her.

Audrey looked up, blinking as she took in what the woman was saying.

"So, we are going to accept every invitation that comes in no matter how poor, and we will find someone, anyone, to offer for you. This will not end in disaster. I will not have my daughter remain unwed no matter how unfortunate her appearance."

In all her life, her mother had never come right out and said it. It had always been hinted at, but never said so plainly. The modiste was instructed to choose favorable colors and styles. Her maid was instructed to dress her hair as if to distract from her less desirable features. But never before had her mother called her appearance unfortunate.

Audrey felt...nothing.

She blinked and rooted around inside of herself, looking for the anger and resentment that should have been there.

But there was nothing.

Because the person who had spoken the insults no longer meant anything to her. This woman who had dominated Audrey's life seemed small and petty now that Audrey had seen the barest glimpse of the world beyond the four walls of Dartford House.

She felt so many pairs of eyes on her. Aunt Verity and Grandmother Regina. Caroline and even Ethan, though he pretended to be reading the paper in the corner. And where was Gavin? How odd her brain should pick that out just then.

"Audrey, I shall request an appointment with the modiste. We will order the finest gowns to distract from your visage, and we will see you married."

Audrey stood, her heart suddenly quiet, her breathing deep and even. She smiled and tilted her head as she considered her mother.

And then calmly folding her hands in front of her, she said, "Go stuff it, Mother."

The gasp did not come from Eugenia D'Arcy nor did the shout of triumph. The gasp came from the maid who had the unfortunate timing of bringing in a new tea cart, and the call of triumph came from Caroline on the sofa behind her.

Audrey advanced on her mother. "My visage is not unfortunate, and it does not require something with which to distract people's attention from it. I have it on good authority that my face is captivating." She flung the word at her mother as though it were a bullet.

Her mother didn't flinch.

"I do not know who would think such a thing," Eugenia sneered.

Dimly, Audrey heard the rustling of paper and knew Ethan had lowered the newspaper and was watching them. But it didn't matter.

Audrey leaned in, feeling the power that was still so new to her. "The man who took my innocence does."

There were no cheers of triumph, no gasps. There was only deathly silence.

Audrey smiled now, power radiating through her at the ashen pallor on her mother's face.

"There will be no visit to the modiste, Mother. There will be no invitations. No more balls, no musicales, no more dinners. Unlike you, I don't need society to validate my existence." She leaned in. "Because no matter what you think of me, I know the truth."

Her mother blinked, her lips parting without sound.

"I know that you're afraid of what people think of you. That one day someone will find you lacking, and you will no longer be the social queen you think you are." She gestured to the side. "You force Aunt Verity to keep Grandmother quiet for fear someone will discover your mother is less than perfect." She gestured to the other side of the room. "You hide invitations from Ethan because you don't want people to see his face." She pressed her hands to her chest. "And you would pawn your daughter off on whatever eligible bachelor should offer for her because you cannot wait to be rid of her and her unfortunate face. Because for some strange reason, you really believe the rest of us reflect poorly on you." Audrey shook her head. "But that's not the truth. You don't need us to reflect poorly on you, Mother. I already know what a terrible person you are."

She took a step back and brushed at her skirts. "I shall no longer be attending balls unless I should choose so. The same for the rest of the invitations. Now if you'll excuse me."

She was almost to the door when she heard the word her mother hissed behind her.

"Harlot."

Ethan shot to his feet, but Audrey stopped him with a raised hand.

"No, Mother. I am not a harlot. Unlike you, I don't

choose to hide behind some silly facade. I was offered love, and I took it." She shook her head. "I'll never regret it."

She left the room, feeling Aunt Verity's gaze on her.

He had heard that losing oneself in a complex task was a means of forgetting one's woes. Four days after the night at the musicale, Dash was happy to say this was a load of rubbish.

He was up to his elbows in plans for the new stables at Evers Park, and he couldn't have told anyone the difference between a door and a paddock. Every time he looked at the plans he saw Audrey's captivating face, and despair smothered him again as if for the first time.

He'd already removed his cravat and coat thinking perhaps it were the tightness of his dress constricting him, but he knew the truth.

He couldn't get her out of his mind, and he knew he never would. He'd lost the one thing that mattered to him because he had been too caught up in the past. That was the last time. He swore to it. He would no longer allow David's ghost to determine his future.

His mother had left without a word that night, and he had heard through his man of affairs that the dowager cottage at Evers Park had been opened. He could only assume that his mother had taken residence there. He felt no pity or guilt for relegating her to the depths of the country. It was better than most widows could attest to, and it wasn't as though he had pushed her out completely. Her annual allowance was more than generous, and that would be all. She would no longer command him the way she once had.

But what did it matter?

Only Audrey mattered, and she was beyond his reach.

He picked up his pen again, determined to see to the notes the builders had left on the plans when a knock at the door drew his attention. His butler, Udall, entered and extended a silver salver with a single linen card on it. He was not surprised to see the name Ethan D'Arcy, Baron Grays in neat black letters across the pristine finish.

Dash snatched up the card and stood, telling Udall to allow the man entrance.

He had only managed to don his coat by the time the baron marched into his study and without permission, closed the door behind him.

Dash waited, his hands still on the lapels of his coat as Grays approached.

"You've probably guessed that I'm here to speak to you about my sister."

Dash dropped his hands. "I assumed as much. Would you care for a drink?"

He had no idea of the time. One hour melted into another excruciating one, and he'd left off figuring them out.

Grays shook his head, and Dash could easily see the soldier still in the man. He stood stiff and upright as though he may be called into battle at any moment. Not for the first time, Dash felt a pang of guilt over not being there to fight with the rest of the men his age.

"I'd like to address the matter as quickly as possible."

Dash nodded. "I understand. Then we should start with the fact that your sister no longer wishes for my company."

"I thought as much, but seeing as how she's in love with you, I would hope you would come up with a way to overcome that."

Everything inside of Dash stopped. "In love with me?"

Grays nodded once, succinctly. "I would venture to say she's madly in love with you. Emphasis on the mad." He took the seat in front of Dash's desk, again without being asked. He leaned back in the chair and crossed one leg over the opposite knee. "Yesterday she informed my mother in a family gathering that she no longer had her virtue."

Dash sat, blinking furiously. "She told your mother what exactly?"

For the first time, Dash saw a small smile play at the baron's lips. "It was rather well done of her. Our mother is a cruel woman, but she's a sad one too. She hides the perceived flaws of her family or pretends they do not exist. Audrey chose to point out these facts to our mother yesterday by way of exposing her own secrets. Secrets she was rather proud of, I might add. Which can only bring me to the conclusion that she's madly in love with you."

Audrey had stood up to her mother, and he hadn't been there to see it. Perhaps they were both mad with love.

Dash relaxed back in his chair, defeat dispelling despair for the first time in days.

"I hope you have brought some ideas with this news you carry. I've tried everything I can think of, but I'm afraid she has other designs for her life. She even refused my suit to court her."

Grays lips thinned. "I figured she would do something like that. I fear she may have some grand illusions about spinsterhood. I overheard her speaking of such to our cousin Caroline."

Dash wondered how much he should tell the man of his sister's designs on her future and decided perhaps the whole truth may help them find a way through Audrey's defenses.

"Audrey wishes to be a spinster for the freedom of it, but upon my questioning, she didn't know what freedoms it was she sought. When she refused my courtship, I offered to help her discover what it was she planned to do with her freedom."

Grays face transformed into something hard, and Dash held up a hand.

"My intentions were honorable even if the present circumstances suggest otherwise. When your cousin Caroline ensnared Audrey in that house party invitation, I made certain to gain an invitation myself so I could protect her. Your mother obviously was not up to the task."

The hardness in Grays's face softened somewhat, but a twitch started in his cheek. Dash thought this likely due to the mention of his mother and her lack of motherly attentions.

"The house party at Stonegate? I was aware of the invitation. I take it my aunt Phyllida was also not an adequate chaperone."

Dash recalled seeing the woman on occasion the week they were at the house party, but she was more of a ghost than anything. Dash only shook his head.

"So, you set out to protect my sister, and then you ruined her."

The words hurt, but they were the truth no matter how much he didn't like it.

"I had every intention of marrying your sister, Grays. It's only that my past got in the way of my future."

"And have you managed to eradicate your past now?"

Dash sat forward, his elbows on his desk. "I've obliterated it, but it doesn't matter. Audrey doesn't wish to see me."

Grays dropped his foot and leaned forward, his face intense. "If I can arrange for you to be alone with Audrey, do you have the proof she will require to accept your offer of marriage?"

Dash's insides tightened with anticipation. "I do, but I can't say that she will even think of listening to me."

Grays stood, his expression decided. "She will listen. I won't give her the option not to."

Dash stood as well. "That seems rather draconian."

Grays smiled truly for the first time in their meeting. "Sometimes one must take rather extreme measures when it comes to one's sister."

18

Her mother hadn't spoken to her in a week.

The season was in full swing now, and Miles, their butler, was often weighed down with two salvers of invitations when he came to the breakfast room each morning. Her mother selected each one carefully and opened it with great ceremony in front of Audrey but never spoke a word.

Audrey wished she could have enjoyed it more.

Instead, the numb feeling that had become so familiar seemed to have taken up permanent residence inside of her. It was strange to exist, and yet know that you weren't really existing. She was truly just doing the bare minimum. The very least she could do to make it from day to day.

Was this what her freedom had earned her?

It suddenly didn't seem so grand.

She was finally out from under her mother's disdain, albeit through rather unconventional means and certainly not how she had meant to do it. But even that had not brought her the joy she had expected.

Because nothing really mattered without Dash.

It sounded pathetic when she thought of it, and she wished it weren't true. She wished she were the vixen she had believed herself to be. She wished she were powerful and self-sufficient, and if she really thought about it, deep down she was. She was all of those things or else she would not have spent that night with Dash. She wouldn't have done any of it with Dash had she not had the courage to do it.

For that she was proud.

But the rest of it...

Her life would go on. She knew that. It just wouldn't be as bright or wide without him by her side.

Could she forgive him?

She didn't know.

Perhaps it had been a misunderstanding with Breedlove. The man had seemed the very sod Caroline had said Hawk called him. That she could get over, but the rest of it?

What was she to do about a man so controlled by his past?

She didn't wish to change him. The very thought was absurd. If he wished to change, he would need to do it for himself.

Just as she had changed.

She could admit that now in the safety of the Dartford House drawing room, the space quiet around them. She fiddled with an embroidery pattern she had no interest in while Ethan read the papers opposite her.

Gavin was once more mysteriously absent, and her mother had likely accepted an invitation somewhere without deigning to bring her daughter along.

Audrey's reputation was no worse the wear in society for no one else knew of what had happened at the Stonegate house party. But within the walls of Dartford House, Audrey was a fallen woman.

And she reveled in it.

She couldn't help the small smile that came to her lips as she stabbed at the linen with her needle. At least there was something in her life that could bring her joy even if it were only her memories.

There was a quick knock at the door, and she nearly stabbed herself in the finger.

She looked up as Miles entered and gave a nod to Ethan. "Lord Grays, would you like calling hours to commence?"

Audrey darted her gaze between the two men, settling finally on Ethan who had set down his paper. "Calling hours? What is this about? I'm not receiving callers."

Ethan had already stood and brushed at his coat, and—

By God, he was smiling. It was harder to tell now as one side of his face was a labyrinth of tight scars, but she could almost see his teeth. She set down her embroidery and gained her feet. Whatever was happening, she was not engaging in it sitting down.

"Thank you, Miles," Ethan said, his gaze still on her. "Lady D'Arcy shall be receiving callers."

Miles nodded. "Very good, my lord."

Audrey watched the servant retreat before moving her attention back to her brother. "Ethan, what is going on?"

A tightness had begun to coil deep in her stomach, and she pushed her hopes down. This couldn't possibly be—Ethan didn't know who—

He nodded. "If you will excuse me." He headed to the door.

"Ethan." Her voice was a pitch higher than normal, and she swallowed. "I have no chaperone."

There was that smile again. "It didn't stop you the last time, did it?"

Her face heated instantly, but there wasn't accusation in his eyes. Only understanding. He was gone before she could respond.

She paced to the window that overlooked the street, hoping to see a familiar carriage even though every one of her senses knew who was here. What was she going to say? What was she going to do?

Did she know whether or not she would forgive him? Did she know if she could...

This was useless. He hadn't asked her to marry him. He hadn't even told her he loved her.

Perhaps he was only here to ask her to be his mistress.

Why did the thought suddenly seem so empty and cold?

"Hello, Audrey."

Her hand stilled against the curtain, her body frozen in front of the window. Slowly, so achingly slowly, she made herself turn around.

And her heart shattered.

He was so utterly handsome. So utterly perfect. So utterly...Dash.

His smile was soft and beguiling, and he stood so casually just inside the door, one foot in front of the other, the knee slightly bent as if he'd spent the whole of his life walking into her drawing room.

"Dash." Her voice was steady even as her hands shook, and she let go of the curtain lest she give away her nervousness.

"I trust you are well." He didn't try to come closer to her, and she noticed he held a rolled piece of paper in his hands.

"I am, and you?"

He nodded. "Very well. Thank you."

The stilted conversation broke what remained of her heart, and she swallowed down a sob that tried to escape. How had they come to this? What had happened to the man who had embraced her in the dark cloakroom? What had happened to the woman from the temple who dared to play with fire?

"I don't want you to think I've come to ask you to court me again." His smile was sheepish and self-deprecating. "I think I've learned my lesson on that score."

Another piece shattered. How did she have any left?

"I just came to tell you I'm leaving London for a time, and I hope you enjoy the remainder of the season."

"Leaving London?" There her voice went up an octave. She swallowed, hard. "Does business require you elsewhere?"

For one horrible moment, she pictured he and Lady Wilson running away to the continent together.

But then he held up the rolled paper in his hand. "I'm away to Evers Park actually. The construction on the new stable is beginning, and I wish to be present."

It was happening again. Once more she stood on the edge of something, unsure if she should step forward or back, but knowing each way contained danger.

"The stables?" Her mind was suddenly filled with memories of that rainy afternoon in the temple.

He took a single step forward and bent, placing the rolled piece of paper on the small table where she had discarded her embroidery. "Yes, I'm moving forward with the new stables. That is a copy of the building plans. I know how much architecture interests you." He said this last part with a small grin, so achingly familiar it made her stomach twist.

"But your mother," she said before she thought better of

it. “Does your mother approve of the plans?” she asked, knowing it was too late to stop now.

He straightened and put his hands behind his back, once more bending his knee casually. “My mother has removed herself from the Amberley residences and is now living in the dowager cottage at Evers Park.”

She must have stepped over the edge because now she was falling. Surely the floor could no longer be at her feet. The world was tumbling about her, and she must have moved.

But she hadn’t, and neither had he. They both still stood there in the quiet drawing room, not more than a square of carpet between them.

And yet everything had changed.

His mother...he had made his mother leave? She couldn’t form the question. She couldn’t ask. But the stable plans. If he were building the stables then...

“Your mother must not approve.”

He laughed softly. “It matters not if she approves. She is no longer in a position to make decisions for Evers Park.” He paused, his gaze so intense on hers she almost wanted to look away. Almost. “Or for me,” he said so softly she almost missed it.

Her eyes widened, and suddenly it became hard to breathe.

“Audrey, I meant what I said. I’m not here to ask to court you. I’m not here to ask you to forgive me. I know how you feel, and I respect that. I only wished for you to know why I was leaving London and to know the time that we had together, well, it means everything to me, and I will always look back on it fondly. And on you.”

The drawing room around them dropped away, and it was as though they were back in her rooms at Stonegate

Manor, nestled in the dark just the two of them, the rest of the world held at bay. She didn't know how long she stood there thinking of what she was supposed to say to this.

But then he took a step forward and another, and he stood so close she could smell him, that glorious smell of sandalwood and soap, and for one sickening moment, she thought this would be the last time she would smell it.

"Audrey, I love you. I don't expect that to change anything. I just wanted you to know." He smiled. Oh God, he smiled, and she couldn't breathe. "I love you, but I respect the decision you've made. I'm sorry this world hasn't given you more choices, but I know you will make a wonderful spinster." He laughed, but the sound was wet as though he were trying not to cry.

She needed to say something, but she still couldn't breathe. She couldn't remember how to speak.

But then he was backing away. He hadn't even touched her. She wanted him to touch her.

"I hope I will get to see you again one day, Audrey D'Arcy. If only to see your captivating face once more." He bowed then and turned to the door.

He took two steps. Her heart pounded against her ribs. Her throat was so dry, so terribly dry. She had to say something.

"No."

The word hardly came out; it was really not more than a whisper, but he stopped as if she'd pulled him physically back.

"No. Dash. Don't." She couldn't form complete sentences. Tears were in her voice and in her eyes, and then they were spilling down her cheeks, and he was turning, and she was running—running in the small space of the drawing room—and finally, *finally*, she was in his arms, and he was kissing her.

"Don't go," she said between kisses. "But if you need to go, take me with you because I love you. I love you, Dash."

He kissed her lips, her cheeks, her temple, and she kissed him back, her arms tight around his neck as he lifted her off the ground.

"I'm a ruined woman now. You can do whatever you please with me."

He laughed softly against her lips. "What I would like to do with you is marry you, but I'm afraid that would take away your adventures as a spinster."

She pulled back far enough to look him in the eye. "Being married to you will be the greatest adventure," she said and kissed him.

EPILOGUE

"Do the bride and groom always hide in cloakrooms in order to avoid their wedding breakfasts?"

Dash pushed his way through the cloaks and wraps to the farthest corner of the room, pulling her behind him until they were ensconced in a pile of furs.

"If they don't, they are truly missing a wonderful opportunity."

Her husband pulled her into his arms and kissed her until she thought they would need to find a more private place than even the cloakroom.

She let him nibble along her jaw, down her throat as she said, "I didn't think our mothers would get along, but this... this is like..."

"Waterloo," he said against the sensitive spot by her ear.

She sighed and sank against him, letting his arms hold her up as she reveled in the feel of his hard body pressed against hers.

"I fear Waterloo was a great deal more civilized than what is happening between our mothers right now."

He pulled back, and she lamented the loss of his attention, but his expression was serious, and she met his gaze.

"Haven't you ever found it curious?"

She tilted her head. "What is curious?"

His eyes became unfocused as though he were considering a problem. "It's just that we're rather suited for one another, you and I."

She couldn't help a smile as she said, "Then I'm very glad you married me."

He laughed but shook his head. "No, it's not that. It's rather more that we were meant to be together. Almost as though someone planned it."

The lightness she always felt in his arms dissipated, and she considered his words. It was rather odd that they should have encountered each other the way they had, and that they were rather suited for one another, each carrying the scars their mothers had given them.

"What do you mean that someone planned it?"

He shook his head, his eyes still wondering. "I don't know. Almost like someone was playing matchmaker."

She wrinkled her nose. "Well, who would do that? Is there anyone that you and I knew before we knew each other?"

Finally his eyes focused on her. "Do you mean a common acquaintance? Someone who would know that we were suited?"

"Yes, something like that." She snuggled closer to him, enjoying the feel of him even if their conversation was rather serious.

"I think the only people we both knew were Hawk and Philip, and they don't seem the matchmaker type."

"Well, they would be the only ones who would know us well enough, wouldn't they?"

Dash shook his head though, his eyes unsure. "Unless it was someone that would go unnoticed."

"Do you mean like a wallflower?" she said, unable to stop a grin.

She hadn't meant to distract him, but suddenly his own smile split his face.

"You know perfectly well, Lady Amberley, that I never fail to notice a wallflower," he said and kissed her.

ABOUT THE AUTHOR

Jessie decided to be a writer because there were too many lives she wanted to live to just pick one.

Taking her history degree dangerously, Jessie tells the stories of courageous heroines, the men who dared to love them, and the world that tried to defeat them.

Jessie makes her home in New Hampshire where she lives with her husband and two very opinionated Basset hounds. For more, visit her website at jessieclever.com.

Made in the USA
Columbia, SC
19 March 2022